Unconditionally

BOOKS BY ERIN LYON

I Love You *Subject to the Following Terms and Conditions*

Unconditionally

Unconditionally

A CONTRACT KILLERS NOVEL

ERIN LYON

A TOM DOHERTY ASSOCIATES BOOK
NEW YORK

UNCONDITIONALLY

Copyright © 2017 by Erin Lyon

A Forge Book
Published by Tom Doherty Associates
175 Fifth Avenue
New York, NY 10010

www.tor-forge.com

Forge® is a registered trademark of Macmillan Publishing Group, LLC.

Library of Congress Cataloging-in-Publication Data

Names: Lyon, Erin, author.
Title: Unconditionally : a contract killers novel / Erin Lyon.
Description: First edition. | New York : Forge, 2018. | "A Tom Doherty
   Associates Book."
Identifiers: LCCN 2017039438 (print) | LCCN 2017045083 (ebook) |
   ISBN 9780765386137 (ebook) | ISBN 9780765386120 (trade pbk.)
Subjects: | GSAFD: Romantic suspense fiction.
Classification: LCC PS3612.Y558 (ebook) | LCC PS3612.Y558 U53 2018
   (print) | DDC 813/.6—dc23
LC record available at https://lccn.loc.gov/2017039438

Our books may be purchased in bulk for promotional, educational, or
business use. Please contact your local bookseller or the Macmillan Corporate
and Premium Sales Department at 1-800-221-7945, extension 5442, or by email at
MacmillanSpecialMarkets@macmillan.com.

First Edition: January 2018

Printed in the United States of America

0 9 8 7 6 5 4 3 2 1

This is for you, Stephen. Because you speak our secret language of movie quotes and Jim Gaffigan jokes, taught me to appreciate the beauty of both Rush and MST3K, and, you know, because you're the love of my life.

Unconditionally

CHAPTER *1*

Move-in day. A new beginning. I looked out the window at my new rental and got a rush of excitement at the thought that I finally had my own place again. My parents are amazing, but moving home with Mom and Dad at thirty-four, after an unexpected breakup, is definitely *less* amazing.

Dave and I pulled up in front of my new apartment with his truck loaded with my belongings and my parents parked at the curb behind us in Dad's truck packed with the other half of my stuff.

Dave and I hadn't really talked since he picked me up at the bar last night. You know, after my irrational and unexpected little bout of jealousy sent me running at the thought of Adam's (potential) hookup with another woman. When I'd met Adam, he pursued me because I was unavailable. And when I suddenly became *available*? I no longer fit his criteria—no attachment—but he still wanted us to be friends.

At first, sure, Adam was beautiful, but he didn't really get to me. Until we became *friends* and I was treated to a whole new, amazing Adam that I seemed to find slightly irresistible.

So I left with Dave last night, leaving Adam standing on the sidewalk, watching me climb into Dave's truck. And he just let me go.

So I woke up this morning with a new resolve to do the same.

I looked over at Dave with a big, silly grin and danced around a little in my car seat.

Dave chuckled. His blond hair was perfectly styled, as usual, but he had some sandy-blond scruff on his face like he'd skipped his morning shave. He smiled at my excitement, displaying his overly perfect teeth (which, Dave had clarified, were necessitated by his brief foray into youth hockey and not by the vanity that came with being a well-known local news sportscaster, as I had first suspected). He was very all-American-boy handsome today, which always made me think of a wolf in sheep's clothing. Jury was still out on that one.

A Mercedes belonging to my landlady, Sandy, was already parked on the opposite side of the street. Sandy was standing on the front steps, managing to look crisp and vintage even when she was in jeans. She had on a white blouse with the wide cuffs turned back and she was wearing brown loafers that were just old enough to look classic rather than dowdy. Her dark hair with its streaks of gray was pulled back from her face with a headband. The distinctive combination of dark hair and light-green eyes made it hard to forget that she was Adam's mother. Damn.

I walked up to her and she wrapped me in a big hug. My parents followed me up the walk and I made introductions.

Sandy unlocked the front door and we all trailed in behind her and stood in the foyer. I had a foyer now. A teeny, tiny foyer, but it was mine.

"Oh, Kate," Mom said. "This is perfect."

I smiled at her and draped an arm across her shoulders. "I know!" I said, not masking my excitement. She wrapped an arm around my waist and smiled back at me with her matching light-blue eyes. As much as Adam and Sandy were definitely mother and son, I was my mother's doppelgänger. Sure, I was a little taller and leaner, but our brown hair and light-blue eyes made our link unmistakable.

We headed back out and started unloading the truck with the big items first. Dad and Dave went back inside with my mattress, heading straight upstairs. I grabbed the closest box marked "Kitchen" and figured I could start getting the boxes to the right rooms while the guys lifted the heavy furniture. I walked inside, holding the big box a little awkwardly.

I smiled to myself as I headed for the kitchen. Life was good.

And then it happened—one of those pure Wile E. Coyote moments. One minute my feet were under me, and the next, I could see them straight out in front of me. It's awesome the way time slows down when you start to fall . . . because you would hate to miss a moment of this. I seemed to have ample time both to admire the air I'd managed to achieve and to ponder how much it would hurt when I crashed to the wood floor.

It hurt a lot. Thankfully, I had the foresight to push the box aside so that it didn't land on top of me. *Whoosh.* The wind was completely knocked out of me and I could see little gray spots in my field of vision. And I just lay there, stunned.

The first thing I saw was Sandy dropping down to kneel over me, her green eyes wide and shocked.

"Oh my god! Kate! Are you okay?"

Kate can't come to the phone right now—you'll have to leave a message.

Then it was Mom, Dad, and Dave, freaking out, talking about calling an ambulance. *Say something, Kate. Before someone tries to give you CPR.*

"I'm okay. I'm okay. I'm okay." Perfect. Why say something once when you can say it three times?

Dad was looking down into my face, his bushy eyebrows lowered over his gray eyes. "Are you sure?"

Mom put her hand on my dad's shoulder. "Maybe we should still call the ambulance, Jeff."

Shit. Time to nip this hysterical little situation in the bud. I took a deep breath and lifted my head off the ground. So far, so good. When I got my shoulders off the floor, Dad and Sandy reached arms under me and helped me to a sitting position. Dave was positioned by my feet and reached out and took one of my hands, once I was sitting up. He was frowning, his lips pursed tight.

"I'm okay," I repeated.

"Are you sure?" Sandy asked, sounding on the verge of tears. "I think you should go get checked out."

I shook my head—and wished I hadn't. I had a quick throbbing in the back of my head and a few more spots danced in front of my eyes.

"Really," I said. "I'm fine. I'm just a klutz."

"I am so sorry, Kate. The housecleaners must have used some kind of wax on the floor. I'm *so* sorry."

I grasped her hand and smiled. "It was my fault." I wiggled my well-worn Chuck Taylors. "These shoes are so old, they are worn completely smooth on the bottom. I should have worn different shoes."

Sandy shook her head, unconvinced.

"Maybe we should take you to the hospital," Dave said. "You could have a concussion."

"I don't have a concussion," I said, although I was careful not to shake my head this time.

Dad waved Mom down to his side. "Deanna, sit here with her. Dave, let's go get the sofa so she has somewhere to sit and we can get her off the floor."

"I'll give you my homeowner's insurance information," Sandy said.

"Sandy, please don't blame yourself. I am totally accident prone."

"She really is," Mom chimed in.

Sandy reached out and gently brushed my hair back from my forehead and looked into my face intensely. The act was so sweet and maternal, I had a complete *Awww* moment, and I tipped my head at her, smiling. She finally smiled back.

The guys brought the sofa in, and apparently all four of them were determined to help my sorry ass off the floor.

"You guys. I really am okay," I repeated, feeling like a broken record.

Mom settled a pillow behind my back when I sat down, and Dave picked my feet up and put them on the couch so I was semi-reclined. I think I would have fought it more if I didn't feel a little queasy all of a sudden.

"Knock, knock," Logek, my best friend, chirped from the doorway. Her long blond hair was pulled back in a ponytail and she was wearing a plain pink T-shirt and jeans with holes in both knees. She walked in and saw me stretched out on the sofa and her eyebrows went up. "What did I miss?"

"Kate took a bad fall," Dad said.

"It wasn't that bad," I said.

In response, my mother turned to Logek and nodded agreement with my father.

"You know I can see you, right?" I asked her.

Mom shrugged.

Logek looked down at me and down to my feet. "I told you to throw out those Chuck's, Kitty Kat. They're like ice skates."

Since apparently this crowd was going to need some hard proof, I put my feet down on the floor in front of me and sat upright. My fingertips were still a little tingly, but I definitely was fully functional. I didn't want to stand up just yet, since I felt like there might be a fifty-fifty chance I'd swan dive to the floor. That's okay, though. They seemed satisfied with me sitting up, looking alert and cheerful.

Everyone seemed to be feeling better, except for Dave. He was still frowning at me, thoughtfully.

"You could have a concussion," he repeated.

"I don't have a concussion."

He shrugged but still didn't look happy. Tough shit. The emergency room was so not happening today.

I smiled brightly for everyone. "Okay. Enough slacking. Let's get me moved in."

I got a couple of chuckles, some smiles, and everyone started moving with a purpose again.

Logek walked over to the box I'd lobbed away for my well-being. It was on its side and it was a little lopsided now. She righted it, broke the tape, and opened the box. She looked inside and made one of those inward sighs where you suck air in through your teeth.

"Do I want to know what was in there?"

"Nope."

Wonderful. I raised my eyebrows at her. "Hit me with it. I can take it."

She pulled some newspaper off the top and laid it out flat next to the box . . . undoubtedly for whatever broken pieces would be laid out on it. I sighed.

She held up a large piece of glass that it took me a moment to identify. Part of my wineglass. My favorite wineglass. The goblet with the giraffe spots on it. So cute. Damn.

She continued plucking out pieces of broken wineglass until we'd counted five broken out of my set of six. Her face lit up then. She pulled lucky number six unscathed from the box. I guess I didn't pack them well enough. Then again, I hadn't really expected to be chucking the box six feet in the air.

"We have a survivor," I said, as Logek twirled the stem of the wineglass between her fingers.

"Oh no!" Sandy said, when she realized we were inventorying the damage from my fall.

"No biggie," I said. "I got them at Pottery Barn. Not exactly fine china."

"You must be Sandy," Logek exclaimed, jumping up to shake her hand. "I'm Logek, Kate's best friend."

"Very nice to meet you," Sandy said.

"So, I understand you are Adam's mother."

Shit. I was kind of hoping to make it through the day without hearing his name. I guess I sort of assumed Logek would come to that conclusion, given that she knew I bailed at the bar last night after seeing Adam in "contract killer" mode. I had another flash of the petite hottie that had her arm around Adam's waist, a token dangling from her bracelet announcing her signed status. I really needed to work on that *letting him go* thing.

"Yes," Sandy said, smiling like a proud mama. "You know Adam, too?"

"Just through Kate, but yes."

"I wonder where he is," Sandy said, with a glance toward the front door. "I told him I wanted him to help with the move."

Logek must have (finally) caught the chilly look in my eyes, because she quickly replied, "I'm sure he was just busy today. But it looks like we have plenty of help."

Sandy sort of shrugged. Adam was so going to get it later. Mama was not happy that he was a no-show.

"Well, I guess I should start helping," Logek said.

"Me, too," I said, about to push myself to my feet.

"Oh no you don't," Sandy said.

"You do still look a little pale. Just sit a bit longer and see how you feel," Logek said.

So I leaned back on the sofa and watched the bustling activity as everyone (but me) put my little apartment together. My furniture fit perfectly. The decor looked like I'd bought it specifically for this apartment. My tastes were much like Sandy's, apparently. My things were a blend of vintage and rustic, which went perfectly with the wood floors and old-school appliances in the kitchen. No wonder this was Sandy's favorite of her rentals. It was her—classic, lovely, and perfectly stylish. I had a moment of disbelief that this was really my apartment. And I don't think it was falling on my head that gave me the disbelief, thankfully.

Dad and Dave came down from upstairs. "Done with the furniture up there," Dad said. "Logek is putting your clothes away. I assume that's okay?"

I laughed. Silly question. Logek knew my clothes as well as her own and had been familiar with my closet for twenty years. You pick up a lot about someone's organizational techniques in twenty years. Dad winked at me, and he and Dave disappeared outside again.

I'd stopped leaning my head against the back of the sofa, since I was pretty sure I was developing a pretty good goose egg on the back of my head. My phone was sitting next to me on the couch, and it buzzed.

I heard you fell and might have a concussion?

Adam. I ignored the butterflies in my stomach since they had no business being there.

I don't have a concussion.
You sure?
No. Yep. *I'm fine.*
I leave you alone for a day and you practically split your head open.
Pretty sure I still would have managed to fall on my ass even if you had been here.
That's comforting.

Who told you?
Mom.
She feels so bad. Totally not her fault. Tell her.
I did. I told her you're one of the clumsiest people I know.
Thanks?
Lol. Well, you did trip on the rug on your way out of the bar last night.

Wow. Really? We're talking about my hasty (and inept) departure last night? I stared at my phone. I can't do this. I can't talk about last night.

Kate?

Nope.

Dave walked through the door carrying my coffee table. He set it down in front of the sofa and sat down next to me.

"Thank you," I said.

"You're welcome," he said, and he leaned in and kissed me. Nothing indecent, since my parents were walking around the apartment, so he just pressed his soft lips to mine and held them there a moment. When he pulled back, I glanced into the kitchen and saw Sandy watching us. She looked bummed, so maybe Adam was right when he said she'd had hopes of matchmaking the two of us. She may be in for a lot of disappointment if she thinks she's ever going to be successful on matching Adam with anyone.

Logek came bounding down the stairs with a spring in her step and sat down on the coffee table, facing Dave and me.

"Your closet is organized, my lady," she said, with a slight bow of her head.

"Much appreciated."

"Next time I have to move, I am totally spraining my ankle," she said with a decisive nod.

"Yes, my humiliating fall was all part of my master plan to avoid my own move."

She chuckled. Then looked at Dave. "So, Dave, how's it going?"

"Good." He checked his watch. "I've got to head to the station pretty quick."

"It was nice of you to help," she told him.

He tipped his head toward me. "I spend so much time pissing her off—I have to do something to stay in her good graces." And he kissed the top of my head, like he frequently does, I've realized, when he's trying to be sweet. And pacify me.

Logek laughed. "Maybe try pissing her off less and you won't have to work so hard."

"Now there's a thought." Dave looked at me, then back at Logek. "Don't you think we'd make a great couple, though?" he asked her, putting his arm around my shoulders.

When I met Dave, two weeks ago, he struck me as an unrepentant playboy who likely bedded women like it was an Olympic sport. But once I caught on to his BS (and called him on it), we ended up kind of liking the unfettered honesty that we were left with. So we sorta started seeing each other. And despite things kicking off with his open declaration of having the goal of getting me into bed, he did an about-face a week ago and now claims to want an exclusive relationship, which is wrong in more ways than I can count. Not the least of which is that I'm not totally sold on his sincerity. I can't help but wonder if it's part of his game. So, at his mention of the relationship thing again, my eyes rolled back in my head.

Logek smiled. "Wow. You really are good at pissing her off."

Dave quickly looked back at me to catch the spectacular glare I was giving him. Then he made matters worse by going all sweet and sensitive (and yes, probably totally fake) and saying quietly, "I just want to be with you. I don't know why that's a problem." All his sweet gesture did was unleash a flood of contradictions in me, making me somehow flattered and suspicious at the same time.

He pulled me against him, kissing me again, but with added enthusiasm this time. Before he could get too carried away, I leaned away, tipping my head to Logek, who was just sitting in front of us with an amused look on her face. After I pulled back, he released me and stood up.

"I have to get going, baby. Logek," he said, leaning over and giving her a quick hug, "always nice to see you."

"You, too," she said, with a somewhat speculative smile.

I heard Dave kissing ass—I mean saying good-bye—to my parents and Sandy and, with a final wave, he headed out the door.

*

My parents had left, along with Sandy, hours ago. Logek and I were sitting in my kitchen with a glass of wine.

"Congratulations, big girl," she said, with a quick look around my new home.

I grinned. "Thank you very much."

"How's the head?"

"A little sore. Tell me the truth. Did my parents tell you to stay with me tonight and keep me awake in case I have a concussion?"

"That is one possibility."

"I figured. Did you have plans tonight?"

She played with her wineglass . . . part of my mismatched set, now that my one complete giraffe set was busted all to hell. And her evasiveness meant one thing: Derek. Derek, as in the once love of her life, turned heartbreaker, Derek. Derek who breached their contract by sleeping with another woman Derek. And now he was back, full of sincere apologies and regret. And it seemed he was still Logek's kryptonite.

"Logek. I'm not going to judge."

"I know," she said with a sigh. "I'm judging myself."

"Don't. Old habits die hard."

"And that's why I'm still in love with him?"

Well, shit. I nodded.

"It feels like more than habit."

"Did anything happen last night?"

"A kiss. One kiss, and I didn't return any of Daniel's texts today."

Daniel was a new guy she'd recently started seeing, who was apparently about to further the stereotype that nice guys finish last. I didn't know what to say.

"I'm a terrible person," she said matter-of-factly.

"No," I said.

"Yes. I'm going to break Daniel's heart. For no good reason."

"Come on. How serious could you really have been about

Daniel if you were this ready to push him aside? Maybe it's for the best that you figured this out now rather than stringing him along for another six months. And besides, maybe Derek *is* different."

"He seems different. But we know I've never been a good judge of character when it came to him."

"So take it slow. Text. Talk on the phone. Try not to jump back into a physical relationship with him. See how dedicated he seems."

She took a long drink of wine and her blue eyes were shiny. I reached out and grabbed her hand.

"Why are you crying? The love of your life just waltzed back into your life and wants to be with you. It could work." I wished I believed that. *Prove me wrong, Derek. Please, please, please.*

She sniffed. "It could." I could hear it in her voice. She didn't believe it any more than I did. Yet she accepted that she would get drawn back in, as though he were a hurricane she might not survive—brutal, dangerous, and beyond her control. Love sucks.

Her phone buzzed and she checked the screen. She tapped in a reply and looked up at me. She smiled. "I told him I'm on concussion watch."

"I'm glad my clumsiness could be there to save you from yourself tonight."

"Yeah, so what's planned for tomorrow?"

I laughed. "We'll think of something."

"You know, I could ask you the same question. The love of *your* life wants to be with you. What's holding you back?"

The love of *my* life, Jonathan, had turned my world upside down a month ago by informing me that he didn't want to re-up our contract at the end of our seven years, which I'd foolishly taken as a given. I hadn't even considered life without him. Apparently, he'd somehow convinced himself that I'd be willing to take a *break* from our contract for a few years and then reunite and grow old together, or something like that.

After a couple weeks of nursing my broken heart and planning for my new single-girl life, he threw me for another loop when he declared that he'd made a huge mistake and asked if I would sign with him again.

I looked at Logek and shrugged. "I have no answer to that. Having trouble letting go of the hurt and disillusionment, I guess."

"I have no idea what that would be like," she said, heavy on the sarcasm.

"Yeah," I said with a grimace. "Sorry. Your breakup totally wins. Or loses. Whatever. So how are you over it?"

"Derek is my crack. Terrible for my health but irresistible. And I'm not over it."

"But you're still willing to give him another shot?"

"Did you miss my crack metaphor?"

*

Since I'd taken my spill at about 9:30 a.m., by 2:00 a.m. Logek and I figured I was safe from any concussion side effects and she went home (happy that I was now only five minutes away from her place instead of forty).

I climbed the stairs of my new apartment and went into my room. My bed was set up exactly where I would have put it, and all my trinkets were already perfectly arranged on my dressers. I'm not saying people should *try* to get a concussion at the start of moving day . . . I'm just saying, it's crazy the way everything gets done perfectly with zero help from you.

After brushing my teeth, I climbed into my crisply made-up bed. Occasionally, I could hear the sound of a car passing down my street. Welcome to the city. No after-hours traffic in the suburbs where my parents live, that was for sure. But I wasn't in the 'burbs anymore. And there was something exciting about that—about being back in the city.

Of course, that excitement contributed to me staring at the ceiling (and the clock) at 3:00 a.m. It was about 20 percent new-apartment insomnia, 30 percent work related, and 50 percent what-to-do-about-boys. And I missed Jonathan. In my own bed in my new apartment and I missed him more acutely than I had in the month we'd been apart. Whenever I was confused, he was always the one thing that just made sense.

I picked up my phone from the nightstand and stared at it, debating. Screw it. He won't see it till morning anyway. No harm.

I started typing a text to Jonathan, then the phone buzzed in my hand with an incoming text (and it may have scared me enough to drop the phone—so sue me).

It was Dave. Naturally.

Hey beautiful. Can't sleep tonight. Got home from the basketball game I was covering, worked out, watched some TV, thought about you. I know you're probably asleep and won't see this till morning, but just wanted to say I wish you were here. I think if I could wrap my arms around you right now, I'd be able to fall right to sleep.

I lay there in the dark, looking at that text, trying to make sense of things. Obviously sleep found me before any sense did.

CHAPTER 2

The next morning, I got up and started making coffee. There was a little door off the kitchen that led out to a small deck and a postage stamp–size backyard. I opened the door and let the morning air into the kitchen.

I poured some coffee into a mug and wandered from the kitchen into the living room and looked around. I've never lived alone. Logek and I were roommates up until I signed with Jonathan . . . then, from Jonathan, it was back to my parents. It is a little strange being a thirty-four-year-old woman who is just now living by herself.

There was a knock at the door and I looked at the clock above the fireplace. 9:15 a.m. I was in my usual yoga pants and a tank top—no bra. To open the door or not to open the door, knowing that I probably had more than a little nipple show-through happening. Screw it.

I opened the door, and shock undoubtedly registered on my face. Adam. Standing there, frowning a little, looking perturbed. And totally delicious. His hair was a little overgrown, just enough that you could tell he had a little curl in it, and his eyes looked so green against his tan skin. He was in a plain white T-shirt that clung to him in all the right places, jeans, and black leather shoes. His hands were tucked into his front pockets and he was looking down at me, which, when I'm barefoot, seemed like a long way down, even though I'm five foot nine.

"Good morning," I said, cautiously. Not really sure what I did to piss him off. Well, aside from giving him the silent treatment yesterday.

"Good morning."

And then some awkward silence.

"Would you like to come in?" I asked, finally, stepping out of the doorway.

He walked past me and looked around the living room, before turning back to me.

"Looks very nice," he said coolly.

"Thanks."

And silence. Well, this is fun. Apparently we were having a battle of wills to see who could be more stubborn. PS I suck at stubborn.

"You seem upset," I said.

"Good guess."

"Because I never texted you back yesterday?"

"Because you ran away Friday night and *then* ignored me yesterday."

"Oh."

"Care to tell me why?"

Nope. No desire to go there. "No reason."

"Kate. You are a terrible liar. Don't bother."

I shrugged and, regrettably, felt a little choked up. Thinking about him. And that girl. And my stupid, stupid crush.

"Let's sit," I said. I sat on the sofa, leaning forward with my forearms on my thighs.

He looked at me a minute and his mouth quirked a hint of a smile. "You really can't sit like that in that shirt."

I looked down and realized I was giving a splendid view of the goods, clear down to my belly button. I immediately put my hand to my chest, holding the neck of my tank top in, and sat back on the couch. And then, as a bonus, I turned beet red.

"Oops," I said.

"I'm not complaining. And I think I forgot why I was annoyed with you."

I laughed, but I could still feel the heat coming off my face. Adam walked around the coffee table and sat down next to me, turned slightly so that he was facing me.

"I feel like there was more to say Friday," he said. "But you just left. Then you stopped responding yesterday. I'm not okay with you just avoiding me."

Big sigh. My heart started beating faster. It always does that when I'm about to be uncomfortably truthful with someone. Because the truth is scary. I put my hands to my cheeks and they were still flushed.

"Kate."

I turned to him, tucking my feet up under me.

"Adam. I blew it. You were very clear. You couldn't have been *more* clear about not wanting a relationship. Or emotional entanglements. That you just wanted us to be friends." He was starting to frown, his brow lowering over his eyes. "But it didn't work. This," I said, gesturing with my hand between us. "This didn't work. I can't be friends with you."

He just kept frowning and remained silent.

"I care about you, Adam."

"I care about you, too, Kate."

"No. I care about you *too* much. Think about you too much. Want you too much." My chest was getting tighter with every word, and my eyes were burning. I was pushing him away and it hurt even more than I thought it would.

"I think about you a lot, too. I'm obviously attracted to you. That doesn't mean we can't be friends."

"It does for me. I want more, but I can't have more. That makes you confusing and frustrating . . . and painful."

His turn to sigh. "I never wanted to hurt you, Kate. I'm just not capable of that kind of relationship. I'm not wired that way. That's why I was so careful to be up-front about everything with you."

I reached out and covered his hand with mine. "And you were. I knew the rules. Well, my head did. My heart is sort of a pain in the ass who doesn't listen." I smiled. "This isn't your fault. You were fair. But we don't always get to choose whether or not we develop feelings for someone."

He turned his hand over and held mine, caressing it gently. He looked sad and like he didn't know where to go from here.

"I'm sorry, Adam. I wish I could stay friends. I just can't."

He pulled on my hand firmly, drawing me toward him. I didn't exactly fight it. Because, let's be real, it was Adam.

Once I was close enough, he wrapped his arms around me and held me against him. I breathed him in, knowing I'd never be able to smell this soap (or aftershave or whatever the hell it was) again without thinking about him.

It was strange being this close to him and understanding his internal conflict, all the while knowing he wouldn't change. That type of surrender just wasn't an option.

He gripped my chin and tipped my face up to his. Oh, this is all bad. Crossing this line while we're both all emotional like this has the potential to go seriously awry. Probably should stop this. Not gonna. Just saying, I probably *should*.

He kissed me with his typical strength and aggressiveness, holding my face firmly while pressing me against him with his hand on my back. His hand was big enough that it covered most of my cheek and still wrapped firmly beneath my jaw. His tongue ran along my lips before entering my mouth and caressing my tongue. He bit my lower lip lightly between his teeth and pulled it gently between his lips before plunging his tongue back into my mouth.

I moved my hands up his wide shoulders to his neck and slid my fingers into the back of his hair. When his tongue came into my mouth again, I sucked on it, and when I did, things started to escalate. I heard a small grunt escape his throat and he pushed me back down onto the couch and lay down on top of me, never breaking the connection between our lips. His hands slipped under the bottom of my tank top, and before I knew it he was cupping both of my breasts in his hands. The kiss was becoming more intense by the second, and when he pinched my nipples between his fingers, I gasped and arched against him.

In one swift movement, he stripped off my shirt and immediately had his mouth on me. He was rough and passionate in a way that made me dizzy. I could barely catch my breath as he started sucking firmly on one nipple and then the other, but I held his head against me anyway. When I heard the first moans escape my lips, my first thought was to stifle them, but then I remembered that I lived alone now. No risk of Mom hearing me from down the hall.

He moved off me so that he was lying along my side. Just as my head started to clear enough to think about what he was going to do next (and to remind myself that I needed to stop this), he sucked my nipple into his mouth again and bit down lightly, and instantly I was lost again, moaning, writhing, and basically not stopping shit.

He spread his hand across my stomach and slid it beneath the band of my yoga pants and inside my underwear. I could feel his fingers finding their way, and once they did, he slid one big, long finger inside me, forcefully. And I almost came. And that was before he started moving it in and out.

I was falling for him.

Shit. That was a sobering thought. *Because, news flash, Kate: this is going nowhere.*

I pulled his hand out of my pants and scooted away from him. Purely from reflex, I crossed one arm across my bare breasts. *Little late for modesty, genius.* I looked around for my shirt and found it on the floor next to the sofa. I quickly slid it back over my head and sat upright on the couch again. All without looking at Adam. *Come on, girl, sack up.*

I turned and faced him. His eyes were still heated, and I could see the rise and fall of his chest, telling me that he was still breathing heavily. He looked like he hadn't completely given up on the idea of this going further, but after a moment he ran his hand through his hair and sighed.

"Shit. Sorry. I shouldn't have started that," he said.

"Don't be sorry. We both seem to have a problem with getting carried away in the moment sometimes." I shook my head. "I just can't let that happen. Not with you," I said.

"It was happening just fine for a while."

"I know."

"I'm thinking I may have been too hasty in rejecting your suggestion of us being friends with benefits." He smiled at me but he still had the intensity of the moment in his eyes.

"No, I'm pretty sure you called that one right when you said I wasn't a 'meaningless sex' kind of woman." I tucked my shoulder-length brown hair behind one ear. "Adam . . ." Pause. *Out with it, Kate.* "You must have realized by now that I'm falling for you. And if that happened between us—if I slept with you—I'd be gone. And you would break my heart."

He was back to looking sad and stoic again.

At the risk of history repeating itself, I reached out and took his hand again. "I know that I mean something to you—something you don't even really understand. I know that you don't want to hurt me. And sleeping with you would devastate me because I'd fall in love with you. And you wouldn't love me back. You couldn't. So you really don't want to sleep with me, because it would hurt me—and you don't want to do that." I looked down at our hands and felt the first tears prick my eyes. "Because you're you," I said, looking up at him. "And, despite your tough shell, you're a marshmallow inside," I said, pressing my forefinger to his chest. I gave him a smile, but I knew he could see the unshed tears in my eyes.

He nodded. "I wish . . ." he said, but trailed off. I waited.

He started again. "I wish I was different."

"I kinda like you the way you are."

He shook his head.

"I can't be your friend," I said softly. "Why couldn't you have just stayed that arrogant, aloof prick that was trying to get in my pants because I was signed?"

He smiled. "Oh, I'm still that guy."

I laughed, but shook my head. "I just need to remember that you're not *all that* and then I'll be fine."

"I'm *not* all that."

"I know, but you've been doing a damn fine impersonation of it."

He squinted at me like he was going to say something, but decided against it. He just continued watching me in a way that was making me nervous. I couldn't trust myself around him.

"You should probably go."

For a second I didn't think he was going to listen, but then he pushed himself up to his feet and headed for the door. I followed him. He stopped at the door and faced me.

"Good-bye, Kate."

I looked up at his beautiful face and gave myself kudos for somehow managing to push him away before I was completely in over my head. Because I wasn't yet. I think.

I wrapped my arms around his waist and hugged him tightly for a minute. He did the same. I stepped back and he released me.

"Good-bye, Adam."

After a beat, he went out the door, closing it behind him. I leaned my forehead against the cool wood panels of the door and the tears started. I suspected they would last a while.

*

By noon, I'd stopped crying. I'm going to call that a win. I'd called Logek and asked her to come over. She asked no questions, just said she'd be over in an hour. I showered, did my hair, did my makeup. I looked in the mirror when I was done.

Whenever I cry, my eyes look too light, because they contrast against the red around them. Basically, I looked weird. Thankfully, not quite zombie-esque, but not too far off. The makeup helped, but it wasn't magic.

Logek knocked twice and walked in. She came into the bathroom as I was putting my makeup away and unplugging the flatiron.

She gave me a pouty face. "Uh-oh. What's up, Kitty Kat?"

"I'm okay."

"You've been crying."

Yep. Anyone who knew me could tell.

"I broke up with Adam," I said, following it up with a decisive nod.

She smiled, amused. "You broke up with your *friend*?" I nodded again. "And how did he take it?"

"Well, we almost had sex on the couch."

"And?" she asked, loud and animated.

"And I stopped it. I'm falling hard without all the intimacy and mind-blowing sex. Could you imagine if I actually slept with him?"

"How do you know it would be mind-blowing?"

I gave her my best *what a stupid question* expression.

She held up her hands. "Fair enough. So, did you tell him why you were ending it?"

I gave her a nod. "There is absolutely no way for me to stay friends with him without ending up completely . . ."

Logek nodded in agreement with my unfinished statement.

"So," I said, raising my chin up. "My friend, we are officially saving each other from ourselves. Since clearly neither of us has the sense God gave a goat, we are going to stop each other from jumping into the fire."

"Well, you managed to kick your problem child to the curb. I haven't been able to do that."

"Have you slept with him since you left here eleven hours ago?"

"I have not."

"There you go. You're a walking success story."

"I'm supposed to have dinner with him tonight."

"I'll go with you."

Logek had a brief moment where I think she wanted to strangle me. Luckily it passed quickly. "Fine. Derek won't think your tagging along is strange at all."

"I could bring a date?"

"Who?"

Sort of a silly question. There were only two possibilities. And I still didn't trust myself to spend an evening with Jonathan without having a contract signed by the end of the night. "Dave?"

"What is his deal?"

"I have no idea."

"Do you think he's serious about the relationship thing?"

"He's certainly persistent as hell. But who knows. I guess he could be completely faking it."

"But you're usually pretty good at detecting bullshit."

"Usually. Doesn't mean always."

"He definitely treats you like his girlfriend."

"Whether I agree to it or not."

"He's the exact opposite of Adam."

"Tell me about it."

"So, if you love Adam—you know—at least a little, then I'm guessing you are *not* falling for Dave?" she asked.

"I am not. Although I have brief moments when I think

I am falling in *like* with him. He's tall, good-looking, good job."

"Adores you."

"Or is pretty good at pretending he does."

"And has a knack for irritating the shit out of you."

"Oh, that's right," I said. "Sometimes that slips my mind."

"But he also makes you smile."

Just the thought of that did make me smile. I laughed. "True. When he isn't acting like a spoiled brat."

"Have you talked to Jonathan?"

I shook my head.

"Maybe you should bring *Jonathan* tonight and we can both sulk over our good loves gone bad while they attempt to woo us back into the spider's web."

I laughed. "Woo us? Well, that's tempting, but I think Dave is the easier choice. Uncomplicated. I don't worry about it blowing up in my face, like everything else lately."

"Ah. The only one that can't hurt you because you don't care enough. That doesn't sound like much to build a relationship on."

"Good point. But I could start to care. I mean, it's not completely implausible that Dave could eventually get under my skin."

"Then he might stop being the uncomplicated choice."

I shrugged. "I can ram that iceberg if I come to it."

"That's the spirit."

"All I know is that I managed to end one very complicated relationship today. I'm spent. I can't think about spending the evening with Jonathan—I don't have the energy."

"Works for me. Sold to the lowest bidder."

I scowled at her. She deserved it.

*

Dave and I were on our way to the restaurant to meet up with Logek and Derek. When we were close, he started looking around for parking spots. No way I could parallel park this beast. I have enough trouble with my little car. He glided into a snug spot that didn't leave much room in front or behind, but I guess they really don't make spots that would leave much room for this truck.

I turned around and looked over my shoulder at the car behind us. "That's a pretty tight fit," I said.

"Just the way I like it," he said.

I rolled my eyes. "Charming."

"You bet your cute little ass I am."

And I had no response to that so I just got out of the truck.

When I met him around the other side of the truck, he immediately reached out and grasped my hand, smiling down at me.

"You're in an awfully good mood," I said.

"You asked me out on a date. A double date with *your* friends. Of course I'm in a good mood."

I laughed. "Settle down. You didn't win an evening with the Backstreet Boys. Just me."

"Then I did win."

Ugh. So sweet. Too sweet. It was starting to give me a headache.

We walked into the restaurant and headed over to the table where Derek and Logek were already seated. I made the quick intro for Derek and Dave and we all sat down. Derek and Logek, sitting next to each other, had a distinct Barbie and

Ken quality, in that they were both blond and surreally good-looking. Derek's hair hung down to his shoulders and he was just as fit and annoyingly perfect as when he cheated on Logek and breached their contract. Tonight, neither of them seemed able to keep their eyes off each other.

"We took the liberty of ordering a bottle of red and a bottle of white. Hope that's okay," Derek said, as the waiter returned to the table and started uncorking the bottles. He did the typical splash in a glass and waited for Derek to approve. Derek sipped from the glass, uncomfortably, and then nodded at the waiter. Apparently Derek hates that little ritual as much as I do. All I know is that the bottle would have to be pretty bad for me to tell the waiter to take it back, so instead I just feel put on the spot while he stands there waiting for me to taste it.

After the waiter poured the wine for the rest of us, he said he'd give us a few minutes with the menu and left.

There was a tap on my shoulder and I turned to see a familiar face smiling down at me. Neatly trimmed beard, Brawny Man face . . . Oh crap. He was familiar because he was the cheating ex of our client Mario, who (inadvertently) decked me on my first day at the firm, while taking a sloppy swing at this guy. Note to self: when you're in a room negotiating a breach between an angry couple, be ready to duck.

"Ms. Shaw, right?"

"Um. Yes. John?"

John nodded and extended his hand and I shook it. Pretty sure this is a no-no. Opposing counsel, represented party. Definite no-no.

John gestured to a handsome Middle Eastern man next to him. "Fared, this is the attorney Mario punched in the face."

Pretty sure my jaw was hanging open at that intro. Yeah,

John. Right after you admitted to screwing this guy. And now we're all up to speed.

"Glad to see he didn't cause any lasting damage to such a lovely face," Fared said in a deep voice. Wow. Mario and John weren't kidding—Fared was a gorgeous man. He looked past me and his eyes settled on Dave. "Aren't you Dave Hunter?"

Dave immediately went into TV mode and stood, smiling, extending his hand. They shook.

"You are the sole reason I watch channel forty," Fared said. Hm. I wonder how Dave's gaydar is. Is he going to take it as the flirty comment I know it to be or assume Fared is just a die-hard sports enthusiast?

Dave's face was unreadable, but he gestured to the table and asked if they wanted to join us. Damn it all.

All my newbie-lawyer alarms were going off. "Oh, I'm sorry guys," I said, putting up my hands in an attempt to stop everyone in their tracks. "We really can't socialize." I looked at John. "You're represented, and I'm opposing counsel . . . sort of. We really aren't supposed to talk at all without your lawyer present."

"Okay," John said. "I understand. I really figured after punching his own attorney he would have settled this rather than dragging it out longer."

I shrugged. Can't have this conversation with you, John. Pretty sure I covered that.

"You didn't press any charges or anything after he knocked you out?"

"He didn't *knock me out*."

"You were still on the floor when I left."

I cringed. Really? Tact, John. Look it up. "I was fine. It was an accident."

"Well, hitting *you* was an accident."

Sigh.

John leaned in close to me and lowered his voice. "Maybe you should tell him that if he doesn't drop this case and waive the damages for breach, I'm going to go to the DA and tell them I want to bring charges for assault, since he was *trying* to hit *me*."

I touched my finger to the corner of my eye, because I'm pretty sure it was starting to twitch. "That's sort of extortion," I said quietly.

John frowned at the word *extortion*. Most people would. "Well, I'm just saying—"

I cut him off. This was getting out of hand. "Just *don't* say, John. *We* can't talk. This really isn't appropriate."

He made a slightly disgruntled sound and turned and walked away. Fared gave Dave one more long look, smiled at me, and followed John across the restaurant.

I looked at my dinner companions with wide eyes. Turning to Dave, I said, "If it ever seems like I know people through my job, please don't *ever* ask them to join us."

"Sorry, babe. I guess I didn't think." He reached out and covered my hand, which was resting on the table.

Logek was grinning. "I'm *so* glad you went into signing law. You were never this much fun to bring out in public before."

*

Two hours later, Dave was pulling up to my apartment.

"That was fun," he said.

It was. The four of us got along great. Dave and Derek

were both funny, and Dave was only minimally overbearing tonight, so that was a plus.

Dave leaned over and started kissing me, but before he got too far into it, I turned my face to the side a little. Adam was too fresh in my mind to be kissing another guy tonight. After I turned my face, he started trailing kisses along my jawline, and he whispered, "Maybe we should go inside."

Pretty sure that is a bad idea. "Things tend to escalate quickly when we're alone, Dave."

"Mm-hm." He continued his slow, sensual path to my ear before moving to my neck.

"Dave." I pulled back slightly.

He sighed. "I'm crazy about you, Kate, but I can't wait forever."

That made me uncomfortable in an unidentifiable way . . . part pressure, part threat, part compliment. Mostly it pissed me off.

I tilted my head at him. "Excuse me. I'm pretty sure I'm not begging you to hang out with me. If you aren't getting what you need, you are free to do whatever you want, with who-ever you want. I didn't think I needed to remind you of that."

"Well, joke's on me then, because I only want you," he said, narrowing his blue eyes at me.

I raised my eyebrows a little. "It is really irritating the shit out of you to find a woman that's immune to you, isn't it?"

He frowned. "First off, you so are not *immune*. Second, can we drop that bullshit? Yes, I wanted to get you into bed, but I've been pretty clear since then that I have very real feelings for you."

"I don't know what 'real' is to you, Dave."

He shook his head, looking wounded, and I felt bad.

"I'm sorry. That was uncalled for," I said, putting my hand on top of his. "But don't pull that 'can't wait forever' shit on me. I don't appreciate it."

"Fine. I'm sorry, too."

I climbed out of the truck, and by the time I reached my front door, he had driven away.

After climbing into bed, I stared at the ceiling for an hour or so. About ten minutes of insomnia was devoted to Dave's unpredictable temperament, and the rest was a heartbreaking, repetitive replay of my morning with Adam. Good times.

CHAPTER 3

Monday morning at the office I did my typical booting up and logging in and then I went in search of my coworker Brad. He represented Mario, so I figured I should let him know that John had ambushed me at the restaurant last night, plus Brad had agreed to help prep me for taking my very first deposition. I'd been at the firm, Manetti Markson and Mann, for two weeks. Aside from my law school internships, I was an excruciatingly green attorney, so pretty much everything I did was a first for me.

As I reached his office, he was just setting his things down.

He looked up and smiled, pushing his oversized glasses further up on the bridge of his nose. "Hey, slugger." Yet another nod to his client clocking me my first day on the job.

"Hey. How was your weekend?" I asked.

He shrugged. "Uneventful. I'm kind of a homebody." Mags,

my paralegal (and friend), had mentioned that to me, when she finally came clean last weekend about her former liaison with Brad. "How was yours?"

"Interesting. I went to dinner with friends last night and Mario's ex started talking to me in the restaurant."

Brad chuckled. "Uh-oh."

I grimaced. "Is that a major problem? I told him we shouldn't talk, since he was represented and all."

Brad made the universal *eh* expression and shrugged again. "As long as you told him you shouldn't be talking. I'll let Beth know when I speak with her again."

"Okay. And he sort of suggested that he wanted me to tell Mario to drop the case and waive the damages or he'd go to the DA and try to press charges for Mario taking a swing at him."

Brad raised his eyebrows. "Nice."

"Yeah. I may have mentioned that that could be considered extortion."

Brad laughed. "Okay. In that case, I'll give Beth a call today and let her know what her client is up to."

"That was my thought."

"So, when is your depo?"

"Oh. Tomorrow morning."

"Okay. You want to spend some time this afternoon going over it?"

"That would be great."

"Okay. We'll use your office. Your view is better." Pretty sure he's talking about my secretary and not my skyline.

I got back to my office and started going through my email. By the third time I checked my phone to see if I had any texts, I gave myself a mental head slap and put my phone in my purse. In my desk. Stop the madness.

My desk phone buzzed.

"Kate, Rochelle Britton is on the phone," Mags said.

"Okay." Rochelle was my first client, who I was supposed to represent at her child support hearing against her serial philanderer ex, until they suddenly made up. Five minutes before the hearing. Up against the wall outside the courthouse.

I put on my phone headset. "This is Kate."

"Hi, Kate. This is Rochelle Britton."

"Hi, Rochelle. How are you?"

Pause. Uh-oh. I think I heard a sniff. "I don't know. Am I an idiot?"

Pretty sure I'm going to need a little more detail to answer that question. "What's going on, Rochelle?"

As an afterthought, I went into my time sheet and started Rochelle's clock running. I *hate* billable hours, by the way. Me and every other attorney out there who has to clock and charge for every minute of their time.

"I'm worried Richard is cheating."

That's got to be a record, right? One week after getting back together? And thinking that is probably naïve.

"Have you signed a contract?" I asked.

"No. Did Richard's attorney email you a draft?"

"I haven't received anything yet."

"Well, he moved back in, and he *always* has his phone with him."

"Okay," I said. "But lots of people have their phones at all times."

"No, like *always*, Kate. He brings it in the shower with him. He tucks it in a towel and puts it on a shelf so it won't get wet."

"Odd."

"Exactly. He's afraid to leave it lying around where I could look at it."

"Are you sure that's why?"

"Why else would someone take their phone in the shower?"

I got nothing. "I see your point. Well, it's not too late to change your mind."

Now she started crying. I guess I should have seen that coming and been a little more evasive with my response.

"But I love him!"

I sighed and looked down at her timer. Brad was right when he said clients should realize that a therapist would be cheaper than calling your attorney when you're upset.

Rochelle continued sobbing and talking. I wasn't sure how to cut her off. Or if I should.

"Maybe he's not doing anything," she said with a sniff. "Maybe I'm being overly suspicious. But last time I wasn't suspicious *enough,* and look where I ended up . . . with his screwing half the neighborhood! I just want to be able to trust him again. But instead I end up watching his every move— looking for signs."

"Rochelle . . ." I began, but she steamrolled right over me.

"I mean, Kate, I smell his clothes when he's in the shower to see if I smell another woman." Ew. Didn't need to know that. "But I'm worried he's going to see me do it and get upset that I don't trust him."

"Okay, Rochelle. That's not fair. You have every reason not to trust him, and if he's really sorry, he'll work to prove that you can trust him again, not get mad at you for being suspicious." I'd lowered my voice. Not sure how much relationship advice I'm allowed to give out in this job. I'm guessing I shouldn't be playing therapist.

"Exactly," she said, emphatically. "I should tell him he's going to have to prove himself!"

"Absolutely," I said. And it *absolutely* was never going to happen. It would take a miracle for her to ever actually stand up to her ex.

She must have come to the same conclusion, because there was more noisy sobbing after that. I had no idea what else to say. I waited a minute. Gazed out my window. Reached into my purse and checked my cell phone for messages. (Yes, I'm weak. This is not news.)

"Rochelle, maybe give it some time before signing another contract. We can always go back and schedule the child support hearing again and go forward with that."

She sniffed. "Maybe. Maybe we should just proceed. I don't think I can go through this again."

"I understand."

"Go ahead and schedule the child support hearing. I'll tell him I'm not signing again."

"Are you sure?"

She sniffed some more. "Yes. I can't live like this."

Alright. Go, Rochelle. "Okay. I'll call you once we have a hearing date."

"Okay. Thank you, Kate."

"You're welcome, Rochelle. You take care. I'll talk to you soon."

"Bye."

After I hung up with her, I buzzed Mags. "So I guess we're going to need to notice another child support hearing."

"Nice work," Mags said. "I'll update the motion and let you review it. I'll get it served on Dr. Dickhead's attorney today." Mags knew that my uncle Tony (who was also my boss) had nicknamed Rochelle's dentist ex "Dickhead" in all his hand-written notes in the file. Given the list of women Dr. Pope had been sleeping with before Rochelle finally caught on, it did seem fitting.

"Great. Thanks."

Before clocking out of Rochelle's time, I sent a quick email to Dr. Pope's attorney, Doug Simpson, letting him know that it didn't look like the new contract was going to happen and that we were going to go ahead with the child support motion. I wanted to give him notice. I'm guessing surprise attacks don't make friends.

I picked up the Trainor file for my upcoming deposition and started reviewing the notes.

"Kate?"

I looked up, and didn't hide my surprise at seeing Sandy standing in my doorway. With a big box. Oh no.

"Hi," I said, standing and walking over to her.

She set the box down on one of my chairs and gave me a quick hug.

"I'm sorry. Is it okay for me to drop in on you like this? I told Rita at the front desk that I was your landlady and she just walked me over here." Sandy seemed to be channeling Audrey Hepburn today, wearing a black pencil skirt and moss-green blouse that matched her eyes.

"Of course," I said, with a smile. "No problem at all. So . . . what's up?"

"My attorney is in this building and I was there signing some lease documents on some commercial property I have. And I had something for you, so I figured . . . what the heck."

"That is so sweet of you," I said, shaking my head.

She grinned at my approval, picked up the box, and set it on my desk. It was oblong and wrapped in white paper. So sweet. *So* awkward.

I ripped off the paper and opened the box to see items wrapped in brown paper. I plucked one out and carefully unrolled it from the paper. It was a wineglass. A gorgeous wineglass, finely etched with a tiger print design. That, by itself, undoubtedly cost more than my entire broken set.

I looked up at her with wide eyes. "Sandy . . ."

"I'm sorry. I looked. I couldn't find your darling giraffe ones anywhere. But these seemed to have a similar . . . personality." She was smiling, eager for my reaction.

"It is so beautiful. You *really* didn't need to do this."

She waved her hand in front of me in that *no biggie* way. "They're actually different," she said, reaching into the box and unwrapping another glass. She held it up to me. It was etched with a leopard print. Oh my god. So darling.

"These are the cutest things I've ever seen," I said. "They're so much nicer than the ones I had, Sandy. You really shouldn't have."

When I hugged her, she hugged me back hard. I really liked her. Damn you, Adam.

"I'm so glad you like them," she said, her hands still on my arms. She was touchy like that.

"And who's this?" I heard Tony ask.

Shit. Uncle Tony. My inappropriate uncle, who I've wanted to gag on more than one occasion (since you never knew what un-PC thing might come out of his mouth at any moment), and who also happened to be the Manetti in Manetti Markson and Mann. I looked up and he was darkening my doorway, smiling at Sandy. His salt-and-pepper hair was brushed straight back from his forehead and temples and he was more broad than tall in his fancy navy suit.

Ugh. I guess it would be a little difficult to smuggle her out now without them meeting. Maybe he'll be polite and *not* embarrass me. Miracles happen, right?

"Tony, this is Sandy, my landlady. Sandy, this is my uncle, Tony. He's my boss. One of them, anyway."

Tony moved forward to Sandy, extending his hand, doing his charming goombah thing.

They shook hands, but Tony didn't let go right away.

"Very nice to meet you, Tony," Sandy said with a lovely smile.

"The pleasure is mine."

And this is why I need to start keeping a flask in my desk drawer.

"So, you're Kate's landlady?" Tony asked, with a brief glance at me.

"I am." She smiled at me. "I feel so lucky to have her."

"I'd say she's pretty lucky to have you, too," he said, still holding on to her hand.

Ew. Mayday. No flirting. Sandy is perfect. Tony is icky. Must stop this.

"Sandy," I said, stepping between them. "Again, thank you so much for the glasses. You really shouldn't have."

"I'm just so glad you like them, sweetie."

Tony eyed me with a raised eyebrow. He was not appreciating the interference.

"So what do you do, Sandy?" Damn. Tony would not go gently into that good night.

"I used to be a real estate broker, but now I just manage my rental properties. Good lord. At my age, it's enough."

"Your age? What are you? Forty-five?"

Shoot me.

Sandy laughed. "I appreciate the thinly veiled attempt at flattery, but I turned sixty this year."

"It was more than an attempt. You are a beautiful woman."

I need to leave my office. Out the window if necessary. Watching my uncle put the moves on anyone would give me nightmares. Watching him put them on Sandy . . . might give me a seizure.

"Oh my. Thank you, Tony. That is very kind of you."

"I'm sorry. I realize I lost all subtlety some years ago. Life is too short to beat around the bush."

Sandy nodded at him.

"Are you signed?" he asked.

"Um. No."

"Would you have dinner with me?"

Sandy looked at him, wide-eyed.

"I'm sorry," he said, grasping her hand again. "Like I said, I'm no good at subtlety. But if you left and I were foolish enough to not ask . . . I know I'd regret it."

"Well. Um. Okay, Tony. That would be nice."

No! No, it wouldn't be nice. It would be creepy. Like accepting a date from the ice-cream man who also happens to be on the sex-offender registry. Wrong.

Tony was grinning, looking all genuine and un-assholey for once. "If you were on your way out, I could walk with you, get your number so I could call you and set a time."

"Okay," Sandy said. She smiled at me.

Sorry, Sandy. I accept no responsibility for this. If anything, I tried to run interference. But no. You two went right ahead with it like two dumb teenagers. *Yeah. Keep telling yourself that, Kate. Damn right you feel responsible. Sweet Sandy never would have met Lecherous Tony if she hadn't been* here *to see* you. Have I mentioned that I *hate* that my conscience never lets me pass the buck? Like, never?

Sandy reached over and gave my shoulder a tight squeeze. "Talk to you soon, honey."

I smiled weakly and watched them walk out of my office. Crap.

I sat at my desk, thinking about that train wreck I just witnessed. I can't say I know a ton about Uncle Tony's love life, but I know enough to have the impression that he is an unabashed womanizer. And I definitely don't want him womanizing Sandy.

I pulled my phone out of my purse and texted Adam.

I have a valid reason for texting. Not an effort to reopen a can of worms.

I wouldn't have called it a can of worms exactly. How are you Kate?

Oh, Adam. Even through texts you overuse my name, making everything feel more intimate . . . and meaningful.

I'm okay. You?

Okay, true. That's not why I was contacting him. I shouldn't have asked. Hoping that he would say he was just awful and missing me terribly. Definitely not that.

I'm fine.

Damn. That was disappointing. *Okay, Kate. Stop the self-centered thing and get to the point.*

> *So, I just wanted to let you know that your mom came to my office today to bring me a gift (because she is so ridiculously sweet and still felt bad about me falling and breaking my wineglasses) and she sort of met my uncle.*
>
> *Uh oh. Uncle Tony?*

Okay. Can I stop for a second to melt? Because I only complained to Adam about Tony once and he remembered. Of course he did. He's Adam.

> *Yeah. He's kind of a . . . well, shit. I don't really know what he is. But I'm pretty sure he shouldn't be going out with your mom. Your mom is so sweet. I tried to run interference but failed. And they made a dinner date.*
>
> *I see. Well, she is a grown woman, Kate.*
>
> *I know but she's a very sweet grown woman. And Tony is . . . crude. Sexist. Arrogant. Nowhere-near-good-enough for your mom . . .*
>
> *Haha. Sounds like you do know what he is. Okay. I'll touch base with her. I promise. Can't guarantee I can stop it, but maybe I can at least put her on guard.*
>
> *Thank you.*
>
> *Thank you, Kate. It's sweet of you to worry about her.*

I closed my eyes. Counted to ten. No problem.

I may have dropped my forehead on my desk, dramatically, but I was alone, so that doesn't count as being a drama queen, right?

"Kate?"

Brad. Well, naturally.

"Hi," I said, sitting upright again with a fake smile on my face.

"Everything . . . alright?"

"Yep. Super."

He smiled. "Want to review for the depo?"

"God, yes."

He laughed. "That's a little too much excitement for depo prep."

"And, yet, it's exactly what I need at the moment."

"A little sad, but I'll let it slide."

"Thanks."

"Okay, well let's review the main facts and decide what you need to get her to tell you tomorrow."

I smiled. Then had a brief *aww* moment when he not-so-inconspicuously glanced over his shoulder toward Mags's desk, where she was standing, reading something. Her dark hair was back-brushed into a slight bouffant and she was dressed in her typical take-no-prisoners fashion, all bright colors and curves.

Mags may have ended things, but Brad clearly hadn't moved on. She looked up and smiled at us before sitting back down, out of sight. Brad sighed—or maybe I sighed for him . . . hard to say.

After Brad and I had spent a productive hour or so going through the critical points of the case, he gave me a quick little pep talk about what a great job I was going to do in the depo tomorrow, before heading back to his office.

I made myself a few more notes for the depo, and then picked up my phone when it buzzed.

It was a Facebook notification. I had a friend request . . . from Rochelle. I frowned at the screen. I mean, I liked Rochelle, but it seemed a little odd to be *Facebook friends* with a client. I post pictures of my weekend shenanigans there, for god's sake.

With my phone still in my hand, I walked back over to Brad's office.

"Knock, knock," I said, leaning into his doorway.

"Hey. Did we miss something?"

"Oh. No. I was just curious. What do you do when you get a friend request on Facebook from a client?"

He frowned through his big glasses. "You're kidding. One of your clients sent you a friend request?"

Perfect.

CHAPTER 4

By the time I got home that evening, I was fried. I pulled a bottle of wine from the rack, opened it, and poured myself a glass. I turned on the oven and tossed in a pan that I'd been marinating chicken in all day.

After changing my clothes, I came downstairs again and went into the kitchen. I put my hand against the stove. Cold. Dammit. I just wanted some chicken and it feels like the universe is conspiring against me. I put the chicken back into the fridge and picked up my phone to call Sandy.

"Kate! How are you?" Sandy asked, after picking up on the first ring.

Her delight at getting a call from me melted away some of my grumpiness, and I actually found myself smiling. "Wonderful, Sandy. How are you?"

"Right as rain. So what's going on, honey?"

Now I felt bad, spoiling her mood by just calling with a problem. "Well, my oven won't turn on."

"Oh no! Is your pilot light lit?"

Pilot light. I know *what* it is, I just don't technically know *where* it is. Or what it would look like if it was lit.

Apparently my delayed response gave me away. "Don't you worry, sweetheart. It's probably just the pilot light. I'll send someone right over to check it for you."

"Thank you so much. Sorry to be a pain."

"Oh, heavens. You just moved in and your oven isn't working. I'd say that warrants a phone call."

I laughed. "Thanks, Sandy. I really appreciate it."

"Okay. Call me back if there is any problem getting it fixed."

"I will. Good night."

I sat down on my sofa, feeling immeasurably lighter than when I first got home.

About ten minutes later, there was a knock at my door. I looked down, glad that I'd left my bra on, since it was normally the first thing to come off at the end of a long day. I was in shorts and a tank top, but at least I was "handyman appropriate." If that's a thing.

I opened the door and it felt like the earth literally shifted. Adam was standing there. Looking a lot like he did yesterday when we ended up on the couch. Jeans, white T-shirt. Too beautiful for words.

And he could read all that in an instant, I was pretty sure, by the gentle look on his face.

"Adam." Way to go. No. Seriously. I deserve props for getting that much out, considering I thought maybe I'd just faint, instead. "I wasn't expecting you."

"That much is obvious, Kate. Can I come in?"

The confusion must have registered on my face, because he lifted a black duffel bag in his hand so that I could see it. "My mom said your oven won't turn on."

Oh! Shit. Handyman. Sandy's son. "Oh, I'm sorry. Yes, come in," I said, hastily moving aside. "I had no idea Sandy was going to bother you. I'm sorry."

"It's no trouble. You know I'm always nearby."

Yeah, don't remind me. Because there's no need, since that thought crosses my mind almost daily.

He had a healthy five o'clock shadow going and his hair was a little unruly. But, on him, clean-cut or overgrown, it all worked. It was really just a difference of whether he looked like an Armani model or an Abercrombie one.

He frowned a little and I realized that I'd been staring at him, saying nothing. "So, what's on your mind?" he asked.

I shook my head, gave myself a mental slap across the face. *Snap out of it, girl.*

He gestured toward the kitchen. "Can I take a look?"

I nodded. Seriously. When did I get this tongue-tied around him? I let out a sigh, which for me seems to have the effect of mentally rebooting my brain when I'm flustered.

"Yeah, sorry. So, I came home and turned on the oven for about fifteen minutes, and nothing," I said.

He opened the oven and crouched down in front of it. His T-shirt lifted away from his jeans a little, offering me a glimpse of his smooth, bronzed back. Which I'm totally not allowed to touch. No touch. He fiddled with the knobs on the stove while watching the inside of the oven.

"Yeah. It's probably the pilot light." He reached into his bag and pulled out a few things. He smiled up at me. "I'm out of long matches, so I need to be creative." He took out a screwdriver and a wooden match and proceeded to tape the match around the end of the screwdriver. Then he rooted around in the oven some more and eventually pulled out a small plate over the bottom of the oven. "There it is," he said. Using a second match, he lit the match taped to the screwdriver and reached the screwdriver into the back of the oven. In a few seconds, I saw a small blue flame begin to burn.

"There you go," he said, blowing out the match. Then he replaced the tray he'd pulled aside across the bottom of the oven. He reached up and turned on the knob for the oven, and things lit up and came to life. Adam has a way of making things come to life in his hands.

"Come here," he said.

Huh? I must have looked confused, because he laughed.

"Squat down for a second and I'll show you where you light the pilot."

Ah. Of course. For educational purposes. Stupid educational purposes.

I squatted down next to him. He was broad enough that I couldn't get a view of the oven without our shoulders touching. And our arms. Legs. Not that I was cataloging or anything. He reached in to move the plate on the bottom of the oven, and when he did, I lost my balance and started to fall back.

Adam reached over and grasped my upper arm to steady me and we ended up in a pseudoembrace. That did *absolutely* nothing for me. Promise.

"Oops," he said, steadying me. "Sorry."

"No problem."

Adam's tutorial on where to look for the pilot light and how to light it were reduced to a sort of buzzing in my brain due to our proximity. I just tried to nod at the appropriate times so that it seemed like I was paying attention like a good little student.

When he was done, he stood and reached down for my hand and pulled me back to standing. Standing way too close to him.

I smiled and took a not-so-subtle step back. Well, it was either that or jump him. I took the high road.

"Thank you so much," I said with a smile. "Sorry you came over for something so minor. Guess I should know how to do that, huh?"

He made a slight smile and looked at me a little too intently. "I really don't mind. It's good to see you. Since I apparently need an excuse now."

"Well, I appreciate it. Can I at least offer you dinner? Nothing special, but I was about to make some chicken."

He gave me a skeptical look.

"What?" I asked. "I can totally cook chicken."

He chuckled. "I just wasn't sure me staying for dinner would fit within Kate's Rules of Conduct."

Well, that was definitely true. But didn't showing gratitude to someone who helped you out trump your personal rules for self-preservation?

I'm going with yes.

I smiled. "I'll make an exception, since you did me a favor."

"I accept, then."

"Glass of wine?" I asked, holding up my own glass for reference.

"What are you drinking?"

"No idea. I just grabbed the first bottle I saw and went with it," I said, with a severe look and a raised eyebrow.

He folded his arms across his chest. "Hm. Wine roulette. Look at you, being all reckless and crazy," he said.

"Hey, I didn't choose the thug life—the thug life chose me."

Adam burst into laughter, causing me to grin stupidly, which led us to stare at each other too long. Houston, we have a problem.

He broke the tension for us by clearing his throat and saying, "Whatever you're drinking will be fine."

"Good choice."

I put the chicken back into the oven and adjusted the temperature to 350 degrees. Then I grabbed the bottle of wine and poured a second glass and handed it to Adam.

"Thank you," he said.

"Thank *you*," I said, with a nod at my now-working oven. "So. How's things at work?" Adam was a rock star marketing exec at a large advertising firm downtown called Samson and Tule.

"Great." He looked down at the table, smiling, and smoothed a napkin on the table. "I'm actually up for partner."

"Adam, that's amazing!"

"Thanks," he said, grinning at me. He looked down at the table again, like he was shy—which would be a first for Adam Lucas. Around me, anyway. Then I realized . . . this was big to him. Not just that he was up for this promotion, but that he wanted to tell *me* about it. He wanted me to be proud of him for his accomplishment. This realization tied me up into one big butterfly-encrusted knot. So I just looked at him with a stupid expression for a minute, certain that my face was flushed. I wanted to grab his hand, but we sort of have a dangerous history with spontaneous physical contact.

"When do you find out?" I asked.

"Next couple of weeks."

"I'm sure you've got this. You kick ass over there."

"I don't know. I'd be the youngest partner ever at the agency."

Screw the danger. I reached across the table and gripped his hand. "You deserve it. I'm sure your bosses think so, too."

He squeezed my hand. "Thank you, Kate. So, how's your work going?"

"It's so amazing," I said, doing my best Stepford wife impersonation, complete with wide eyes and a Xanax smile. "Turns out I was completely wrong to not want to go into signing law. I really think it's my calling."

Adam clapped his hands softly a couple of times. "Are they giving out awards for sarcasm yet? 'Cause, I'm pretty sure you're due."

"I'd like to thank the Academy . . ." I said, with a hand to my chest.

He laughed and shook his head. "But," he began, with emphasis, "it's only been a couple weeks. You're going to be so good at it that you may end up enjoying it by accident."

"I like your optimism, even if I don't share it," I said, tapping the edge of my glass to his.

"How's Logek doing?"

I gave a one-lip-curl grimace. "Her archnemesis has returned and is attempting to woo her."

"Her archnemesis?"

"Yes. The one man in Logek's history who she completely lost herself in—right up to the point where he cheated on her and left her for another woman."

"Ouch. And now he wants another shot?"

I nodded.

Adam gave a little head shake. "It's funny. People don't picture women that look like you two having any man trouble. But somehow you manage to find your share."

I admit. I got a slight heart flutter when he lumped me in with "women like Logek," since Logek fell into my definition of drop-dead gorgeous. "Well, in most of Logek's man trouble, she's the one making trouble. But there's *one* guy that manages to repeatedly wrap her around his finger. And she's been burned."

"Just one guy?"

"They say everyone has one . . . that one person that you never get over . . . never get past. Your one big 'what if' in life."

He nodded at me, thoughtfully, in a way that gave me butterflies. "I get that. But if he's the one burning her, maybe he's not *that* one."

"That's an awfully romantic sentiment for a self-declared cynic like you," I said, smiling gently.

"Good point. You're a bad influence on me."

I laughed. "I doubt your mother would agree with that."

"True. My mother is an incurable romantic. Why do you think she sent me over here tonight?"

I raised my eyebrows. "Is she still trying to play matchmaker?"

"Not openly, but I find her motives suspect."

My mouth hung open a little. "She saw Dave over here when I moved in and I figured she assumed we were a thing and had given up."

"Are you a thing?"

That question hit me like a high-speed, sudden freeway exit, like when you've almost missed your turn. It took me a minute to shift gears.

"Um. No. But he's doing his best to complicate the hell out of it."

"How so?"

Really? I'm going to talk about boys? With Adam? Well, sure. This makes perfect sense.

"Uh. I . . ." Can't really talk to you about this, apparently.

"What?"

"It's just weird talking to you about this, Adam," I said, frowning.

"But we're friends," he said. "Regardless of how you've tried to complicate it." When I hesitated, he added, "Come on. Lay it on me."

I sighed. Over many, many things at that moment. "It's just hard. He says he wants a relationship. At first I thought he was just playing his game, but now I'm not so sure. He may actually believe he has feelings for me."

"Not sure why that seems so far-fetched," he said.

"Because he is a player. Like a *play-er*." Not sure why enunciating the syllables changed the meaning, but it made sense to me. "And he's almost as damaged as . . ." Oops. And I may have trailed off before finishing my thought, but it wasn't lost on Adam.

"As me?"

"Sorry."

"Don't be, Kate. I know the score. But if my being damaged doesn't bother you, then why does his?"

"His just seems more . . . mean-spirited. Like, he's got a little bit of a mean streak I catch a glimpse of now and then. You don't have that. You may have all your hang-ups, but you're never cruel. It would never even occur to you to be intentionally vindictive."

I was watching him intently, so he just shrugged. "Don't underestimate me, Kate. I can be *way* vindictive."

I laughed. "Whatever. You're a sheep in wolf's clothing."

He looked at me for a minute. "Pretty sure believing that is the last mistake the sheep ever made."

Then he seemed a little deep and broody. He believed he was the wolf.

I retrieved the bottle of wine from the counter and refilled both our glasses with the second half of the bottle. "So, did you warn your mom about my uncle's questionable intentions?" I asked.

Adam chuckled and took a drink from his newly filled glass. "I told her that you found him to be inappropriate and a little sexist. She didn't seem overly concerned by this discovery."

"Hm. Does your mom date much?"

Adam looked down at his glass. I don't think he cared for this part of the conversation. I wasn't sure he'd answer, but then he looked up at me and shook his head. "I don't think she ever got over my dad."

Oh. Well, if he's anything like Adam, I guess I could understand that. And there's probably a lesson to be learned about falling for a Lucas boy, losing him, and never getting over it. I'll be sure to take that to heart. Since I'm oh-so-good at taking my own advice.

"Kate," Adam said quietly, leaning toward me a little.

"Yes?" I asked, unconsciously mimicking his movements and leaning in a little as well.

"I think you might be cremating the chicken."

Cremating the chicken. Cremating . . . Shit! I jumped out of my seat and went to the oven, which now had tendrils of smoke slipping elegantly from the door. I turned the oven to Off before opening the door and letting the cloud of smoke fill the tiny kitchen. Adam had gone and opened the door to the back porch and propped the door open. He came back and picked up a paper bag from the counter and began fanning the smoke out of the kitchen. I wondered if it would be enough to keep the smoke detector from going off.

Why do I bother to ask myself these questions?

The smoke detector immediately started blaring with alternate high and low tones, both equally annoying. I grabbed a bag and began trying to help Adam fan the smoke away from the alarm, but the damn thing wouldn't turn off. Adam rushed back into the kitchen and began opening drawers until he found a couple oven mitts. After slipping them on, he grabbed the pan of chicken from the oven and took it out onto the back porch. And, for the most part, the smoke seemed to follow him. He set the pan down on the porch railing farthest from the door and came back inside. He was grinning at me when he grabbed his bag and, once again, began fanning the smoke toward the back door.

I was smiling back at him because I knew I wasn't going to hear the end of this from him and because this was the most fun I'd ever had giving my dinner a Viking funeral. In a moment, the room went silent. After minutes of the deafening alarm, the sudden quiet was equally deafening.

Adam started laughing, and I joined him.

"Okay, note to self," he said, with a relaxed, happy expression. "Kate can't cook."

"Kate can totally cook," I replied. "Just not when she's distracted, apparently."

He gestured toward the stairs. "Go. Get dressed. I'm taking you to a five-star restaurant for dinner."

We looked at each other a minute, and then I turned and headed upstairs. I threw on some jeans and my Converse (not the worn-out white ones—those went to Converse heaven after my spectacular fall) and put on my favorite plain white T-shirt with the V-neck that was a hint of sexy without trying too hard. I headed back downstairs and he chuckled when he saw me.

"Will this do?" I asked, making a flourish with my hands.

"You're absolutely perfect." He gripped my elbow lightly and guided me to the door.

"Oh. Let me grab my purse."

"You won't need it."

"Okay. How about at least my keys, so I can lock up."

"Fine. Hurry up. I'm hungry."

I dashed back to the kitchen table, grinning like a twelve-year-old. I grabbed my keys and started to reach for my phone. Nah.

I followed him outside and locked my front door behind me.

"Oh! Did you lock the back door?"

"Yep," he said, opening the passenger door of his black Audi for me. I slipped into the soft leather seats and couldn't help but recall the last time I'd been in his car . . . the night he'd rescued me from the signing party and I'd spent the night on his sofa. Which was obviously the start of all of my Adam woes. And, right now, I couldn't seem to mind. Woes, shmoes.

He got into the driver's seat and started off into the night. I didn't ask where we were going. I can honestly say I didn't care. Which for an overthinker like me was a pretty big deal.

I turned my head a little and realized that I could smell smoke on my hair. "Uh-oh."

"What?"

"My hair smells like dinner. I mean the dinner I killed."

"Don't worry. Where we're going, you won't be able to smell anything else."

I narrowed my eyes at him but still didn't ask. Still didn't care.

A few miles away, Adam pulled in to In-N-Out Burger and headed for the drive-through.

"Drive-through, huh?"

"Best food in town."

"No argument here. Glad I dressed appropriately."

"I told you you were perfect."

We smiled at each other.

"My treat. Whatever your heart desires," he added.

No, Kate, he's not offering that. Pretty sure he's not on the menu. Damn. "Double-Double with fries, please. And a chocolate shake."

"I love a woman that doesn't hold back," he said with a chuckle. When he got to the speaker, he ordered the same thing, but with a vanilla shake.

"You're right—this will be perfect. I'll smell like In-N-Out for days."

"Be sure to carry your mace," he said. "You know how guys are when they smell In-N-Out Burger."

"Good point. Thanks for the reminder."

We got up to the window, he passed over some cash, and we were handed our bag of delicious-smelling hamburger-heaven goodness along with a couple of icy milkshakes. Adam knew how to show a girl a good time, that was for sure.

I peeked inside the bag, out of habit. Two burgers, two fries. Gotta be sure not to get screwed at the drive-through.

"So," I said, rolling the top of the bag down to keep the food warm. "Are we eating at my place?"

"Nope. I have something more scenic in mind."

Not to overdo it or anything, but the view in this car right now? Pretty damn scenic.

We drove in silence for the next several minutes, until Adam turned down a quiet, dark road that dead-ended at a space along the river with a great view of the bridge.

"Ooh, pretty," I said with a smile.

"I agree," he said, smiling at me. He held out a hand to me. Come on, give me a little credit. I knew he was just asking for his burger.

I opened the bag and handed him his half of the order. We both chowed down and enjoyed the starlit view in silence.

Adam took a napkin and swiped it across his mouth before talking. "I'm a little surprised my mom hasn't called you yet to make sure we got your oven working."

"Oh. I didn't bring my phone. Then again, she might not want to interrupt, in case we were in the middle of proclaiming sweet, sweet love for one another."

"Good point," he chuckled in a low voice. "She's probably thinking no news is good news." Then he tipped his head a little at me. "So, no phone, huh? Aren't you worried some of your adoring fans might be trying to get in touch with you tonight?"

"They can wait till I get home. You're my only adoring fan tonight."

"Works for me," he said with a quiet laugh, and rested back against the headrest.

I crumpled up the paper from my burger and put all the

trash back into the bag. Took a quick swig of my milkshake and relaxed into the seat, watching the bridge.

Adam reached over and took my hand in his, interlacing our fingers. "We're not going to overthink this," he said quietly.

So I said nothing.

"And we're not going to ask what it means," he added, turning his head to me. It was too dark in the car to see the green of his eyes, but his face was beautiful, nonetheless. His voice was low and a little husky. "Because I know we're just friends. Or not friends. Or whatever the hell we're supposed to be. But we're here. And I don't know how to sit here in this car with you, like this, and not hold your hand."

In response, I just gave his hand a light squeeze.

He turned his eyes back toward the bridge. I tried to focus on the view, as well, but his thumb was tracing soft circles on the back of my hand and that was making it hard to think of anything else.

Except "mayday," that is. *This, Kate. This is why you told him you could not be friends with him. Nothing has changed.* And I'll be damned if my useless little attempt at distancing myself from him yesterday didn't just make my stupid little heart even fonder. All bad. Okay. One night. After this, things will go back to the way they were and I won't be hanging out with him. Or falling hopelessly in love with him. Or any of that stuff.

So just enjoy tonight, because who knows when you'll see him again.

Then I realized he was looking at me. "So much for not overthinking this, huh?" he asked quietly.

"Not really a strength of mine," I said.

"I have noticed that."

"Sorry."

"Don't be. If people start apologizing for *thinking,* it could mean the downfall of our entire civilization."

I laughed. "I don't think I can handle that responsibility."

He smiled. Then sighed. "So, you're still determined that we can't be friends?"

I held up our clasped hands between us. "More than ever."

"Dammit, Kate," he said softly, putting a finger and thumb to the bridge of his nose. "Can't you just . . . *not* . . . fall in love with me?"

I laughed again. "And that seems like such a simple request, right?"

He smiled somberly. "It should be."

"Have you met *you*?"

Now he laughed. "Have you met *you*? You could do *way* better."

"Well, that's probably true," I said with a chuckle.

"Ouch."

I leaned my head against the rest again and turned toward him. "So, I could do better, huh?"

He nodded.

"I'm not sure what 'better' looks like."

"Someone who adores you."

"Adam. Are you kidding me? You freaking *adore* me."

"Shit. That is true. So how about someone who believes in commitment as much as you do."

"Easier said than done," I said, narrowing my eyes. "*Or,* you could just fall in love with *me* and then that would also solve our problem."

He smiled at me in a way that knotted my insides. "If I was capable of falling in love, Kate, which I'm not, it would be with you."

I frowned. "Oh. Well, that's sweet . . . and depressing all at the same time."

He let go of my hand and reached out to push-start the car's ignition. "I'm not giving up on our friendship, though."

Perfect. That should make my goals of self-preservation a piece of cake. I am so screwed. And not the *Oh yay, sexy time* kind.

CHAPTER 5

I walked into the conference room at 8:30 the next morning to meet with Jim Trainor prior to his ex and her attorney arriving. Jim was tall and bulky with the ruddy complexion that suggested he might be a heavy drinker. He stayed seated and watched me walk to the table, squinting at me like he was about to guess my wrestling weight class.

"Jim? I'm Kate Shaw. I'll be working with Tony on your case."

"You look a little young."

"Looks can be deceiving." Which was true. For all he knew, I could have been practicing for nine years already. Clearly I *haven't*. But I could have.

"Fair enough."

"So. I've reviewed your file and it seems like this thing sort of hinges on time line."

"Yeah. Jennifer is trying to say that she only started fucking her coworker because she was terminating the contract, but she didn't know she had grounds to terminate when they started hooking up."

"And you're sure of when they started?"

"Yeah. It was about the time she stopped having sex with me."

"Did she admit it to you?"

"Of course not."

"So do you have any proof of when it started?"

"She started working longer hours."

"Well, probably still not definitive proof for us to use. So, since the contract has a provision allowing a partner to cancel the contract and receive damages if the other partner is convicted of a crime, she's claiming that she only started sleeping with the other guy since she was canceling the contract based on your breach."

"Obviously."

"And you were convicted of driving under the influence?"

"No."

Okay. Sarcasm. "Jim, I'm just reviewing the facts to make sure everything in the file is correct."

"Fine. Yes. DUI."

Gee, he's pleasant. "So you didn't tell Jennifer about it right away?"

"Fuck no. I've got five years left on this contract, and the damages are set for each year remaining. That's a lot of fucking money."

"So when *did* you tell her about it."

"I didn't. She went through my mail and saw a certificate of completion for the DUI course I had to take."

"And then she confronted you?"

"Yeah."

"When?"

"About six weeks ago."

"Okay, so if she started cheating more than six weeks ago—"

"She did," he interrupted.

"Right. As long as we can *prove* she started cheating more than six weeks ago, you'll be in good shape."

I heard Rita's voice behind me.

"Kate, Jennifer Roma and her attorney are here. Shall I bring them back?"

"Yes. Thank you, Rita."

The court reporter came in ahead of them and apologized for being late. She handed me her card and busied herself setting up her equipment.

Jennifer Roma walked into the room ahead of Rita, with Doug Simpson trailing behind her.

"Kate," Doug said, extending his hand to me. "Good to see you again."

"You, too." Doug Simpson and I met for the first time when our clients went MIA at their court hearing (which pissed off the judge), and we found Rochelle and Dr. Pope making out against the courthouse building like horny teenagers. So, although Doug and I were opposing counsel, we obviously bonded over that fiasco. In team building, I believe they call that the "severity of initiation."

"This is Jennifer Roma."

"Nice to meet you, Ms. Roma," I said.

Once the court reporter gave us the go-ahead, I went through my checklist of admonitions. For good measure, I also told her that, given the nature of the conflict, I was going to have to ask some very personal questions and she was going to have to answer them truthfully.

Brad walked in and I introduced him around and he sat at the end of the table. His being here made me both more nervous and more calm. Nervous because I had an audience if I was going to look like an idiot, and calm because I'd have someone telling me during break which questions I missed and needed to ask. Let's hear it for double-edged swords.

I took Jennifer through the standard history—her education, jobs, stuff like that—then got into the time line for the contract with Jim.

"So, Ms. Roma, when did you find out about Jim's DUI conviction?"

"A couple of months ago."

"So, March?"

"I don't remember exactly."

"Do you remember if it was before or after Easter?"

She seemed to think about it. "Before."

"So . . . March?"

"Yes."

"How did you find out?"

"I saw a receipt for a DUI class he took."

"Was it this receipt?" I slid the paper across the table to her.

"Yes. That's it."

"Madame Reporter, please mark this as Exhibit A." The court reporter took the receipt and affixed a sticker to it and logged it into her book. Once she was done, I passed it back to Jennifer.

"Okay, so this is the receipt you found that alerted you to Jim's DUI?"

"I already said it was."

"Could you read the course completion date at the top, please?"

Jennifer scanned the document. Then her expression turned sour. "April eleventh."

"So would you agree that this was probably mailed after that date?"

"Yes."

"So you found out about Jim's DUI sometime *after* April eleventh?"

"I guess so."

"Well, you did say you found out based on this document, right?"

"Right."

"So it would have had to have been after April eleventh, right?"

"Yes." Yes! The elusive unequivocal yes (that you rarely ever get from deponents)! *Okay, don't get cocky.*

"And, based on that, you determined that you were going to end the contract?"

"Yes."

"Do you currently have a physical relationship with one of your coworkers?"

"You know I do." Charming. Shame these two crazy kids couldn't work it out, because they seem to deserve each other.

"I realize that, but I do need it on the record," I said, politely, nodding toward the court reporter. "Who is that coworker?"

"His name is Anthony Muir."

"How long have you worked with Anthony?"

"I don't know."

"You said that you have worked at the company for eight years, correct?"

"Yes."

"Was Anthony there when you started?"

"Yes." Asshole.

"So . . . again . . . how long have you worked with Anthony?"

"I guess about eight years."

Don't let her rile you. That's her goal. I glanced at Doug, and he looked like he might doze off. Not exactly a rigorous advocate.

"When did your romantic relationship with Anthony begin?"

"I wouldn't say it's all that romantic."

Mental sigh. "When did your *sexual* relationship with Anthony begin?"

"I don't remember." Of course you don't.

"Which of you instigated the physical relationship?"

"I don't remember."

"Have you ever been signed before?"

"No."

"Have you ever had boyfriends in the past?" I glanced at Doug to see if he was going to object to my little fishing expedition. Guess not.

"Yes."

"Have you had sexual relationships with other men while you had a boyfriend?"

"Never." Perfect. That was exactly the indignant response I was looking for.

"So this is the first time you've had a sexual relationship at the same time you were in a committed relationship?"

"Well, I knew my contract was over."

"Had you told Jim your contract was over?"

"No, I don't think so."

"No? Or you don't think so?"

"No."

"So you really hadn't *ended* your relationship with Jim when you started having sex with Anthony, correct?"

"Not really."

"Did you feel guilty?"

She stared at me. "No. He breached first."

Hm. Sticking with that story.

"Where were you the first time you kissed Anthony?"

She glanced over at Doug, but he just watched, expressionless.

"At the office."

"And where were you the first time you had sex?"

"I don't remember." Oh, please. As if.

I raised my eyebrows. "Were you in a bed?"

"Yes."

"Your bed?"

"No."

"His bed?"

She pressed her lips together. I could see on her face that she was concerned she had just cornered herself.

"Ms. Roma, were you in Anthony's bed?"

"No."

"Were you at a hotel?"

"Yes." There it was. Paper trail. That's what she's panicking about.

"Which hotel?"

"I don't remember." Naturally.

"Did you pay for the room?"

"No."

"Did you drive there together?"

She frowned at me. She was unsure about giving away so many details. "I don't remember."

"You don't remember if you met him there or drove with him?"

"No."

"Did you plan to have sex once you got there?"

"No."

"So, you were going to a hotel, but you didn't think you would have sex with him once you were in the room?"

"I don't know. I guess I knew it was a possibility."

"So when you were in the room, did you initiate the physical contact?"

"I don't remember."

"Then it could have been you who initiated the sex?"

"No. I mean, I don't think so. I really don't remember."

"Did you kiss?"

"Yes."

"And then did you take off your clothes or did he?"

She was back to frowning, trying to figure out where I was going with this. "I don't remember."

"So it may be that you stripped off your clothes after the kissing?"

She looked confused, but, as I'd hoped, she didn't want to look like the aggressor in the scenario. It was basically irrelevant to her claims, but she didn't know where I was going with it—only that I seemed to *want* her to be the aggressor, which made her want the exact opposite.

"No. In fact, he did. Now I remember, because he had trouble getting my boots off. And I had to help him with my shirt because it was a turtleneck and I was afraid he'd tear it."

"Okay. So you were in a turtleneck and boots?"

Her face went blank.

"Ms. Roma? You've just said that you were wearing a turtleneck and boots that he took off of you. Is that correct?"

"I guess. I'm not sure."

"Madame Reporter, could you read back her last statement?"

The court reporter started to read it, but Jennifer cut her off. "I know what I said. Yes. I think that is what I was wearing."

"So perhaps you were dressed for winter?"

Jennifer stared daggers at me.

"Ms. Roma? It sounds as though you were dressed for winter weather. Was this perhaps back in January or February?"

"No."

"No?"

"I don't believe so."

"You don't *believe* so. So it *could* have been in January or February?"

"No."

"It couldn't have been?"

"No."

"What are you wearing today, Ms. Roma?

She glanced down at her clothes. "A skirt and a tank top."

"And your shoes?"

"Sandals."

"Nice day today. It's supposed to be about eighty-five degrees."

She shrugged.

"Would you agree that we had an unseasonably warm spring this year?"

"I don't know."

I glanced at Doug to see if he'd object that I was asking her to speculate . . . or any of the several other objections that might have applied, since I was asking Jennifer to give a weather report. He was quiet. Thanks, Doug.

"But if we went back and looked, would you agree if the statistics showed that, since April eleventh, most days have been around eighty degrees?"

"I'm not the fucking *Farmer's Almanac*."

"Of course. That's why I suggest that we actually refer to a record of the daily temperatures since April eleventh of this year."

She was pissed. Her face looked flushed and I think she may have been breaking a sweat.

"Ms. Roma, is it possible that this encounter at the hotel where you and Anthony had sex was actually prior to April eleventh, when the weather was cooler?"

She glanced at Doug, who looked concerned but remained silent. She turned back to me and didn't answer.

"Madame Reporter, could you repeat the question for Ms. Roma?"

The court reporter looked for the spot on the transcript, but, again, Jennifer cut her off before she could read the question aloud. "I heard the fucking question."

"Answer, please."

"It could have been."

"It could have been what?"

"I may have met up with Anthony before April eleventh."

"So you may have had sex with Anthony before you found out about Jim's conviction?"

And if looks could kill, I'd be dead. "Maybe."

"You've said that you don't recall the name of the hotel?"

"No."

"Was it in town?"

"I don't recall."

"You don't recall if you drove out of town or not to have sex with a man who was not your partner?"

"I don't have to answer these questions," she seethed.

"Actually, you do. If you don't, I'll get a court order instructing you to answer."

"I think it was in town." She knew that we would be scouring all of the local hotels, looking for their check-in, and that, once we had it, we'd have proof that her affair started before she found out about Jim's DUI. It wasn't going to give Jim damages or anything, but when both partners breach, it means nobody gets damages. And that's the win I was after.

*

Once we'd wrapped up the depo, I got a mumbled "Bitch" from Jennifer Roma and a begrudging "Attaboy" from Jim Trainor.

After everyone left, Brad wrapped me in a big, brotherly hug and pulled back to look at me. "Damn, slugger. You played her perfectly."

"Thanks."

We headed back to my office, and as we passed Tony's office, Brad leaned into his doorway.

"Tony?"

Tony looked up from his papers, eyebrows raised.

"Kate just *nailed* Jim Trainor's ex. It was awesome."

Tony grinned at me. "Good job, Kate."

Oh my god. Tony called me Kate. Not "girl" or his more typical "darling." That in itself seemed like high praise. I felt like I just unilaterally helped advance the women's movement.

"Thanks, Tony."

Brad and I kept walking to my office door. "Thanks for your help, Brad. I really appreciate it."

"My pleasure."

I saw him stop at Mags's desk to talk, so I turned my butt around and went into my office so that I wouldn't overhear.

I dropped into my chair. Hell, yeah. So fun. I felt electric. Okay, so it was no "You can't handle the truth!" moment, but it was still pretty freaking cool.

I wanted to tell Jonathan. He'd be so excited for me. He'd laugh. But mostly, he'd get it. He was there through all of law school, there to hear all about my very first court appearance, there for my first win.

I pulled out my cell phone and looked at it.

I had a text from Dave.

Hey Beautiful. Can I come by after work tonight? It sucks only being able to see you on weekends because of our work schedules. :(

Ugh. He finishes up the late news at 11:35 p.m. so he'd be by no earlier than 11:45 p.m. and I have to be up by 7:00 a.m. Not great scheduling.

I texted Jonathan.

Hey. I just wanted to tell you about my first depo today. I totally got the woman to say exactly what I needed her to say :)

I set my phone down, with butterflies in my stomach, waiting for him to reply.

Just remember, with great power comes great respon-
sibility ;) He always made me laugh. *That's awesome*
Babe. When do I get to hear all the details?

Yikes. Come on. Don't act like you didn't know this might
come up.

Soon? How have you been?
Keeping busy. Miss you.
I miss you, too.

Okay. Sack up. Ask.

Are you dating?
I've gone out once or twice. Nothing major. You?
A little. Nothing major.

We were both using "nothing major" as code for "not
sleeping with anyone." I think.

CHAPTER 6

I'd agreed to let Dave stop by after work but made clear that it would be brief. I'd taken off the makeup, brushed the teeth, and gotten into my jammies by the time there was a knock on my door.

I cracked the door to be sure it was Dave. Once I opened the door, he rushed me and wrapped me in a bear hug.

I pointed over his shoulder. "Close the door."

Without putting me back on my feet, he used his foot to push the door closed.

He kissed me as he walked over to the sofa and sat down, setting me across his lap. Once settled, he continued kissing me and started planting kisses down my neck.

"Easy, cowboy."

He growled. "I don't get to see you enough."

"You're the one with the crazy schedule."

"Well it was never a problem when I didn't have a woman."

"You don't have a woman now," I said through gritted teeth.

He started working his way down my neck again, murmuring against my skin. "Pretty sure I do, even if you don't want to admit it."

I put my hand on his chest and pushed him back and scurried off his lap so that I was sitting next to him on the sofa. "Is it the challenge thing?"

"What do you mean?"

"I have never had a guy be this persistent about wanting a commitment."

He looked annoyed. "And that's what you think? That I only want it because you're playing hard to get?"

"I'm not *playing* anything, Dave." I looked at him in his frustrated silence. He was handsome, but . . . Always the "but" with him. I'd started dating Dave in the wake of Jonathan's whiplash-inducing changes of heart, which left me more than a little hurt and confused. That was coupled with my unhealthy attachment to Mr. Unattainable himself, Adam Lucas. But now that Dave was making things more complicated, I needed to figure out why I was still seeing him. Or if I should be.

"Look, I'm not the kind of girl that will string a guy along if I might hurt him and, until recently, anyway, you certainly did not seem like the type to suddenly fall for a girl. But even looking at you now, I still have alarm bells sounding in my head, making me question your sincerity.

"I like you. I do. But I'm not looking for a relationship, and the more you keep pushing it—the more I just think we need to stop seeing each other."

He looked a little stunned. "So that's what that conversation feels like from this side."

I laughed softly and shrugged. "Sorry."

His expression softened, but he still frowned. "So, are you dumping me?"

I put my hands up between us, exasperated. "See? That's exactly what I mean! We aren't *together*. I *can't* dump you!"

Now he smiled and started laughing. "I know. Shit. Calm down. I'm just messing with you."

I blew out a sigh and scowled at him.

"Okay. It still sounds to me like this is more of a trust issue, since I used to be a player."

"Used to be?"

"Exactly. So, the way I see it, with some time, you'll realize I'm sincere. And once we clear that hurdle, you'll be madly in love with me." He finished with a dangerous smirk and pulled me onto his lap again.

I kept a hand against his chest in an effort to keep some space between us. He looked down at my hand and raised an eyebrow, then leaned forward and gave me a quick kiss on the lips. When I smiled at his annoying-as-hell determination, he leaned in and gave me another, slightly longer kiss. He snaked his arms around me and pulled me in a little closer to him.

This feels a little too good, considering that I still have no idea what I'm doing with him.

"It's late and I have to get up early, Dave. I said you could stop by, but that was it."

"Maybe I should spend the night."

"Not sure that would help with me making my bedtime."

"I plan on putting you to bed."

"Dave."

He let out the big, whiny sigh I'd heard on more than one occasion when he didn't get his way. "Okay." He slid me off his lap and stood up. He pulled me up by the hand and hugged me. He gave me another long kiss.

"Saturday you're mine."

"Are you asking me or telling me?"

He smiled, displaying those too-perfect teeth. "Both?"

I laughed. "Fine."

"You could sound a little more excited."

I gave him an exaggerated smile and threw out some jazz hands for good measure.

He frowned at me and swatted my behind before heading to the door. "You're such a smart-ass," he said on his way out.

"Good night," I called to him as he headed to his truck.

He waved without turning around, and I closed the door.

*

When I got to the office, I leaned over Mags's cubicle, where she was booting up her computer.

"Hey," she said with a big smile. She was wearing black. All black. Which would seem really subdued for her if she didn't look like she was channeling Catwoman. Her dark hair blended with the snug black sleeveless sweater and black pants she had on, and the only spot of color was her bright red lipstick.

"You look like you're in a good mood," I said.

She raised her eyebrows innocently. "Not sure what you're alluding to, boss."

I cut my eyes back to Brad's office and back to her. "Saw Brad chatting with you yesterday."

"Yep," she said, still grinning at me.

When she didn't elaborate, I grunted. "Fine. Don't tell me."

Mags laughed and pointed into my office. I walked into my office and Mags trailed behind me.

Once I sat down in my desk chair, Mags took her usual position, perched on the edge of my desk with her legs crossed.

"It's possible that Brad and I had dinner last night," she said. When I busted out an overly hopeful smile, she held a hand up to me, complete with long fingernails, painted red to match her lipstick. "Just dinner."

I nodded and toned down my grin.

After a pause, Mags leaned down closer to me and added, "Well, and sex."

I started laughing and she joined in.

"Bravo, Brad," I said. "So? What happened to the whole 'he's too much of a homebody for me' thing?"

Mags looked at me with her usual directness. "Remember that guy I danced with at the bar last weekend?"

I nodded. I'd found it ironic that she managed to find the one guy in the bar that looked the most like the guy she had dumped.

"Well, Sigmund Fucking Freud I am not. I didn't even realize until I saw Brad on Monday that I was basically out picking up Brad clones. And, let's be real, it's not like I was going to be able to replace Brad with someone better than Brad." She finished with a broad smile that had "smitten" written all over it.

"I am so happy for you guys. And, I agree—Brad is pretty awesome."

"I know. So I was fashionably late to the party, as usual, but I got there."

I leaned an elbow on the desk and rested my chin in my palm. "Lucky for you he just sat around pining for you instead of moving on."

Mags hopped off my desk and turned sideways to me, with a hand on her hip. "Sweetie, luck had nothing to do with it." She finished with a hand flourish down her substantial curves.

"Damn straight," I agreed.

A few hours later, I'd just finished tucking my Tupperware back into my drawer after eating lunch at my desk when Mags buzzed me. "Dr. Shaw?"

"Shit. Rochelle?"

"Yep."

"Does it sound like she's been crying?"

"Maybe a little."

"Awesome. Put her through, I guess."

I heard Mags chuckle before she hung up. I put on my headset and started Rochelle's time clock. "Hi, Rochelle."

"Hi, Kate. I need advice."

Please let it be about law this time. Or cheese. Those are really my two fields of expertise. And who are we kidding; I don't know that much about law. "What's going on?"

"I think we might need to put the child support hearing on hold again."

I rolled my eyes, even though I was alone and no one was there to enjoy it. "Okay. I can cancel it again, but we really don't want to keep taking it on and off the court's calendar like this."

"Right. When is it?"

"Two weeks."

"Should we leave it?"

Seriously. I am not equipped to answer these types of questions. "Well, from a procedural standpoint, we have to notice the hearing. So once we notice it, the hearing won't be for at least sixteen court days—meaning no weekends or holidays.

If we cancel and then you change your mind, we have to notice a new hearing, meaning sixteen more court days . . ."

"Oh. I see what you mean." And now she was sobbing.

"Rochelle, you don't sound definite. We can wait a few
more days."

"I just love him, Kate," she said, in between sobs. Funny, I
kinda hate him.

"What did he do when he was served with the notice for
the child support hearing?"

"Oh, he completely lost his shit." Of course. What a prince.
"But then we had a really good talk and I feel like we're really
on the same page for the first time in a long time."

"I can't tell you what to do, here, Rochelle. I work for you.
We'll proceed how you want to."

More sobbing. "Please, Kate. I really need your opinion. As
a woman."

You *so* don't want my womanly opinion. "I'm sorry, but I
just don't know either of you well enough to give advice on
the matter."

More sniffling. I looked at the clock. We'd been on the
phone for over fifteen minutes already. I looked over my texts
from Jonathan again.

"I just want to be able to trust him again. To feel safe with
him again."

"I get that." And I'm right there with ya, sister.

She gave a halfhearted laugh. "If I kill him, can you represent me?"

I laughed at her joke. What I hoped was a joke. "Nope, I
don't do criminal, so let's keep this in signing court, okay?"

"Yeah, yeah. Sure, *now* you have advice." We both laughed.
Yes, she was a mess and had an asshole for an Achilles' heel,

but I liked the woman. She *knew* she was a mess. I can identify with that.

"Okay, shit. Leave it on the calendar for now. I'll make a decision for sure in the next day or two."

"Sounds good," I said.

"Well, as much as I'd like to keep talking to you, I can't really afford it."

I laughed. "I understand that, too."

"Alright. I'll be in touch," she said, before disconnecting. Somehow I didn't doubt that.

And thankfully, no mention of the troubling Facebook friend request, which meant I could continue to pretend I never saw it.

Not long after I'd gotten off the phone with Rochelle, my most "senior" boss, Joe Markson, came into my office for the first time. And I felt bad that he'd made the trip. His back was slightly stooped as he walked, and his head was bald and shiny over the dome. He was basically a TV grandpa. And he was smiling like a grandpa, too. Part of me felt like he might try to steal my nose and then give me a butterscotch hard candy.

"Mr. Markson," I said, standing and coming around the desk to meet him.

"Joe."

I nodded at him, smiling.

"Kate, I'd like you to take a case over for me. These two people have been arguing over a settlement for two and a half years and I'm starting to think their fight is going to outlive me." We both laughed. "I don't really have the energy for them anymore, and maybe a new voice of reason will get through to them."

"I'd be happy to give it a shot."

"I knew you would." He put a large accordion file in my

hands. "Don't let them get the upper hand on you," he said, pointing that grandpa finger in my face to drive his point home. "Once you lose it, you'll never get it back."

I smiled. "Thanks for the advice."

"I told her I was bringing an associate in on it, so she's expecting to meet with you when she comes in today."

"Okay. What's the settlement hung up on?"

He smiled. "Elvis."

"Elvis. What is it? A collectible?"

"A guinea pig."

My mouth dropped open. "A guinea pig."

He nodded.

"They've been fighting over a guinea pig for two and a half years?" I asked, astonished.

"Well, they started fighting over Frank Sinatra, but he got hit by a car."

"Do I want to know what Frank was?"

"The Siamese cat."

"Oh. Well, guinea pigs don't live that long, do they?"

"They can live for five years, apparently."

"And Elvis is how old?"

"About two and a half years."

"Oh."

He patted my shoulder. "Good luck."

I smiled. "Thanks, boss."

He chuckled as he left my office. Certainly more charming when he's dumping problem clients on me than Tony is.

I looked at the clock. The client would be here in about an hour, so I figured I'd call opposing counsel and get their take on settlement negotiations before she got here. According to the file, opposing counsel was Beth Erickson, who just happened to be the attorney who had a front row seat to me getting punched out by our feisty little client. At least now I know how to cover up a black eye in case I ever decide to quit the law and become a female boxer.

"Beth Erickson's office," the female voice said.

"Hello. This is Kate Shaw with Manetti Markson and Mann calling in regards to the Lewis–Hamilton matter."

"Let me see if she's available. One moment."

"Beth Erickson."

"Hi, Beth. It's Kate Shaw."

"Kate. How's the eye?"

"Better. Thank you. So, I'm not sure if Mr. Markson mentioned it, but I'm taking over representation of Dot Hamilton."

"Yeah, he told me. I'm jealous. I don't have an associate to dump this case off on."

I laughed. "Well, I'm meeting with my client this afternoon, so I was hoping to get a better idea from you on how negotiations have gone in the past and to find out if there were upcoming motions or trial dates."

"Nope, no trial dates. Good god, could you imagine? Taking the case to trial over a goddamned guinea pig? That would be one pissed-off judge."

"Very true."

"Ironically, the rest of the settlement went really smoothly, until we got to the damn cat and things got ugly. Then Sinatra went and got hit by a car and Dot blames Daryl and suddenly he was unfit to take care of the rat."

"Guinea pig."

"Like it matters."

"And Daryl refuses to give up Elvis?" I asked.

"Yeah, but mostly on principle, I think. These two seem like they're in it more for the fight than anything."

"Super. What about money? Can she buy the guinea pig from him?"

She laughed. Not encouraging. "Neither of these people needs the money. And if they give up fighting over the rodent, then they get to move on with their lives, and neither of them wants that for the other. I just keep hoping the stupid thing will die."

Harsh. "Okay. So basically you're saying that an offer of anything other than giving up Elvis is pointless?"

She sighed loudly. "Probably, but bring an offer anyway. We have to keep trying."

"Have they mediated?"

"Way back when. Before Sinatra died. The mediator threw them out when they started chucking coffee mugs at each other's heads."

"Well, alrighty then. Sounds like a good time. I'll be in touch."

"Good luck," she said, in a slightly wicked, singsongy voice.

That afternoon, I sat down with Dot in one of the conference rooms. She was midforties, too thin, and had a pissed-off expression that I was guessing was permanent by now.

After the usual get-acquainted chitchat, I decided to dive in. "Well, let's see if we can be creative. There really is nothing else you want from him? Aside from the guinea pig?"

"Nothing."

"There must be something."

"I'd take his Maserati," she said, with a bland tilt of her head.

Sigh. I stopped myself from hitting my head against the

conference table, because I thought that might be a little un-professional. "Okay. Anything else?"

She appeared to think about it, then shook her head.

"Okay. What are you willing to *give* to get Elvis?"

She grunted. "You know, I'm the one that always took care of it. I resent that I need to give him anything for it."

"I understand that, but surely you are ready for this to be over? This settlement has been in the works for *two years*. You don't want your life to pass you by because you are fighting over an animal."

"Elvis."

I nodded. "Elvis."

"Okay," she said, leaning toward me across the table. "I'll give him the grandfather clock."

I nodded. "Alright. That seems like a reasonable offer. I'll call his attorney this afternoon and see what she has to say."

Dot stood, shook my hand, and marched out of the room. I don't blame Joe for wanting to unload this. I'd only spent thirty minutes with the woman and I felt as though she'd somehow sucked months off my life.

*

That night, as I was changing out of my suit, my phone buzzed.

It was from Jonathan.

Hey. I was wondering if I could swing by? I have a box of your things that you missed.
Sure.

I hadn't seen Jonathan in more than a week, since I told him I needed to some space to figure out where we were at— and whether we had a future.

You know, I don't actually know where you live any-more. Are you going to tell me? Or are you in witness protection?

I am, but as long as you call me 'Sally' and talk in a southern accent, we should be fine.

I typed in my address.

Hahaha. See you soon.

A few minutes later, there was a knock on my door. I opened it to find Jonathan, dressed in his usual work attire of khakis and a polo shirt. He shifted the box he was holding to one hand and reached in to do the one-arm-hug thing. I hugged him back. Then he set the box down on my coffee table and made a slow circle of the downstairs, peeking into the kitchen, before coming back to stand in front of me.

"Very nice. Very you," he said.

"Thank you. I agree," I said with a nod.

He had his customary five o'clock shadow, since, for him, a morning shave was only good till early evening. His whiskers seemed to accentuate his Latino blood; he had the dark scruff to match his dark hair and bronze skin.

"So, how have you been?" he asked.

"You mean in the week since we last went out?"

"Well, technically it's been twelve days," he said with a se-ductive smile, narrowing his warm brown eyes at me.

See, the tricky thing with Jonathan is that we have too much history. Too many laughs, too much great sex. And all that history made him an all-or-nothing scenario. I either needed to take him back or end things clean. Not really anything in between. This *all or nothing* seemed to be giving me heart palpitations.

"Keeping track, huh?" I asked with a smirk.

"Like a fifteen-year-old girl marking off the days till prom."

I laughed. "Except you're counting the days *since*."

He stepped in toward me, near enough that it felt like the sliver of space between us was being compressed. "Well, I *hope* I'm counting down to something."

My brain did a quick run-through of what it would be like right now to just say *Okay—let's get back together*. It would be so easy. So comfortable. I'd finally get laid again, for the first time in weeks. And I was happy with him. I could be happy again.

But I couldn't do it. There was some indefinable barrier that seemed to make the words impossible to say.

Jonathan put his hands on my shoulders and chuckled. "Okay. Just stop. You look like you're trying to make Sophie's choice instead of just deciding whether or not to give me another shot."

I gave him a little smile, appreciating his interference. "Sorry."

He shook his head. "I'm not trying to pressure you." He brushed a thumb across my cheek. "I just miss you."

"I know," I sighed. "I miss you, too."

We stared at each other quietly for a few seconds. "Okay," he said. "Rather than give you the chance to follow that up with a 'but,' I'm just going to go." He gave me a big smile, but it lacked his usual sincerity. As he turned to leave, he let one of his hands slide from my shoulder to my hand, and he held it on the way to the door.

When he turned to me before leaving, I wrapped my arms around his waist and squeezed him tightly. When I pulled back and looked at him, his old smile had returned.

"Talk to you soon," he said.

"Absolutely." I smiled at him, watching him walk toward his car. And 50 percent of me wanted to stop him from leaving, hold on to him, and never let go. Unfortunately, the other 50 percent felt like I was dragging things out and that I needed to let him go for good. Well, they say admitting you have a problem is always the first step.

CHAPTER 7

"Hello, Kate."

I looked up the next morning and Jared Mann was standing in front of my desk, hands in the pockets of his slacks. Jared was the youngest partner in the firm, with a superhero jawline to go with his handsome face and a villain's reputation for making his paralegals cry when they didn't meet his high standards.

"Hey," I responded.

"Keeping busy?"

"Pretty busy. I've got one client that seems to be calling for a daily therapy session, and Joe just gave me a couple that has been fighting over a guinea pig for two years."

He laughed. "Elvis. Well, I hate to ask last minute, but could you possibly cover a child support hearing this afternoon?"

"Sure. I assume it's pretty straightforward if you aren't worried about sending in the newbie with no prep time?"

He smiled. "Well, yes it is straightforward, but I have no doubt that you'd be able to handle anything I threw at you." Then he just stared. Weird habit of his.

"I appreciate the vote of confidence."

He set a file on my desk. "Candice Mariani. Her mother, Lois, has been our client for years. Candice is twenty, never signed, has a nine-month-old baby. Lois is a great lady. I'm not sure how she turned out a screwup like Candice."

"Well, accidentally getting pregnant doesn't necessarily make you a screwup," I said with a shrug.

Jared gave a faint smile and tapped the file. "The guy we filed the motion against is in custody. Possession with intent to distribute. And then he peed on the arresting officer."

I grimaced. "Gotcha. So, the jail ships him over for the hearing, I'm assuming?"

"Yep. He'll be there. Remember, Lois pays our bills, but Candice is the client. Watch what you say in front of Lois or you can destroy attorney–client privilege."

"Right. Thanks for the reminder."

"Thanks, Kate. You're a lifesaver."

I read through the motion quickly to get a feel for the case. The baby daddy was named Matthew Taylor, thirty-eight years old. Hm. That would have put Candice in the "barely legal" category while hooking up with a much older man. Lovely.

I got to court with plenty of time to spare that afternoon so that I'd have extra time to track down Candice before the hearing. This time, at least, I'd seen a picture, so I was able to spot her right away.

From looking at her, I'm thinking she may have met her drug dealer ex as a buyer. Which makes me a little sad, considering that she's got a little baby to take care of. Candice was really skinny and dressed up for court by throwing on some holey jeans and a T-shirt that slipped off one shoulder. This was coupled with a bright pink streak in her dirty hair and a ring through her nose. Lois was standing next to her, looking tired. I see Jared's point. Lois looks like a middle-aged soccer mom. The apple fell far from the tree. And rolled into the gutter. And maybe got peed on by a homeless guy.

I shook their hands and introduced myself.

"So, this should be pretty straightforward. We'll get a child support order in place, but obviously the award will be little to nothing at this point, since he's in custody and not making any money. But once you have the award in place, it's a lot easier to go back to court for adjustments when he does become employed again in the future," I said. "And his child support will accrue, so if he ever comes into any money, it will go to pay off what he owes you first. Tax returns, anything like that."

"Thanks, Kate," Lois said.

"He's still making money. Even in there," Candice muttered with a frown.

Well, crap. No one gave me a crash course on how to get child support paid from illegal endeavors. "But I'm guessing the money is cash and there's no paper trail?"

"Yeah," Candice said, tucking her pink streak of hair behind her ear.

"If he had a bank account or something, we could go after that, but cash will be nearly impossible to prove. Or find."

"Asshole," Candice surmised.

Not going to argue with you there.

We filed into the courtroom and sat down. Within a few minutes, Judge Warner appeared, once again channeling Mark Twain. Nice to see he hadn't trimmed his bushy white mustache. I quickly reached into my bag and pulled the battery out of my phone. I'd made my stellar first impression on Judge Warner by allowing my phone to ring. In court. I feel pretty certain that it was only our mutual affinity for the *Law & Order* theme song that saved me from being removed by the bailiff that day. When I looked over, Lois was watching me, smiling.

"Bad experience," I whispered.

We were third on the calendar, but I was guessing we'd go first because we had an in-custody defendant.

"I understand we have an in-custody, so we'll start with that matter," Judge Warner said. "Candice Mariani and Matthew Taylor."

Candice followed me through the gate and stood next to me at the table.

"Kate Shaw for Ms. Mariani, Your Honor."

"Good morning, Ms. Shaw. Does Mr. Taylor have counsel?"

"Here, Your Honor," a voice said. I looked over my shoulder, and a thirtysomething guy with a beard and glasses was walking toward the table. "Thomas Stein, appearing as court appointed parent advocate."

"Thank you, Mr. Stein."

A door at the side of the courtroom nearest to Stein opened and the bailiff brought in Matthew Taylor, who was wearing a bright orange jumpsuit and wrist shackles.

Holy. Shit. He's *that* Matt Taylor. The years had not been kind. He didn't look thirty-eight; he looked fifty. His hair was overgrown and hanging in his eyes and he had multicolored whiskers covering his face. My heart started beating faster and my palms got sweaty. I love my life. Please don't recognize me. Please, please, please.

Matt looked down the table, right past Candice, and his eyes rested on me a moment before recognition hit him. Then he lit up like a damn Christmas tree. "Katie?"

Shoot me. No, really. Now would be a good time. I dated Matt when I was sixteen and he was twenty. And not a felon.

Judge Warner looked at me, bushy eyebrows raised. "Ms. Shaw, do you know the defendant?"

"A little, Your Honor."

Matt chimed in. "She's my ex-girlfriend, Judge." Dick.

"Not exactly," I fumbled. "Briefly, Your Honor, when I was a teenager. I haven't seen the defendant in nearly . . . eighteen years."

I got the feeling Judge Warner was doing his damnedest to hide his amusement.

"Any conflict?"

"None, Your Honor," I said, careful to not look back in Matt's direction. Or Candice's. I didn't want to see how she was taking the news that we'd dated the same guy. I would deal with that little fact later, with a bottle of wine and a hot shower.

"Ms. Mariani, do you have any problem with Ms. Shaw's involvement in this matter, in light of her prior knowledge of Mr. Taylor?"

She glanced at me a second and responded, "Nope."

"Mr. Stein?"

Stein just shrugged.

"Okay, let's begin, then," Judge Warner said. "Your motion, Ms. Shaw."

"Your Honor, Mr. Taylor is the father of Ms. Mariani's nine-month-old child. We're asking the Court to put a child support order in place at this time, based on whatever income Mr. Taylor has available."

"Mr. Stein?"

"One moment, Your Honor." Stein went over to Matt and leaned down and the two of them whispered for a couple of minutes. "Your Honor, we're requesting the child's birth date."

The judge looked back at us. I looked at Candice.

"August twentieth, sir," Candice responded.

"Was that near the due date?" Stein asked.

"A couple days late," Candice said. I tried not to notice the way she started rubbing her palms against her jeans and fidgeting.

Stein tapped something into his iPad, then he walked back over and whispered to Matt. Matt laughed and nodded.

"Your Honor, based on the child's birth date, Mr. Taylor cannot be the father."

Close your mouth, Kate. Deep breath. I shot a quick look at Candice, but she just looked confused.

"Your Honor," I asked, "how can Mr. Stein say with any certainty?"

"Mr. Stein?" Judge Warner asked, raising his bushy eyebrows.

"I have a conception calculator and, based on the birth date, conception would have occurred around November twenty-second of the prior year. Mr. Taylor was in custody on an unrelated charge from October second and was not released until the nineteenth of December." Of course he was.

"Bailiff, could you confirm those in-custody dates?" Judge Warner asked.

The bailiff started typing in his computer and I looked down at Candice. She frowned and looked a little perplexed.

"Your Honor, there are multiple 'Matthew Taylor' inmates. I'll need Mr. Taylor's birth date to find him," the bailiff said.

"November sixth, nineteen seventy-nine," Matt said.

"Nineteen seventy-nine!" Candice shrieked, loud enough so that half the courtroom undoubtedly heard her. "He's almost forty!" she said. "I can't believe I fucked an old guy!" Okay. Clearly Candice had concerns other than the identity of her baby daddy.

I looked at her, gave her a stern "Shh," and put my forefinger across my lips in the universal *Shut your piehole* gesture. To my surprise, she actually listened and stopped ranting about Matt's age.

The bailiff began speaking again a minute later. "Mr. Taylor was in the county jail on those dates, Your Honor."

"Ms. Shaw?"

"I apologize, Your Honor. We withdraw the motion."

"Thank you. Case dismissed."

"Kate!" Matt called out.

Against my better judgment, and, really, because I didn't think before I did it, I looked over at Matt. He was grinning and giving me the *Call me* hand gesture with his thumb and pinky, and he mouthed it to me as well, for good measure, as the bailiff led him back out of the courtroom by the arm. In his spiffy orange jumpsuit. And now my day is perfect.

I looked back at the judge, wide-eyed. He'd given in to his amusement and was smiling at me. My face was probably so red that I looked about ready to have a stroke. I gave him a half-embarrassed, half-apologetic look and slipped out of the courtroom.

Back outside, I turned to Lois. "I'm very sorry about that. It never occurred to me it would be the Matt Taylor I knew."

"It's a common name," she said, shaking her head. "And we should be the ones apologizing," she said, her tone hardening as she turned to Candice.

"So weird," Candice said. "I was so sure it was him."

"And now that it isn't, does that tell you who it is?" I asked.

She frowned. "It narrows it down."

The look of embarrassment and defeat on Lois's face was enough to hush up my baby-maker for a while. Definitely the most effective form of birth control.

"Well, if you figure it out, call me." I gave Lois what I hoped was a consoling pat on the shoulder and left the courthouse.

*

I got into my office and dropped down into my chair. Mags immediately appeared and sat on the edge of my desk. She was wearing a snug red dress, red shoes, red lipstick.

"How was court?" she said, wiggling her dark eyebrows up and down.

"Hm. Tricky question. The part where the in-custody baby daddy turned out to be an ex-boyfriend of mine? Or the part where my client had accused the wrong baby daddy, because he was in lockup when she got knocked up?"

Mags erupted into genuine laughter. "No!"

I nodded. "Unfortunately, yes. On both counts."

"I didn't know you went for the bad boys, Kate."

"Well, I think I dated him pre–rap sheet. Does that count for anything?"

"No. Did he recognize you?"

"This is me, Mags. Has my luck *ever* been good enough that I could make it out of there without him spotting me?"

"No?"

"No. And he informed the court that I was his ex-girlfriend."

"Oh my god!" Mags said, falling into hysterics again. She

dabbed at tears in the corners of her eyes. "Well, how did he look?"

"Like orange is his color. And he asked me to call him, so, you know, if I find myself wanting for male companionship, I've apparently got options."

Mags dabbed her eyes again and hopped off my desk. "I love your life." Funny, I thought the same thing today. But I was being sarcastic.

*

That night, I'd just put some pasta on the stove and poured myself a glass of wine when Logek called.

"Hey," I said, wandering into my living room.

"How's things?" she asked.

"Getting stranger all the time. You?"

"About the same."

"Seen Derek this week?"

"Maybe."

"Hm."

"Seen Adam?"

"Perhaps. I texted him Monday, but it was for a benevolent purpose."

"Which was?"

"His mom agreed to go out with Tony."

"Oh crap. How did they meet?"

"She showed up at the office with new wineglasses for me."

"God, she's sweet. Cute?"

"Adorable. Worth about ten times my giraffe ones. You need to see them."

"And naturally Tony saw her and swooped in."

"And she said yes."

" 'Cause he's Tony."

"Which I will *never* get."

"So you told Adam he needed to warn his mom?"

"Something like that."

"And that was it?"

"Yep. Until his mother sent him over that night to light my pilot light."

Logek laughed. "Um. Excuse me?"

I sighed. "Yeah. Unfortunately, just the pilot light *on the stove*. So he came, fixed the oven, I burned chicken, and he took me to In-N-Out Burger. So, what happened with Derek?"

"Well, he 'lit my pilot light,' too." No fair. Pretty sure her pilot light getting lit was a lot more exciting than mine.

"Uh-oh. As good as you remember?"

"Oh yeah."

"Well, that's something. Talked to Daniel at all?"

"No. He didn't put up with my brush-off for long. Which I respect."

"Good for Daniel," I said.

"So, was there much in-n-outing at In-N-Out the other night?"

I laughed. "As if I could ever, in my life, have sex with Adam Lucas and not call you afterward so we could talk about it."

"And don't you forget it," Logek said.

"Pretty sure we won't be having that phone call, however."

"Never say never."

*

Saturday morning, Dave texted me about our date.

> *How about we go to Lucille's tonight? Good food and they have live blues bands on Saturday nights?*
> Sure. Blues, biscuits and beer. Sounds like a perfect night :)
> *Pick you up at 7:30?*
> *Yep.*

I was dressed and ready for my date when I got another text. From Adam this time.

> *Hi Kate. Just wanted to follow up and let you know that my mom went out with Tony last night. I don't think they are planning on moving in together or anything, so—so far so good.*

I chuckled.

> *That's a relief.*
> *What are you up to?*
> *Going out with Dave.*
> *Where are you two going?*
> *Lucille's. Live blues :)*
> *Have a good time. Talk to you later.*
> *Bye.*

Well, he didn't seem too put off by my admitting that I had a date with Dave. But a girl can hope.

Dave was there by 7:15. I was in jeans and my city slicker cowboy boots (meaning they were a little too clean and I had bought them at Nordstrom). I had an old red Windbreaker

that was lightweight enough for the evening, so I slipped it on
and headed toward the door.

"Are you going to wear that?"

I looked at him, a little confused at first, then glanced down
at my jacket. "I was going to. Why?"

He smiled like he thought he was being funny, but I had the
distinct impression he legitimately didn't want to be seen with
me in my out-of-fashion jacket. "I mean—it's fine," he said.

My mouth may have been hanging open a little. I was no
Tyra Banks, but I'd never considered myself a fashion victim,
either. I looked at my jacket again. Okay, so I'd had it since I
was twenty-five. It just never occurred to me that it had reached
the level of embarrassment. I was offended, of course, but also
second-guessing my own judgment in still wearing the thing.

"Look," he said. "It's just not that cold. I don't think you'll
need it."

I slipped it off and headed out the door, probably looking a
little like a kicked dog. I was quiet on the way to the restaurant.

"You look beautiful," he said, taking my hand.

As long as I'm not in my hideous Windbreaker, apparently.

"Are you mad at me?" he asked.

I frowned at him. "I guess I just never realized you were
such a snob."

"What? I'm not a snob."

I looked at him. His hair was perfect, his jeans undoubtedly
cost more than mine, his truck was top of the line. Yeah, guess
I should have picked up on this sooner.

"If you say so," I said.

He sighed loudly like I was being moody and high maintenance. Which I *so* wasn't. But I was pretty damn annoyed.

We got to the restaurant and headed inside to the bar area.

We grabbed a high-top table and ordered a couple of beers. The band was already playing. They were five guys in their fifties, of all different races, tearing it up on the guitar, harmonica, and drums. I'm a blues fan, and they were really good, so it sort of diffused my annoyance, and before I knew it I was smiling and tapping my feet.

"So, how's work," Dave asked, leaning close and speaking loudly so that I could hear him over the music.

"Good, actually. I can't believe I've been there three weeks already."

"That's right. We've been dating for three weeks."

"We've *known* each other for three weeks."

He frowned at me. "Our first kiss was three weeks ago tonight."

Yay for Kate kissing total strangers within hours of meeting them! Tramp. "That's right. It was."

He smiled. "I still think we should agree to not see other people."

He was right back to harping on this subject again. I did like Dave, though. He was cute and sexy and made me feel good about myself. Well, he *had,* anyway. Until he decided to be a dick about my clothing choices. But regardless of whether I liked him or not, I was uncomfortably aware of the fact that he was still placing a distant third among the men in my life. I just couldn't see him pulling some dark horse comeback where I'd find myself madly in love with him.

Dave reached over and grasped my hand, which was resting against my beer mug, and brought it to his lips, kissing the back of it.

I sighed. "Dave . . ."

"Kate," I heard, from behind me.

Holy shit. After a moment of paralysis, I turned around to find Adam standing behind me. "Hi. What are you doing here?" Because when he told me to have fun on my date, he certainly didn't sound like he was thinking of crashing it.

He smiled his glorious smile. He was in jeans and a blue button-down shirt that he left untucked. He pointed toward the band. "There's live blues, Kate." Like that should be sufficient explanation for everything.

"Good to see you, Dave," Adam said, reaching over to shake Dave's hand.

"You, too, buddy. So what brings you here?"

"The owner's a client. He's been telling me to come by for months, so I finally decided to."

"No other reason?" Dave asked.

Adam looked at him a moment, expressionless. "No other reason."

"Oh," Dave said, turning back to the band.

Adam raised his eyebrows to me but I just shrugged. I had no idea what crawled up Dave's butt, either.

"Um. Do you want to join us?" I asked. Dave may be acting like an ass, but I still had manners.

"Well, uh, I don't want to interrupt your evening."

"It really isn't a problem," I said casually.

"Dave?" Adam asked, his eyebrows raised.

Dave turned on a little TV Dave and faked a smile. "Sure. The more, the merrier."

I felt like there was a decent chance I was going to hear about this later. Oh well. It would have been rude to blow Adam off. Even if I was physically capable of doing so—to which, let's be real, all evidence is to the contrary.

Adam pulled out the stool next to me and casually perched

on the edge of it, giving the impression he didn't intend to stay long.

"So, any more problems with the oven?" Adam asked.

"Nope." I could feel Dave focus on me, but I ignored him. "Any word on the partner front?"

"Nah. Not yet. Hopefully I'll hear by next week."

"Well, I'm keeping my fingers crossed for you."

He smiled. "I know you are."

Dave was not taking Adam's intrusion into our date well—or the fact that we had clearly been in communication recently—so he was quiet. And being obnoxiously obvious about it.

"Well, I think I'll let you two get back to your date," Adam said, standing up from his stool.

Now Dave perked up. Ass. He reached over and shook Adam's hand. "Thanks, man. Take care."

Adam smiled. If he was offended, it didn't show. He gave my shoulder a brief squeeze. "Good to see you, Kate."

"Good night, Adam."

Once Adam was gone, Dave turned to me with an annoyed expression on his handsome face. I didn't care for the combination.

"What?" I asked.

"You really couldn't stay away from him for even one night?"

"What are you talking about?"

"You're supposed to be on a date with me."

"I *am* on a date with you," I said. Which feels kind of unfortunate at the moment.

"I just think it would be nice if you didn't invite other guys out on our date."

"What?" Okay, I sounded a little shrill. "Just because I invited him to sit with us?"

He raised his eyebrows at me. "Just asked him to sit down?"

"Okay. I'm really confused. What the hell are you talking about?"

"Sure, sure. Just another famous Kate Shaw coincidence."

"I have no idea what you are talking about, but I don't care for your attitude."

He rolled his eyes at me and shook his head.

"We should go," I said.

"Fine," he replied. He tossed some cash onto the table for our drinks and headed outside, with me a step behind him.

We drove in silence back to my place. He didn't turn off the truck, so he obviously wasn't thinking about coming inside. Fine with me.

"Good night," I said, as I climbed out of the truck.

" 'Night."

Once I was out and the truck door was closed, he drove away. Wow. He's really pissed. And I was entirely at a loss as to how I'd managed to do it. It was giving me a weird mix of anger and hurt feelings.

By the time I was in my comfy clothes with a glass of wine, my phone was buzzing with a text from Dave.

You know—part of the reason I liked you so much was that you didn't play games. Guess I was wrong about that.

What the hell?

I honestly don't know what you are talking about.
Seriously? I'm talking about you having Adam meet us tonight.

I did NOT ask him to meet us.

Yeah. Just a coincidence I'm sure.

He texted me earlier about something else and then asked what I was up to. I told him WE were going to Lucille's. He said have fun. End of story.

Of course. Because telling him where we'd be wasn't because you wanted him to meet up with us.

It wasn't. I never suggested he come out and he didn't sound like it crossed his mind.

You tell yourself that.

He didn't believe me. That revelation made me a little queasy. Beyond the occasional *No, Mom, I love your haircut* little white lie, I'm super honest. The number of times I've had anyone accuse me of lying, I could count on one hand. And those occasions always tie my stomach into knots. But the hard part was that I *did* tell Adam where we'd be . . . what Dave doubted was my reason for doing so. And how do you defend your intentions when only you know what they were for sure?

Dave I'm telling you—I did not mean for Adam to show up. Really.

Okay.

You think I'm lying?

I don't know. Maybe you're lying to yourself.

I was sitting on my sofa, staring at my phone. I was breathing a little rapidly and my face was flushed. He didn't *believe* me. Okay. I was trying to muster up enough anger to overshadow the hurt and confusion, but it wasn't working. Yeah, yeah, I know I should be pissed. And I am. But I couldn't seem to stop the knots in my stomach or the fact that my eyes were welling up with tears.

I set the phone down. I'm not about to plead with him to believe me. I've already done more of that than he deserves.

CHAPTER 8

By Monday, at work, I was still spending too much time thinking about my fight with Dave. I wasn't trying to get Adam to show up at Lucille's and I was still mad at Dave for not believing me when I told him so. I'd also realized that, given how cynical Dave was about women, how could I not think he'd question my motives? But screw that. He was not supposed to question my intentions, because I had told him, sincerely, what they were. I was definitely letting it get to me too much, considering I wasn't all that serious about Dave, but the questioning my honesty thing was bugging me like having a popcorn kernel stuck between my tooth and gum.

Mags to the rescue. She trotted into my office in a little yellow, vintage-looking suit, which, if the skirt hadn't been short and snug, would have seemed a little out of character for her.

I smiled at her. "Love the suit."

"Thanks, boss," she said, hopping onto the edge of my desk. "How was your weekend?"

I shrugged. "It was okay. How was yours?"

"Pretty good," she said, smiling and making her eyebrows go up and down suggestively.

"Mm. Sounds better than mine."

"Because?" she asked, doing the drawn-out, upward inflection at the end of the word.

I sneered a little. "Stupid fight with Dave. He's pissed at me because Adam showed up while we were out on a date."

She grinned but she looked like she was trying to subdue it. "You poor thing. But you have to expect accidentally double-booking once in a while when you keep spares lying around."

"Brat."

She laughed, climbed off the desk, and headed out to her cubicle.

A few minutes later, Mags buzzed me. "It's Rochelle."

"Okay. Wait! Is the hearing on or off right now? I can't remember."

"On. It's next Tuesday."

"Thanks."

Mags connected the call.

"Hi, Rochelle."

"Hi, Kate."

"So, what's up?"

"The hearing is on, right?"

"Yep. A week from tomorrow." Please say good. Please say good.

"Perfect." Even better.

"Well. That sounds fairly definitive. I'm thinking the new contract is off?"

"Way, way off. I will never understand how that man managed to keep reeling me back in."

"Good for you. What changed?"

"No idea. I looked over at him at the dinner table last night, with his receding hairline and his stupid face, and I realized that I really just wanted to punch him."

"But you didn't, right? 'Cause I don't practice that kind of law."

Rochelle laughed. "No, I was a model of restraint. But I did tell him to get the hell out of my house."

"Wow. How did that go over?"

She laughed. "I think he saw me—really saw me—for the first time. I'm pretty sure he's never been as in love with me as when I was dumping him for good last night."

I laughed. "Rochelle, I am really happy for you. You'll have to give me some tips on this whole female empowerment thing you've got going."

"Once I get it figured out, I definitely will."

"So, I guess I'll see you next Tuesday, one thirty p.m., Department Six."

"I'll be there. Thanks, Kate."

"Bye, Rochelle."

After I hung up, Mags stood up over her cube, facing me, and held out a fist with her thumb sticking up. Then she rotated it to her thumb pointing down.

I gave her a thumbs-up.

"Yes!" she said, before sitting back down, out of sight.

A little bit later, Jared stopped into my office.

"Good. You're in a suit. Busy?"

"Not too bad. What's up?"

"I can't believe I'm asking again, being that you just covered for me, but could you possibly cover a hearing for me this afternoon? I've had a client emergency crop up that I need to take care of."

"Uh, sure. Nothing too complicated?"

"It's a motion to compel discovery." He set a file on the edge of my desk. "Just read their motion to compel and my opposition. Then let me know if you have any questions. The hearing is at two p.m."

"Will do."

"Thanks. I really appreciate it."

Cool. The boss really appreciates it.

I read through the motion and the opposition. This would be my first hearing on a motion to compel, so I was a little nervous coming into it three hours before the hearing. And going solo.

The fight was over our client's business records. Apparently she was the main breadwinner of the two and this guy was trying to argue that her business was an asset of the partnership, despite it being left out of the contract. Our client had started the business with her own funds before she met the guy, and the contract laid out nicely that what's hers is hers and what's his is his. My favorite kind of contract.

Jared's opposition was awesome. Naturally. Pretty sure he used every euphemism for *asshole* while explaining in undisputable terms that our client's business was *not* subject to discovery. And then he listed the twenty-five provisions of the contract that backed up that argument. This should be fun.

I ate my lunch and headed out early to court to give myself plenty of time. Unfortunately, I was in front of Judge Warner again, and I wasn't entirely done blushing from the ex-boyfriend fiasco on Thursday. I pulled the battery from my phone and headed into the courtroom. I signed myself in and looked around the room. I'd checked out a picture of Beatrice Adams, our client, so thankfully I found her, no problem. I sat down next to her and introduced myself.

"Hi, Kate," she said. "Jared told me he wouldn't be here but that I was in good hands." Beatrice had long, straight dark hair and reminded me of Elvira, Mistress of the Dark, a little. But she was also friendly and professional, despite her Goth vibe.

"James is over there," she added, pointing across the room. I followed her gesture, and it looked like she was pointing at an eighty-year-old man with a bushy beard.

"Um, with the beard?"

She laughed. "No, that's his attorney. James is on the other side of him."

I leaned over a little farther but still couldn't get a look at him. I shrugged so she knew he was still blocked. "So, I feel good about this hearing. I've reviewed all the moving papers and they have a very weak argument. The nice thing is that this judge is very no-nonsense and I think there's a good chance he's not going to be happy about this motion."

"Good. I'd love to see him get the smack-down."

Judge Warner entered and immediately started going through his calendar. There was one other motion to compel ahead of ours, but the issue wasn't nearly as black and white and the judge ordered the information be produced. My stomach started to twist into knots a little, like it did every time I was about to be in front of a judge. Do all attorneys feel this way, or does it eventually become old hat? I'm kinda thinking I'm always going to want to yack when I first start to speak.

Our matter was next, so Elvira—I mean Beatrice—and I headed up to the table.

"Good afternoon, Your Honor. Kate Shaw for Beatrice Adams."

I glanced down the table and the elderly attorney was no longer blocking James Harris. Now I seriously felt like I was going to be sick, but not from nerves anymore. This isn't happening.

"Gregory Lancaster for James Harris, Your Honor."

James looked over at me and stared a minute before recognition dawned. Then he smiled and gave me a little wave. Unlike Matt in the orange jumpsuit, James was well dressed and had held up well over the years. I dated him in high school. Briefly. Have I mentioned that I didn't date that much? How is it possible that I keep running into ex-boyfriends in court when there really aren't that many of them? There aren't. Honestly.

Can you die of embarrassment? I think I might be about to test that theory. My face felt like it was on fire, so I can only guess what shade of red it was.

"Ms. Shaw?"

"Yes, Your Honor?"

No efforts at hiding his amusement today. "Are you acquainted with Mr. Harris?"

"Yes, Your Honor. A *very* long time ago."

"I take it you did not realize he was the opposing party?"

"I did not, Your Honor."

"Ms. Adams, are you okay proceeding?"

Beatrice looked at me, confused. I leaned in to her and whispered, "I know James from high school. We dated. The judge wants to know if you feel there's a conflict."

Beatrice let out a sharp bark of laughter before whispering back, "Is there a conflict?"

"None."

"As long as you're on my side, I'm good."

"I am one hundred percent on your side."

Beatrice smiled. "Sounds like he was an asshole back in high school, too."

"Yep. He was."

"Alright then. Let's kick his ass."

"Your Honor," I continued, "Ms. Adams does not feel there is any conflict."

"Okay. Let's proceed. Mr. Lancaster, your motion."

Lancaster basically laid out the same weak argument he'd made in his moving papers.

Judge Warner cut him off. "Mr. Lancaster, I have read your motion. Do you have anything to say beyond simply reading your argument to me?"

"Just that during their seven-year contract, partnership resources went into supporting Ms. Adams's business, and that entitles Mr. Harris to some interest in that business."

"As you stated in your motion," Judge Warner snapped. Luckily, I'd gotten the very good "don't just rehash your motion to the judge—assume they've read it" advice and had taken it to heart. "Thank you, Mr. Lancaster."

"Ms. Shaw, is the matter submitted?" The other great advice I'd received is that when a judge doesn't give you a chance to argue and just asks if the matter is submitted, you're winning and you should shut up.

"Submitted, Your Honor."

"Very well. The motion is denied."

"Thank you, Your Honor," I said. "And, Your Honor, we included a request for monetary sanctions in the amount of attorneys' fees in our opposition?"

Judge Warner flipped through his file. "Attorneys' fees in the amount of three thousand four hundred seventy-two dollars are awarded to Ms. Adams."

"Thank you, Your Honor," I said again.

"Thank you, Your Honor," Lancaster said, sounding significantly *less* happy saying it than I did.

I picked up my file and satchel and Beatrice and I headed out of the courtroom. Once we were outside, she turned to me, wide-eyed.

I glanced over my shoulder and saw James and his attorney walking out of the courtroom. I put a finger to my lips to get Beatrice to hold her comments till they had passed us.

Not surprisingly, James was not smiling when he looked at me this time. As he started past me, he said, "So nice to see you again, Kate." Pretty sure I detected a note of sarcasm.

"You, too."

He stopped in front of me with his arms folded across his chest. He did a quick up-and-down glance at me that I'm pretty sure I was supposed to notice. "So, sweet little Kate Shaw ended up as a bloodsucking lawyer, huh?"

I did my best to hide my surprise at the remark, since I knew that was his goal. "Well, I just wanted a job where I get to stand up to bullies and assholes, you know?"

He chuckled. "Okay, maybe not so sweet anymore." As he turned to leave, he added, "Looking good, Shaw."

"Good-bye, James," I said, in my best none-too-friendly tone.

Once they had disappeared down the stairs, I smiled at Beatrice.

"That was awesome!" she said in a loud whisper.

"It was. We'd obviously won before we even got here, which is what I was hoping for. Jared's opposition was really good."

"Clearly!" Beatrice said, beaming at me. "What were the sanctions for?"

"Oh. When an attorney brings a motion to compel discovery and loses, the other party is entitled to attorneys' fees associated with defending the motion. Jared had calculated the costs of defending against this motion to be a little more than thirty-four hundred dollars."

"That's great. I didn't know I'd get back any of the money for this. Today turned into a very good day."

I smiled. "I'm glad. Hopefully this will encourage James to stop going after your business now."

"Not likely, but it's a nice thought."

Beatrice and I parted ways and I headed back to the office.

I was back at my desk, checking emails, when my phone buzzed with another Facebook notification. It was a friend request from Beatrice. I grunted. Just like Rochelle, she fell into that *cool but client* zone. Hm.

I went to Jared's office. He was flipping through one of five stacks of paper on his desk. I tapped on his door frame and he looked up.

"Hi," I said. "I know you're swamped, but I wanted to let you know your opposition killed it. By the time Warner got to me, he just asked if the matter was submitted."

Jared smiled, looking tired. "Great. Thanks for covering that for me."

"No problem. Didn't even have to argue. Oh, and we got our requested sanctions, too. Beatrice was thrilled."

"Awesome. Now if I could just magically get through these five thousand documents by Wednesday, life will be perfect."

"Let me know if I can help."

"If only. It's just that I've worked with this client for ten years and I know it inside and out, so it would take anyone else twice as long just to figure out what they were looking at. Thanks for the offer, though."

"Quick question," I said, before heading back out. "How do you handle when a client tries to friend you on Facebook?"

He tipped his head to the side and smiled. "I'll let you know if it ever happens."

Well, crap.

I sat down at my desk and checked my phone. One text from Logek.

Call me.

Hm. Usually not a good sign.

I dialed and she answered on the second ring.

"Hey. Got your text. What's up?"

"Derek never stopped seeing Hannah." Hannah was Logek's nemesis—simply by being the girl Derek apparently *had* to sleep with while he was still signed to Logek. Logek's voice was quiet, and I knew her well enough to know it was because she'd been crying and was trying not to get going again.

"Oh, honey. How? What happened? How did you find out?"

She sniffed. "Well, she called me. Because she wanted me to know that he was staying with her part of the time."

"Oh, god."

"And I guess she went through his phone and saw our texts and gathered that we were seeing each other and felt certain that I didn't know they were still together." And at that point, crying was game on again.

My eyes misted over. Son of a bitch! Dammit, Derek!

"I just feel so stupid," she said, in a quiet, breathy voice.

"Logek, no. He's stupid. Not you."

"But I fall for it *every fucking time*."

"Because you love him. That doesn't make you stupid—it makes you human."

More crying.

"Are you home?"

She sniffed. "Yes. After the phone call, I faked a migraine and went home."

"I'll be over right after work. Do you have wine?"

Now she laughed for a minute before falling back into tears. "Of course I do."

"Are you hungry?"

"Not in the least."

"I figured. I'll see you soon."

"Thanks, Kitty Kat."

"Love you."

"Love you, too."

At five o'clock on the dot, I was walking past Mags's desk.

"Look at you, sprinting out of here," she said with a smile.

I frowned. "I'm on *best friend's heart just got stomped into a million pieces* duty."

"Oh no! Logek's man that I met when we went out last time?"

"Yes. And that asshole is a repeat offender."

Mags gave me a pout. "I'm sorry. And I'm totally available if you guys need someone to break his kneecaps," she said, looking disconcertingly sincere about her offer.

I smiled at her and headed out the door.

After swinging by my apartment to change out of my suit and grab a box of Girl Scout cookies (because she may not feel like eating, but that really has nothing to do with whether or not she'll be in the mood for Girl Scout cookies), I pulled up to Logek's.

I knocked once and went inside, since the door was un-locked.

I poked my head around the corner, into her bedroom, and there she was, my Logek, curled up on her side on top of her bedcovers. I crawled onto the bed and lay down behind her, draping my arm around her and giving her a squeeze.

And, as seems to be the case with women and emotions, that show of support completely wrecked her. She broke down into loud, wet sobs. They lasted a while. I couldn't help but think of the first time we'd been through the Derek Debacle. There was more anger, less heartbreak. This time, apparently, she was buying into the whole "fool me once, shame on you; fool me twice, shame on me" school of thought and felt she had no one to blame but herself. I didn't have that problem. This was all Dick Derek's fault. I wonder if Mags was serious about her offer?

Logek's phone buzzed. She looked at it but didn't reach for it.

"Do we know who it is?"

"Yep." She picked up her phone and handed it to me without reading the text.

I went into her texts and saw that there were a few unread texts from Derek. I opened the text thread and scrolled back to the first postapocalypse text.

Hannah told me she talked to you. Please hear me out.
I'm done hearing you out, Derek. I'm just done, period.
Logek. Please. There's more to the story. At least let me explain.

When Logek didn't respond to that, he followed up with:

You have to talk to me.

Wrong there.

I love you Logek. I've always loved you.

Dick.

Yes, I've still been seeing Hannah but we aren't exclusive. She made it sound like we're still together. We aren't. I still see her but it's not serious anymore.

Yikes. I kinda hoped she stopped reading before she got to this one.

I'm coming over.

Guessing she definitely didn't read that one.

"His last text said he's coming over."

Logek sat up hurriedly, wiping her face dry. "No, no, no. I do not want to see him."

I scooted off the bed. "I'm gonna go lock the front door."

I went into the other room and threw the dead bolt on the front door before heading to the fridge and grabbing a bottle of wine. Once I had it opened, I brought the bottle and two glasses back into her room.

I sat cross-legged on the bed next to her and poured two glasses of wine. I handed one to her and she sat up to take it, mirroring my position on the bed.

"Fuck!" she said emphatically. I smiled. We tapped glasses and both took a long swig of wine.

"Get it out, girl," I said.

She smiled at me. She was amazing like that. This girl could take hits like nobody's business, but give her an hour to cry, swear, and drink and she'd do you proud every time.

"Fuck, fuck, fuck, fuck, *fuck*." That last one had some serious vigor.

"Attagirl," I said.

"Why do I have so much trouble with men?" she asked.

"Because you're beautiful and they follow you like moths to a flame. So you have plenty of screwup material on hand at all times. And you like bad boys."

She laughed. And cried a little. And nodded. "Shit. I do. Why do I do that? Shouldn't I have outgrown that by now?"

"I guess we could ask Daniel that."

"Ouch. Right," she said with a scowl.

"But bad boys are fun," I added.

"How would you know? You've always gone for good guys."

"Until my last good guy dumped me flat. Since then, I'm pretty sure I'm dabbling on the dark side."

"Mmm. Adam. Still dabbling there?"

"Not really. But Dave is definitely bad boy material."

"Yeah, I'd say so."

We both went quiet and, after a moment, Logek grimaced and some more tears streaked down her face. "I'm so tired of failing," she whispered.

"You didn't fail, honey. You loved and you lost. And that's living, not failing. I'd rather love and lose a hundred times as opposed to never taking the leap."

She nodded. "I just wish I could have one contract go the distance. Feel like someone could love me for a full seven years."

"Oh, they could love you a lot longer than that. Come on, aside from Derek, you've never even been dumped. *Their* longevity has not been the problem."

"True. But the only man I saw myself going the distance with—even re-upping with—is definitely *not* a one-woman man."

"There are others. He's not the only man out there that you could feel that way about."

"My own statistical research proves otherwise."

I laughed. "Then it's time for a new research study."

There was a loud knock on the front door and our eyes went wide like we'd broken into a liquor store and just got caught drinking behind the counter.

We heard Derek's muffled voice. "Logek. Please talk to me. I know you're home. I see Kate's car here."

I looked at her and raised my eyebrows. She could decide if she wanted to talk to him or not without my input.

She wobbled her head side to side, causing her blond ponytail to sway. She blew out a sigh and headed to the front door. I followed her out, thinking it might be time to give her some privacy.

I saw her whisk away a couple more tears before opening the door.

As soon as she opened the door, Derek stepped in, probably figuring he had a small window of opportunity before she slammed the door in his face again.

"Logek, at least talk to me," Derek said. He quickly looked over to where I was standing and then back to Logek. "Kate, could I talk to Logek alone for a few minutes?"

"She can stay," Logek interjected. Oh yay. This won't be awkward at all.

Derek sighed. "Fine." He ran his hand through his wavy blond hair, pushing it back from his face. I knew Logek loved it when he did that. Unfortunately. "I never lied to you."

"Well you sure left out something pretty damn important."

"Hannah and I aren't together anymore."

"You're still fucking her."

"But she isn't my girlfriend."

"This conversation is pointless." I had to agree. Derek genuinely didn't seem to think he'd screwed up royally.

"No, I'm just trying to make you understand," he said, putting his hands out in front of Logek like he was trying to calm a skittish animal.

"I do understand. You *left me* for Hannah. Then you led me to believe you two were over and that you regretted losing me—"

"I *do* regret losing you," Derek interrupted.

"I'm not finished," Logek shouted, pointing a finger at his chest. He immediately fell silent. "You broke my heart when you took off with her. It wasn't that I expected us to suddenly be exclusive just because we started seeing each other again, but you should have known—unless you're the dumbest asshole on the planet—that I would have a problem with you still seeing *her*."

After Logek was silent a moment, Derek said, "Then I must be the dumbest asshole on the planet. Despite the way Hannah made it sound to you, I'm not cheating on her. She knows we aren't exclusive. So, since I'm not living with her and I'm free to see who I want, I thought that would be enough for you."

"This is useless. It's like we're speaking two different languages," Logek said, with an exasperated glance in my direction.

"Well, I never have been able to get inside your head. I wish I could, but I just don't understand the way you work."

"That fact is painfully clear."

"I'm sorry, Logek. I really do love you. We just never seem to be in the right place," he finished quietly.

Logek nodded. "I agree."

"Would it make a difference if I stopped seeing Hannah altogether?"

Logek paused. Based on what she'd told him, logically, it would make a difference. But the fact that he'd proven once again that he's clueless when he's doing shitty things was at odds with her sense of self-preservation. "I feel like we have bigger problems than Hannah at this point."

Derek stood motionless, waiting to see if she'd give in. She wouldn't. You go, girl.

Eventually, Derek gave a slight nod and leaned in, gave Logek a tight, unreciprocated hug, and headed out the door.

When the door closed behind him, Logek whispered, "I did the right thing."

"You did the right thing," I echoed.

"One way or another, he was going to keep hurting me."

"He was."

"And love isn't supposed to be this hard."

"It isn't."

Logek turned her tearstained face to me and quirked her mouth into a half smile. "You're my favorite parrot."

I laughed. "Yeah, well Polly needs a drink."

"Amen."

We headed back into her bedroom, where we'd left our wineglasses, and settled onto the bed once more, sitting cross-legged and facing each other. She sighed. And drank. Wiped away more tears and muttered "Fuck" a few more times.

We sipped our wine and looked at each other blankly. Logek snapped her fingers suddenly and leaned over the side of the bed. When she sat up straight again she was holding a behemoth box of condoms. "Here. Take these with you when you go. In case I have any moments of weakness."

I held the box of Trojans between my hands. "Where exactly does one purchase a box of condoms this big?" I asked with a smile.

"Costco."

"Good to know."

"Not sure they carry the Magnum, though, if that's what you might need . . ." She trailed off with an eyebrow raised.

I laughed. "I appreciate your confidence in me, but I don't need *anything* in *any* size right now."

She shrugged. "Good. Make 'em earn it."

"Oh," I said. "Mags offered to break Derek's kneecaps if you want."

Logek smiled. "Where has she been all our lives?"

"Right?" I glanced at the box of condoms. "You know, just because you won't be having sex with Derek doesn't mean you won't . . . *eventually* . . . be having sex with *someone*."

Logek appeared to consider that. "You're right. I better hang on to them."

We took another sip from our glasses, but Logek's mind was clearly falling back into the Derek abyss, since she started wiping her eyes and sniffing again.

"Oh!" I said, startling her out of her misery. "I forgot to tell you. I ran into Matt Taylor."

She frowned. "High school Matt Taylor?"

"Yep."

"What's he doing?"

"About three to five for possession with intent to distribute."

Logek laughed just as she'd taken a drink of wine, so she quickly covered her mouth with her hand. She fanned her face a little, trying to swallow without spitting wine all over me. "Oh my god. You saw him in court, I take it?"

I nodded, smiling. "And then, because I apparently pissed off God somehow, I saw James Harris in court today."

Logek laughed and shook her head. "Was he there on felony charges, too?"

"No, he actually looked great but apparently is still an ass-hole after all these years. Point is, both of them outed me to the judge, so I'm pretty sure that judge now thinks I was a call girl in my former life or something."

Logek shrugged. "Well, law school *is* expensive."

CHAPTER *9*

When I got into the office the next morning, I swung by Mags's desk. She was wearing a sleeveless black turtleneck with tight black slacks. I was about to ask if she was moonlighting as a cat burglar, when she looked up at me with a smile and picked up a Louisville Slugger she had resting against her cubicle wall. Oh—clearly she's dressed for a little assault and battery.

I laughed and shook my head at her. "Have I mentioned that you are one of my favorite people?"

"Not today, but it's early."

"I did extend your very kind offer to Logek, but I don't think she's mustered up quite enough anger to wish him bodily harm."

"Oh well. One of these days, buddy," Mags said to her baseball bat, then rested it back in the corner. "How's she doing?" Mags asked, turning to me again.

"Taking her broken heart like a champ."

"She seems like the type that would. I got a call first thing this morning on a referral for you."

"For me? Who referred them?"

"The guy whose partner claimed she only cheated after she found out about his DUI."

"Jim Trainor?"

Mags nodded. My excitement fizzled. "He's kind of an asshole. Not sure I really want to be on his friends-and-family plan."

"But it's your first client that *you* brought in. Just by being a badass."

I smiled. "Jim's ex did call me a bitch at the end of her depo."

"Exactly. Badass."

"Okay, then. Maybe birds of a feather don't always flock together. What's the situation?"

Mags bit her lip. Crap. "Well, apparently Scarlett and her ex-partner Rhett—"

I cut her off, waving my hands in front of my face. "You're making this up."

"Kate. You *can't* make this up."

"Scarlett O'Hara?"

"Now you're just being silly. Scarlett *Blutofsky* . . ."

"Lovely."

"I thought so. Was signed to Rhett *Cadavetti* . . ."

"Good Italian name."

"Precisely. And while they were signed, they owned two neighboring parcels. They lived in one and rented out the one next door. A few years in, they both breached, fireworks, et cetera, and they ended up ousting their tenant and each taking one of the parcels in their settlement."

"What could possibly go wrong?"

"Right? And yet, as it turns out, everything," Mags said with a severe expression. "They have temporary restraining orders against each other and the hearing on the actual orders is being heard this afternoon."

I turned a blank expression to her. *"This afternoon?"* I asked.

Mags nodded.

"Do signing attorneys usually handle this kind of thing?" I asked.

"More often than you'd think."

I sighed. "So which one is mine?"

"Blutofsky."

"Awesome."

"She'll be here in an hour."

I thrust my fist into the air, giving my best *yay* gesture, and walked into my office.

Before I'd finished reading through my new emails, my phone buzzed.

"Beth Erickson calling regarding Lewis–Hamilton," Mags said.

"Thanks," I said. I'd made a call to Beth after Dot had told me she was willing to trade the grandfather clock for Elvis. I could hear the distrust in Beth's voice, feeling like it had been a trick somehow. I sort of agreed with her.

I picked up my phone as soon as it rang. "Hi, Beth."

"Hi, Kate."

"So, how'd we do?"

"Better than expected, actually. I'd half expected Daryl to explode when I conveyed the offer, waiting for him to tell me that the clock had been a gift to her from a previous partner or something."

"You weren't alone on that."

"Turns out, he *does* want the clock."

"Good. That's good, right?"

"No, it's good. It's apparently *his* family heirloom that she had her movers take from the house when he was away."

"Oops."

Beth laughed. "Yeah. Big oops. He said 'if that bleepity bleeping thief wants to trade his own bleeping clock back to him,' he'll take it."

"Your ears must have been burning."

"Practice. I know to keep the phone at least three inches from my ear."

"So that's it? The clock for Elvis?"

Beth made a cynical laugh. Naturally. "Of course not. He wants the clock *and* a twenty-five percent reduction in the damages payment."

I flipped through my file quickly, looking for what the damages were calculated to be, and whistled when I found the figure. "That's a lot of money."

"Tell me about it."

"So I guess I can tell Dot she can either accept the reduction and get Elvis back or she can keep the money and buy herself a million new guinea pigs to replace him."

"More or less."

"Did I mention she also said she'd take his Maserati?"

Beth laughed. "I'm sure she would. I have a feeling you'd miss the rat a lot less driving around in *that* car."

"Guinea pig," I said, before I could stop myself.

"Kate."

"Right. Whatever. Okay. I guess I'll take this back to Dot and get back to you."

"My advice? Do it over the phone. And keep the phone at least three inches from your ear."

"Sound advice. Talk to you soon."

I looked at my clock and figured I had time to call Dot about the new settlement offer before my next appointment. Yippee.

Dot picked up after a couple of rings. "Dot Hamilton."

"Hello, Dot. This is Kate Shaw."

"Hi, Kate."

"Well, I took your offer of the grandfather clock to Daryl's attorney."

"I think I changed my mind about that."

Is she effing kidding me? *Okay. Breathe.* "Dot, you can't authorize me to make settlement offers and then just change your mind. It undermines the whole settlement effort."

She sighed. "Fine. Did the ass accept it?"

"Not exactly."

Dot made a dry, cynical chuckle. "I'm surprised, after how much he's whined about that stupid clock."

"Well, he sort of said it was his anyway, so I think he felt like it was more of a dig, you offering it back in exchange for Elvis."

"Too bad."

"So what he did say was that he would give you Elvis for the grandfather clock . . ." *Just spit it out fast, Kate.* "And a twenty-five percent reduction in the damage amount."

Now Dot's laugh was lyrical. And way more disconcerting than the dry, bitter one.

"So he wants me to pay him a million dollars to get back an animal that already belongs to me?" Her voice rose an octave with every couple words, until she was shrill and practically screeching by the end.

"I understand. But, Dot. This is your life. Do you really want to spend years . . . the rest of Elvis's life . . . fighting over this settlement?"

"Are you actually suggesting, as my attorney, that I give up a million dollars to get a guinea pig?"

Oh, hell no. And not just because I'm pretty sure she was trying to trap me. "No, no, no. Of course not. I'm just saying, it seems like deep down you must know what it will take to settle this. I just hate to see someone wasting their life fighting instead of finding an agreement they can live with and moving on."

"I really like Elvis," she said quietly, and for the first time, I actually felt bad for the shrew.

"Dot, have you thought about a dating site? Maybe you just need something to help you move past Daryl."

"The problem is that Daryl was such an ass, I just don't feel like men, in general, are worth it."

"Yeah. I get that. But who knows? You might have some fun by accident."

Dot actually laughed a little at that. "I'll give it some thought. Both suggestions."

"Glad to hear it."

"Besides, it would piss Daryl off to no end if I started seeing other men."

Good talk. Kate Shaw: changing lives for the better.

After hanging up with Dot, I really didn't have time to read Mags's notes about Scarlett before she showed up. Rita from reception buzzed my phone and informed me that she was putting Scarlett into conference room 2 for me.

I picked up my pad of paper and pen, mustered up an unenthusiastic smile, and headed down the hall.

When I got into the room, Scarlett was sitting at the conference table, frowning at the legal services contract Rita typically gives them to review while waiting for the attorney.

When she heard me come through the door, she looked up at me.

"Hi, Scarlett. I'm Kate Shaw."

"Scarlett Blutofsky. Nice to meet you," she said, shaking my hand. Scarlett had big, frizzy auburn hair and was dressed in floral print capri pants and a sleeveless pink shirt. She looked to be about midforties, but she seemed like the type that might just look older from years of hard living. Her face had a leather quality to the skin, like she's a sun worshipper, and she had a smudge of pink lipstick on her front tooth. Which I was going to do my damnedest to not stare at. *Don't stare.*

"So, Scarlett, I haven't really had time to review my assistant's notes, so why don't you just tell me what's going on."

She nodded and let out a big dramatic sigh. "Well, it started small, with Rhett just stealing shit off my porch when it got delivered by UPS. Then he started cutting down my rosebushes. Then he was letting his dog shit on my front lawn. So I put up security cameras so I would have proof enough to have him arrested. I have him on camera flipping me off."

"Flipping *you* off? Or the camera?"

"Well, he did it to the camera, knowing I'd be watching."

"Not really illegal."

She frowned at me.

"Please. Continue."

"So, I got these pink flamingoes on my lawn." Totally not surprised. "And he kept claiming they were on his property. But they weren't. Anyway, I came out and all their heads were missing."

I almost laughed, but luckily stifled it at the last moment so it came out sounding more like an indignant grunt. She approved. "Right? He's such a dirtbag. I watched the video and saw him lopping their heads off with pruning shears. What's to stop him from doing the same to me?"

I frowned. "Well, I don't think decapitating plastic lawn decorations rises to the level of a threat on your life." She narrowed her eyes at me. "Necessarily," I added. "Why don't you tell me what else he's done that led to your request for the restraining order."

"He's pressed his bare ass to his window."

"Which window?"

"His bedroom window."

"How did you happen to see that?"

"I caught it on camera."

"You probably shouldn't have a security camera pointed into his bedroom. The judge may frown on that."

"Well, I gotta know what he's up to," she whined. "My life could depend on it."

"But he could be acting out because you're invading his privacy."

"I thought you were supposed to be on my side."

"I am, but I just want you to understand what the judge will think of the situation, this afternoon in court."

"But he's pushed me. I had to call nine-one-one."

"What happened?"

"I was putting my garbage at the curb, and he always says it's over the property line and is actually on his property and that he has trouble pulling in to his driveway. So, to be an ass, he moves it to where it's in front of my driveway, so that I have to move it when I get home."

"Well, is it on his side?"

"Barely. Anyway, so last week, I got home and had to get out of my car to move the garbage can, and as I was rolling it back to where it was, he came running out of his house. Clearly he'd been watching for me. So he grabs the garbage can and tries to pull it away from me. We wrestle over it a few minutes and he finally comes around and shoves me, calling me a crazy bitch and stuff. So I went and called nine-one-one."

"Did they arrest him?"

"Well, no. On account of us each saying it was the other one that shoved and neither of us having any marks."

"Well, did you shove him?"

"Not that I remember. But I was scared. Anyway, the cop said I should get a restraining order, so I wrote up the application and had my sister serve it on him."

"When were you served with his application?"

"Two days later. He totally just did it to get back at me."

"Do you have a copy of his application?"

Scarlett opened an ancient green Trapper Keeper folder she had in front of her and rifled through some papers.

"Here it is. It's all lies." *Of course it is. I'm sure you're 100 percent innocent in this.*

I scanned down his application looking at his allegations. Blocking his driveway with her garbage can. Placing ugly lawn ornaments on his yard. Angling a security camera in through his bedroom window. Egging his front door. Defecating on his porch.

What the hell? My stomach turned a little at the mere thought of that one.

"Um, Scarlett. This says you defecated on his porch."

"What's 'defecated'?"

"Uh, basically he's saying you . . . pooped . . . on his porch."

"Oh. Well, I'd had a few beers and I was pissed about finding dog shit on my lawn for the fifth time that week. I guess I shouldn't have, but he pissed me off."

I stared at her with my mouth hanging open. I was doing everything humanly possible to not picture this chain of events, but I was failing. The image of Scarlett, her floral capris around her ankles, squatting to relieve herself on Rhett's front porch, was burned into my brain for eternity. Awesome. I shook my head and returned to Rhett's application in my hand.

Chased him into his house with a knife. Attacked him while moving her garbage can out of his driveway. Threatened to kill him if he ever brought a woman home.

"Scarlett," I said, looking up at her severely. "This has some very serious accusations. This makes me think he has a decent chance of getting his restraining order granted. If he gets his restraining order, it will likely be in place for three years, and you won't be allowed to keep or own any guns. Do you own guns?"

"I'm an American, ain't I?" Oh, dear god.

"Well, if this gets granted," I said, holding up the papers in my hand, "you'll be forced to get rid of them all."

"Well, then we can't lose."

I sighed. I flipped to the last page of the application and realized that it was filed by Doug Simpson. "I didn't realize Rhett had an attorney representing him in this."

"Yeah. Once I realized he'd lawyered up, I figured I better do the same."

"Okay. Well, I think our best bet will be to try to settle something to avoid the restraining orders."

"Whatever you think is best. But he's the one being a dick."

I looked back down at Rhett's application. Yep. Clearly he's the only asshole in this scenario.

"Well, I'll meet you at the court at twelve forty-five p.m.," I said, standing up from the table. "I'll keep this and make copies for my file and bring your copies back to you at court."

"Okay. Thanks. See you soon."

I watched Scarlett walk back toward the lobby, her ample rear end swaying back and forth, before I turned to head back to my office.

Mags came in a moment later. "So? Was she everything you hoped?"

"Remind me what I was hoping for?"

"That she was nothing like the guy who referred her."

"Ah. I think she's actually much worse."

"Yikes. Sounds . . . entertaining."

"She admitted to taking a dump on his front porch."

I was treated to one of Mags's rare shocked expressions. "No."

"Yep. She knows she *probably* shouldn't have, but she was pissed about the number of times his dog had crapped on her lawn, so . . ."

"That's not exactly an eye for an eye."

"My thought as well. Would you make copies of these for me?" I asked, handing her Scarlett's stack of documents. "Those are her originals, so I want to return them to her this afternoon at the hearing."

"You got it, boss," Mags said, on her way out of my office.

I sat down at my desk and made a whiny sigh. Totally not because I was feeling sorry for myself that I was adding to my crazy-client quota. Not at all. Because self-pity is super an-noying.

*

I walked into the courtroom right on time and was slipping the battery out of my phone when I spotted Doug Simpson. Today he was in a slightly wrinkled, outdated brown suit, and I'd swear his hairline had receded more since we'd last seen each other. He gave me a little two-finger salute and headed to where I was standing.

"Heya, Kate. How's it going?"

"Good, Doug. You?"

"Better if I was making so much money that I could turn down these shitty cases," he said with a lopsided grin.

I made a noncommittal chuckle. I haven't been doing this job long enough to make those kinds of jokes—I needed to earn my own jaded persona. No cutsies.

"So," Doug continued when I didn't say anything, "both our clients are getting slapped today unless we can stipulate to a truce."

"I sort of had the same thought."

"Okay. Judge Warner typically tries to get parties to work shit out before hearing the matter anyway, so we'll just tell him we want to try to work out an agreement."

"Perfect."

We headed back inside and I spotted Scarlett. I went and sat next to her and watched Doug sit down next to a dark-haired guy with a beard. Beyond the hair, I didn't get a good look at him.

"Well?" Scarlett whispered loudly to me, once I sat down.

"We're going to ask the judge to give us some time to see if we can work out a settlement."

Scarlett pouted. "I guess. If you really think we need to."

"If you don't want to risk being required to get rid of your guns, then yes, I think we really need to."

When she continued to pout, I sighed, but I tried to make it sound like it was an *I hear ya sister; this is so unfair* sigh, and not a *Maybe if you hadn't taken a shit on your ex's porch we'd have more bargaining power* sigh. Even though it was definitely the second one.

Judge Warner called our case and we approached the table.

"Good afternoon, Ms. Shaw," Judge Warner said, with a slight smile. I smiled back, happy he knew me by name. Made me feel like less of a fraud pretending to be a lawyer.

"Good afternoon, Your Honor. I'm here on behalf of petitioner . . . and respondent, Scarlett Blutofsky."

"Thank you. And Mr. Simpson?"

"Good afternoon, Your Honor," Doug said. "Appearing for Rhett Cadavetti," he said, making a slight gesture to the man standing on the other side of him.

"Thank you, Mr. Simpson," Judge Warner said, before turning back toward me. He had a slight grin and raised his bushy eyebrows to me. Shit. What was he asking? We'd stated our appearances. He was looking at me like I'd forgotten something. Then he made an almost imperceptible head nod toward Doug's client. And I died a little.

Or maybe a lot, as I realized that at my last two appearances *in a row* I'd been surprised by the opposing party being an ex-boyfriend. And now Judge Warner was giving me shit for it. A tiny part of me felt like the cool kid, since I had a good enough rapport with the judge for him to needle me like this. But the overwhelming majority of me wanted to crawl into a little hole for the next five years or so. Just until the embarrassment subsided.

I was just about to shake my head no and attempt to resurrect whatever dignity I could scrounge up, when I suddenly had the horrible thought that I hadn't actually gotten a decent look at Doug's client. Erring on the side of caution, I leaned forward over the table, ever so slightly, and tried to sneak a glance at Rhett Cadavetti.

Okay—let's be clear. When the entire courtroom is silent and waiting for something to happen and the judge and one of the attorneys are having some sort of unspoken communication, there is no such thing as *sneaking* anything. Everyone was watching everything like it was an episode of *Court TV*. Except that I felt like I was playing the part of the defendant in this little scenario.

Rhett Cadavetti was super furry. As in halfway-to-a-wookie furry. His hair was overgrown and wavy; he had a full, bushy beard and mustache; and his eyebrows looked like furry little caterpillars having a race to meet in the middle of his forehead. And, thank god, I'd never seen him before in my life. Yes, theoretically I would have remembered if I'd ever dated a guy named Rhett, but guys lie sometimes. Or change their names. Or end up in witness protection. Point being, my recent luck is bad enough that I felt the need to check him out before confirming that I'd never dated him.

I slapped a smile on my bright red cheeks and shook my head at the judge.

"So, Ms. Shaw, I've read the petitions. Would you and Mr. Simpson like some time to see if your clients can come to terms?"

"Yes, Your Honor. We believe we can reach an agreement."

"Very well. I'll trail your matter. If you're unable to reach terms by the end of today's session, come back in and we can continue the matter to another day."

"Thank you, Your Honor."

The four of us filed out of the courtroom. I was hoping the question the judge silently posed to me wasn't as obvious as it felt to me. Maybe it was subtle and no one noticed the momentary lag.

"So, what the hell was that all about?" Doug asked, his face unusually animated. *Stupid, Kate. Of course it didn't go unnoticed.*

"Oh," I said, waving my hand nonchalantly. "I've just run into acquaintances as defendants on my last couple of cases. I think Judge Warner was teasing me. He wanted me to confirm that I didn't know Mr. Cadavetti."

Now Doug looked a little astonished. Damn. Did he see right through my "acquaintances" euphemism?

"What?" I asked, shrugging my shoulders.

"Judge Warner doesn't *tease*. You really are charmed, Shaw."

Yeah. Yay me. That's exactly what I was thinking.

"Okay, well, Scarlett, why don't you stay in this conference room for now," I said, gesturing to a tiny room outside the courtroom. "And Mr. Cadavetti can wait outside. And Doug and I will talk about what each of you want out of this agreement."

Scarlett nodded, still wearing a sulky expression, and went into the room and closed the door. Doug led Rhett outside and then came back in, and he and I went into the other tiny conference room.

Doug pulled out a folder and took out a preprinted stipulated agreement form. Nice. I didn't even know those existed.

"Alrighty," Doug started, as I watched him neatly print the names of the parties and the case names at the top of the form. "So, shall we start with the 'No shitting on each other's porch' thing?"

I gave him a weak smile. "Ha-ha. I don't think we need to be quite that detailed. I guess just the basic 'Parties agree they shall not harass, verbally abuse, or intimidate each other.' "

"That works. And 'No speaking unless through legal counsel.' "

"Obviously. Since they can't speak without getting into a fight. And they need to stay entirely off each other's property. Would Rhett agree to split the cost of getting the boundary line surveyed? I think a lot of issues are arising because they think the other is on their property."

"The issues are arising because they're assholes. But yeah, that's a good thought. I'll check with him."

"And I want them to still be able to call nine-one-one if they feel in danger from the other party, without calling us first."

Doug didn't look up from his writing. "Right. Calling nine-one-one in a perceived emergency is not a violation of this agreement. And parties agree not to call each other's home, work, or cell phone and agree not to attempt contact of any kind."

"Perfect."

"Okay," Doug said, handing the handwritten agreement to me to read through.

"Looks good. Let me run through it with Scarlett while you talk to Rhett about it?"

"Yep."

We left, and I went into Scarlett's conference room.

"Okay," I said. "I think we have a reasonable agreement. Basically, the two of you are not to contact each other, harass each other, or go onto each other's property. On that point, I think you two should really have your boundary line surveyed, since you guys seem to disagree about *where* the line is. Would you be willing to split the cost of the survey? It could be a few thousand dollars."

"Fine. But then, once he realizes that his fence is actually on my property, can I tear the fucking thing down?"

"No. But I'll talk to Doug about provisions, should there be an encroachment. Are you okay with the rest?"

"I'm not sure. So what do I do when his dog takes a shit on my lawn?"

I can't believe I have to say this. "You'll call me. And then I'll call Doug and he'll talk to his client about him being in violation of the agreement." Mental note: add Rhett's dog to forbidden visitors to Scarlett's plantation.

"And that'll work?"

"Yes, it will. If we have an agreement signed by the judge, violation of that order is contempt of court. If he violates it— we'll bring an action against him for contempt."

She lit up a little at that thought. Aww. How sweet.

"Okay, let me go back and talk to Doug about a few more things."

I headed back into the other conference room and Doug was already in there.

"Rhett's good with the splitting the cost of a survey."

"Great. We may need to add something about the parties agreeing to add an addendum to this agreement after the survey is done, so they don't go all Hatfields and McCoys over the boundary line once it's found."

"Yeah, Rhett mentioned that Scarlett thinks his fence is on her property."

"There may have been a little talk of ripping it out."

"Okie dokie," he said, beginning to add to the preexisting agreement. "The parties agree to share the cost of a survey to determine the placement of their shared boundary line, fifty-fifty. Once the boundary is located, the parties agree to meet, through counsel, to discuss any encroachments before exercising any self-help."

"Perfect. Oh—you better add his dog to 'people and things not allowed on her property.' "

Doug chuckled but kept writing. "We'd better just make that a general 'The parties agree not to enter the other's property, let their pets or visitors on the other's property, and agree not to damage or place any object of any kind on each other's property.' Did she tell you about the twenty pink flamingoes?"

"She mentioned something about Rhett chopping the heads off *her* pink flamingoes. But I have a sneaking suspicion that isn't what we're talking about."

"I guess her and some girlfriends got drunk and went around stealing pink flamingo lawn ornaments and relocated them all to Rhett's front yard."

"Wait. She found twenty houses with pink flamingo lawn ornaments?" Okay, so maybe I lost focus a little. But I found that astonishing.

"Don't they normally put those things in pairs? Maybe she only needed to find ten houses with them."

"Still! Ten houses? I thought they only existed in novelty stores!" *Okay, Kate. Get back on track.* "Well, I think that might have been in retaliation for him cutting the heads off her pink flamingoes with pruning shears. How did he know it was Scarlett that created the flamingo garden in his front yard?"

"He has a security camera on his front porch. Oh. That

reminds me. We need Scarlett to change the angle on the camera that's pointed at Rhett's bedroom."

"Are you sure it's pointed directly at it?"

"He seems to think so. Can she access them remotely? If she can pull it up on her phone and show me, I can let him know if it isn't actually aimed at it."

"Okay, let's go see if she has access."

We walked across the hall, and Scarlett glared at Doug when she saw him come into the room behind me.

"Scarlett, we're almost done. But there is a question about your security cameras. Can you pull up the footage over your phone?"

"Of course I can. That asshole works from home. God knows what kind of shit he's gonna pull while I'm at work."

I didn't bother to look back at Doug. We just waited quietly while she logged into her security system and loaded her camera feeds.

"Okay, here's the first one," she said, turning the camera so that we could see it. You could only see her front yard. "Here's the second." She gave us a view of her backyard. Tastefully littered with nylon lawn chairs and an inflatable kiddie pool. Few beer cans. "This is the third." She turned the screen toward us and we had a different view of a backyard. It still had its share of redneck decorations—vehicle tires, ice chests, scrap plywood—but I was pretty sure it wasn't the same yard.

"Is that your yard?" Doug asked. Damn. I was gonna go with no.

"Well, this camera is attached to the corner of my house at the end of the driveway."

"But it looks like it's pointed into Rhett's backyard. That will need to come down. Or be angled somewhere else."

Scarlett shot some eye daggers at Doug and clicked her screen once more. "This is the last one."

It was centered on a window. Taped up in the window was a big piece of cardboard with a hand giving a one-finger salute, drawn in black marker.

"I'm guessing this would be Rhett's bedroom," I said.

"Yeah. But the camera is to view my driveway. I just can't do that without accidentally getting his window."

"Actually, I don't see the driveway—just the window," Doug said.

"Scarlett, that one will need to be moved as well. You just need to change the angle so that you aren't invading his privacy," I said.

"Fuck. Fine."

Doug sat down at the table and scribbled a last line on the agreement. "Is ten days enough time for you to get the cameras moved?" he asked.

"I guess." Scarlett was back to the sulking thing. She apparently just had two settings: pissed off or pouty.

Doug handed the agreement back to me. "I'll give you a few minutes to review it with your client. Once it's signed, I'll take it to Rhett for his signature."

"I already know what's in it," Scarlett said, snatching up a pen from the table and scribbling her signature at the bottom of the agreement. "Here. Go get Dickhead's signature so we can get the fuck out of here." Such a delicate flower.

Doug looked at me for approval and I nodded. "Thanks," I said, a little apologetically.

After Doug left, I turned back to Scarlett. "Okay. It's going to be really important to remember that this agreement gets signed by the judge. That means if you violate it in any way, they can get you for contempt of court, too."

"I get it. If he just keeps out of my way, it'll be fine."

"So, how long were you guys signed for?"

"Six years."

Wow. I raised my eyebrows.

"This time."

Oh god. Serial dysfunction. "How many times have you two signed?"

Her eyes rolled up toward the ceiling. Adding? "I guess it's been five times. There was a sixth, but we didn't sign that one."

"So, how long have you two been on-again, off-again?"

"Since we were fifteen."

I was glad I wasn't drinking water, because I think there'd be a decent chance I would have choked on it. "Fifteen? You signed for the first time? Or you just started dating?"

"No, we started dating when we were fourteen. Signed our first contract when we were fifteen."

"With parental consent?" Stupid question. Minors can't sign contracts. But I couldn't stop myself.

"Yeah," she said with a sly grin. "Well, my mom would have signed anyway, since *Gone with the Wind* is her favorite book and she felt like we were meant to be signed, just like Rhett and Scarlett." Ah, Parenting 101. Let your fifteen-year-old daughter sign because she met a guy with the corresponding literary name. "But we knew his parents wouldn't go for it, so we just told them I was knocked up. Then they were all for it."

"But you weren't, right? I mean, I don't think you mentioned having any children."

"Fuck no. We're pretty sure I can't have kids." After she said that, she pushed her red painted lips together in a way that made me feel sorry for her . . . for the *one* second before she followed it up with, "Probably a good thing, since I really can't stand kids." There it is. The process of natural selection, hard at work.

I nodded noncommittally.

There was a knock at the door a couple minutes later and I opened up to see Doug standing there with the signed paper in his hands. "Ready to head back in?"

"Absolutely," I said.

We walked back in to the courtroom and I saw Judge Warner register our return, so I knew he'd call us when he had a break between cases.

He finished up another case and then reached behind him to grab a folder. "Recalling the matter of Blutofsky v. Cadavetti and related matters."

We stood at the table once again.

"Ms. Shaw, were you able to reach an agreement?"

"Yes, Your Honor. Mr. Simpson has the agreement, signed by both parties."

"Mr. Simpson, please hand that to the bailiff."

Doug handed it to the tall, lean man with gray hair who walked stiffly up to the judge's bench to hand him the agreement.

We were quiet for a couple of minutes while Judge Warner read over the agreement.

"Very well. Ms. Blutofsky, have you had time to review this with Ms. Shaw?"

"Yes, sir."

"And is this your signature here at the bottom?"

"Yes, sir."

He repeated the same question to Rhett and confirmed his signature as well.

"Okay. Do either of you have any questions of the Court before I sign this?"

I looked at Scarlett and she shook her head. Rhett did the same.

"Okay. I've signed the agreement. The clerk will get you both copies. I want to reiterate to you both that this agreement is enforceable by this Court. Failure to follow its terms will be grounds for contempt of court."

Scarlett and Rhett both nodded once again.

The bailiff took two copies of the fully executed agreement from the court clerk and walked them over to us.

"Thank you, Mr. Simpson. Thank you, Ms. Shaw."

"Thank you, Your Honor," Doug and I echoed together.

Once we'd cleared the courtroom, I turned to Doug and held out my hand. He shook it. "I hope *not* to talk to you soon," I said, smiling.

Doug chuckled. "Wanna bet?"

"No. I said 'hope.' I'm not an idiot."

That earned me another chuckle before he and Rhett walked away.

"Okay, Scarlett. Let me know how it goes. And let me know if you have anyone in mind to do the surveying so that I can run it by Doug Simpson. Since you guys are splitting the cost, we need to be sure they agree on the person to do the work."

"Okay. I'll look into it and let you know."

"Remember, don't let him goad you into violating the stipulated order. He knows how to push your buttons to get a reaction from you."

A wistful look came over her face. Ew. *Poor choice of words, Kate.*

"Seriously, Scarlett, don't let him piss you off and make you do something stupid."

"I know. I know. Believe me—he'll do something stupid first."

"That's the spirit. Okay, I'll talk to you soon," I said to her with a pat on her shoulder, and began walking toward my car.

By the time I got back to the office, most of the afternoon was gone. I gave Mags a wide-eyed look as I passed her desk.

"How'd it go?"

"Awesome. Pretty sure Scarlett is my new BFF."

"Super. Speaking of your new BFF, she called for you."

"What? When? I just left her fifteen minutes ago."

"Right before you walked in. She says Rhett flipped off her camera."

"I don't want to sound melodramatic, but maybe you should shoot me. Because I'm thinking, after a couple weeks of playing peacekeeper between these two, it'll be a mercy killing."

Mags nodded. "Well, let's table that idea for now."

CHAPTER *10*

I got home that evening, drained. After I'd changed out of my suit, my phone buzzed. Dave. And all the angst of our unresolved argument flooded back into me.

> *Kate we need to talk.*
> *I'm not sure what else there is to say.*
> *Really? We have one argument and you're just going to end things?*
> *It's not just one thing. It's everything.*

I looked at my phone, waiting for a response, and jumped a little when there was a knock at my front door. I looked through the peephole. Dave.

I opened the door, frowning.

"Dave . . . I'm tired. I had a long day and I don't have the energy to do this right now."

He wasn't smiling. He was in slacks and a button-down shirt, like he was in between newscasts. "Well, I don't have the energy to wait. We need to work this out and get back on track."

I waved a hand through the air. "Fine. But if this is happening, I'm going to need wine."

"Sounds good to me." He followed me into the kitchen.

I pointed to the opened bottle on the counter and he carried it to the table along with the two glasses I handed to him. He poured the wine and I sat down at the table.

He picked up his wineglass and held it out to me. "To us," he said.

I feel like I'm gonna be sick. I gave him a halfhearted smile and took a sip of wine (that may have been more an indelicate gulp).

It was clear that Dave was expecting our talk to be quick and easy and that we would get back into . . . whatever the hell we were into before the fight. He turned his chair so that he was facing me.

"Okay," he said, taking a sip from his glass before setting it back on the table. "Let's get the unpleasantness over with."

"The unpleasantness?" I frowned and focused on my glass. "Dave, I do my best to always be honest with people. Even when it's difficult. So I'm really not accustomed to having people accuse me of being deliberately manipulative and calling me a liar. I wouldn't expect that from an acquaintance, let alone someone who claims to care about me."

"I understand that now. I was wrong. I admit it."

"But why would you want to be in a relationship with someone that you can't trust?"

"I do trust you."

"Really? That's why you assumed I was lying to you?"

"Fuck, Kate," he said, throwing his hands up in a frustrated gesture. As his hand went out, he clipped his wineglass, tipping it over. I watched as it fell, seemingly in slow motion, landed on the table, and broke into several pieces.

"Dammit, Dave!" I said, jumping up and reaching for the pieces of glass. I felt my eyes well with tears.

"Seriously, Kate? You're crying over a wineglass? I'll buy you another one."

A single tear rolled down my cheek as I turned on him, my hand full of the broken pieces. "That's not the point! They were a gift! They're important to me."

He put his hands up in front of him, defensively. "I'm sorry. It was an accident."

We were quiet for a couple minutes as we cleaned up the broken glass and spilled wine. I stepped on the pedal of the trash can to open it and dropped in the pieces of the tiger print glass. After washing my hands and drying them, I stood quietly with my hands on the kitchen counter.

"Kate," Dave said softly. He reached out and grasped my hand. "Let's go talk in the other room."

Yep. Time to rip off the Band-Aid. I nodded and he held my hand and led me into the living room, where we sat down on the sofa.

"I really will buy you another wineglass."

I shook my head. "I overreacted. It was an accident."

He put his hand on my chin and turned my face so that I was looking at him. "You've made your point on the honesty thing, babe. I've learned my lesson. I won't doubt you again."

I sighed. "I'm not trying to teach you a lesson."

"I think you are. Even now."

"I'm not upset with you to punish you. I'm upset because you hurt my feelings. A lot."

"I understand that. But we should be able to move past this."

I shook my head.

"Kate," he said, gripping both my hands in his. "I'm in love with you."

Excuse me. What now?

I pulled my hands back. "No, Dave. You aren't."

"How can you possibly tell me how I feel?"

"I don't know how I know. I just know."

"How could I not fall for you? It's like we were made for each other."

"Why, Dave? If you really believe you do, then tell me *why* you love me."

He frowned, confused. "Because you're beautiful, you're smart."

I shook my head at him.

He frowned and looked more somber. "Because I can be myself around you. Because I feel more comfortable around you than anyone. Because you make me happy. You make me laugh."

Now I nodded. "Everything you just said, do you know what was missing from all that?"

He shrugged, looking perturbed.

"*Me.* Every reason you just gave for loving me had nothing to do with *me* and everything to do with you. You like the way I make *you* feel. When you love someone, you love *who* that person is—not what they do for you."

"I do love you for you. It's not just for the way you make me feel."

I looked at his earnest blue eyes, his chiseled features, and I knew I would never love him. "I don't feel that way. I'm sorry."

He stood up and paced the room, with his hands on his hips. "Why?" he asked.

"Why what?"

"Why don't you love me?"

"Really? Love is complex and difficult to understand. I can't answer that."

"Are you attracted to me?"

I threw my hands up a little. "Of course. You're a beautiful man."

"And I have a good job. Own my own home. Educated."

"Dave, you don't fall in love with someone because of their résumé."

"And I make you laugh. And I'm crazy about you."

"And you hurt me. And you are *moody*. And you're *demanding*."

He raised his eyebrows, looking surprised. "You aren't perfect, either, but that didn't stop me from falling for you."

I stood up from the sofa and walked around the coffee table. "I'm sorry, Dave. I don't know what to tell you. I guess I shouldn't have let this thing with us get this far—not that I thought it had. When we met, I was going through a lot. You know that. You even said you would be a good 'distraction' for me. I just didn't see us hanging out casually somehow getting out of hand." His face was expressionless as I talked. "But apparently it has. I'm sorry for that. But this wasn't what I wanted."

He stopped pacing and squared off toward me, grabbing my

upper arms and pulling me close to him. When he spoke, his voice was low and rough. "You don't know *what* you want."

I put my hand against his chest and stepped away from him. "Maybe. But I know what I *don't* want."

"You don't want me?" He said it quietly, with a slight break in his voice. Holy crap. Is he really getting choked up? My frustration and anger fizzled and I suddenly felt bad for him. Shit. I can't do this, though. This is how he's kept me around this long. These confusing personality shifts, where he goes from bossy to sweet and from sweet to spoiled. Not enough good to outweigh the bad.

I shook my head. "I'm sorry."

He took a deep breath. "I could've made you happy."

"I don't think so," I said gently. "We just seem like oil and water, Dave. A relationship isn't supposed to be this much work. Especially not this early on."

He put his hands back on his hips and stared at the floor. I took a step toward him and put my hand on his shoulder.

Moving so fast, I hardly realized it was happening, Dave wrapped his arms around me, pulling me against him. Putting a hand on each side of my face, he kissed me hard on the mouth. His intensity cleared away the cobwebs in my brain and I tried to step away from him, but he was holding my face firmly between his hands. I turned my face away and he put his lips to my cheek and put his arms around me once more. A moment later he let go and stepped back from me.

"I think you're making a mistake," he said, looking me in the eye again.

"I know you do."

"I'm not just going to wait around for you to come to your senses, Kate."

"I don't expect you to."

He paused, with a frown on his face. I think he still expected this to go his way. Because, let's be real, this must be new territory for him.

I walked toward the front door a few steps. "Take care of yourself, Dave."

Emotionally Vulnerable Dave was gone, and instead he just looked annoyed and slightly smug.

"You, too, Kate," he said, heading toward the door. "Call me when you realize you can't live without me. Who knows? Maybe I'll still be interested."

I opened my eyes wide. "And the player is back," I said with a smirk.

The smug faded for a second, when he looked at me with a slight smile. "Hm. Maybe I do love you for you."

I had no response to that and just watched him walk out to his truck. He climbed in and drove away without a wave or a backward glance.

I closed the door and leaned against it. I had the strangest combination of butterflies from what he said mixed with a profound sense of relief. I did it. I let him go. I didn't get reeled back in. I walked over and flopped down onto the sofa, replaying the bizarre evening in my head. It ended the way it needed to. But, in true Dave form, he left me with the tiniest twinge of doubt that he was right and I was making a mistake. The guy was good. I'll give him that.

*

The next night, after work, I was sitting on Logek's couch with my feet tucked under me. She set a bowl of popcorn on the sofa next to me and handed me a glass of wine before taking up a similar spot on the other end on the couch.

I took a sip of wine. "So, I finally ended things with Dave last night."

She nodded. "Well, good. That needed to happen."

"You thought so?"

"Of course. It was obvious that was never going to work. You don't put up with controlling people for very long."

I raised an eyebrow. "You know, you could have mentioned that to me."

"I knew you'd figure it out on your own," she said, smiling and putting a piece of popcorn in her mouth. "So what happened?"

I shrugged. "He broke one of my new wineglasses, told me he was in love with me." I shook my head at this point to show that I wholeheartedly doubted the truth of the statement. "And told me I making a big mistake."

She nodded. "That's about how I would expect it to go down. An egocentric like him? He is probably *still* in shock that anyone could pass up the chance to be with him."

"No kidding."

"And you are having terrible luck in the wineglass department lately."

"Right? Anyway, I do wish I'd figured out a little sooner that it was a dead-end street. Would have saved both of us some time and energy."

Logek patted my knee. "Live and learn."

I nodded. "So, anything new on the Derek front?"

"He's been texting. I haven't responded. I guess his goodbye at my apartment Monday wasn't as final as I thought."

"Well, you are pretty tough to get over."

"Damn straight," she said, although it was lacking in her usual confidence and sounded more like she was trying to convince herself.

"What's he been saying?"

"That he wants to find a way to make it work. Asking me what it would take."

"Ouch. So, what do you think?"

"That I'd be sleeping with a live grenade."

"Colorful."

"Thanks."

"No desire to respond?"

"Of course the *desire* is there. I just . . . somewhere, inside, I just know he couldn't stay on the straight and narrow."

"You are a pretty hot 'straight and narrow' though."

"Thank you. But, for now, I'm going to protect myself from myself as long as I'll let me."

"Somehow, that makes perfect sense."

Logek looked at the TV and turned up the volume. "Okay. My show is on."

"I can't believe you still watch this," I said, focusing on the sappy legal drama she'd put on.

She shot me a wry look. "Oh, please. Pre-lawyer, you were just as hooked as I was. The only reason you stopped watching it was because you went to law school and never had time to watch television."

"Okay. Fair enough. Well, can you at least give me a quick refresher on the last four seasons that I missed?"

"Yes," Logek said, putting some more popcorn in her mouth.

By the time the intro was over, I was all up to speed on who was sleeping with who, who'd been disbarred, and who had been both charged and eventually acquitted of murder (in one season, no less). Unfortunately, I think I also shed a few IQ points.

"Oh," Logek said, holding up a finger, "and last week, Katrina's client rejected her partner's settlement offer, so she's in trial."

"I thought Katrina was a criminal defense attorney."

"She is, but she does signing law, too."

I smiled and chuckled.

"What?"

"Criminal attorneys usually *just* practice in that single field. Signing attorneys are the same."

After giving me a quick, dirty look (which I probably deserved), Logek refocused on the television.

I watched the Katrina character, who looked more like a Victoria's Secret model, prance into the courtroom in four-inch heels, which may have been longer than the skirt of her snug suit. After a little chitchat with her client, and the judge telling them to proceed, Katrina began making her opening arguments to the jury.

I took another drink of my wine and leaned over toward Logek. "You realize people don't have the right to a jury trial in signing law cases, right? I mean, it's like they didn't even try for accuracy. And it's California *state law*, and the show is set in California."

Logek looked at me with an expressionless face. "Are you really going to do this during the entire show?"

"Absolutely not."

"Thank god, because it's annoying as shit."

"One last thing?" I asked, with a pleading smile.

"Fine. Get it out."

"Just because Katrina's client rejected the offer, they don't just automatically go right to trial—they'd be looking at like a *year* before it actually went to trial. And even then, they would run the risk of getting bumped by a criminal trial and getting rescheduled. I love that they decided to go to trial *a week ago* and—voilà! Like magic, they're in trial."

Logek sighed. "Feel better?"

I nodded.

"Good. Then zip your fucking lip. You're spoiling the show with *reality,* which has absolutely nothing to do with why I watch it."

"Understood," I said, giving her a smile.

She tossed a piece of popcorn into my face, laughing, and went back to watching TV.

I made sure to keep the rest of the show's legal faux pas to myself so that I wouldn't wind up on Logek's Hell No list for TV watching companions.

*

The next morning, when I got to the office, Mags was standing by her cubicle with a sardonic grin. When I reached her, she handed me a small stack of messages. I glanced through them quickly.

Scarlett called. Rhett walked his dog across the corner of her yard.

Scarlett called. Rhett took down the picture of the middle finger from his bedroom window and taped up a naked photo of himself instead.

Scarlett called. Rhett played his TV too loud and he was watching a Steven Seagal movie and he knows she can't stand his movies.

Scarlett called. Rhett barbecued hot dogs in his backyard and burned them and it stunk up her whole house.

I finished reading and looked at Mags in stunned silence. I looked at my watch.

"It's eight oh-seven a.m. How is it possible she's called four times already?"

"Those were on my voice mail. She started calling me when you didn't answer your phone."

"Awesome. Then I can assume I have a few messages as well?"

"Safe assumption," Mags said.

I made an inward, grumpy sigh and went into my office to check my voice mail for more of Rhett's cardinal sins.

Yep. Two messages before she decided to start harassing Mags instead. Rhett also apparently moved his lawn gnome to her side of the property line and flicked a cigarette butt onto her porch.

Okay. Take charge. Time to rein this bullshit in.

I dialed Scarlett's number.

She picked up before the first ring finished. "Hello?"

"Scarlett, it's Kate Shaw. I got your messages."

"Jesus. I thought you were supposed to be helping me in this situation. Rhett has been fucking out of control and I haven't even heard back from you."

"I understand that, Scarlett, but I don't sleep at the office. Now, I'm not sure all of your grievances are actual violations of the agreement."

"Oh my god! He *knows* how much I hate Steven Seagal. The entire time we were signed. Every time. There was no reason for him to blast *Marked for Death* so loud that I had to hear it but to annoy the shit out of me."

"Okay. Well, I'll certainly bring up television volume with Doug Simpson. And about the cigarette butt. Did you catch that on camera?"

"No." Of course not. That would make my life too easy. "But I found a Marlboro butt on my porch. I *don't smoke Marlboros.*"

"But lots of people do. I'm not sure that gives us much to go on if you didn't catch it on camera."

"Goddammit! I know it was him."

"Okay, look Scarlett. Let me call Doug and tell him that you've got complaints that we think are in violation of the agreement. Let's see if Doug can get Rhett to stop needling you. Because you know that's what he's doing—just trying to find ways to annoy you."

"No shit."

Good talk. "Right. So, I'll get back to you after I've spoken with Doug."

"Fine."

"Oh, and you need to move that camera that's focused on his bedroom window. Until you move the camera, I can't complain over the artwork he's hanging in the window."

Big sigh. "I'll do it today."

I hung up the phone, thinking that this was my penance for stooping to the one kind of law I said I wouldn't do. *Time to pay the piper, Kate. No one to blame but yourself.* Well, and Margaret Mitchell, for writing the novel that brought these two train wrecks together.

I hung up the phone and pressed my forefingers against my temples. Immediately, my phone buzzed.

"It's Doug Simpson," Mags said.

"K." My body tensed. This couldn't be coincidence.

I picked up my phone on the first ring. "Good morning, Doug."

"Mornin', Kate."

"I was actually just about to call you."

"No doubt," he muttered sarcastically. "So, the kids aren't getting along."

"Yeah. I've gathered. Do I even want to know what Scarlett has been doing?"

"Stealing his mail, posting stork signs that say 'Welcome Baby' in his yard, and taping up horror movie posters over his windows. What's my boy been up to?"

"Flipping off her camera, flicking cigarette butts on her front porch, taping up a naked photo of himself in his bedroom window, blasting his television, walking his dog on her lawn, and burning barbecue in his backyard." I mumbled that last one, since it was more than a little ridiculous.

Doug immediately burst out laughing. I wish I found it as funny, but I was more exasperated than anything at the moment. "Okay, so we both report back to our clients, tell them we've aired their grievances, reprimand them for their own bullshit, and tell them they're going to wind up in contempt of court if they don't knock it the fuck off?"

"Always a pleasure, Doug," I said, with a smile in my voice.

"Talk to you soon."

"No offense, but god, I hope not."

He laughed again and disconnected.

I called Scarlett back.

"Hi, Kate," she said, answering on the first ring.

"Hi. Just got off the phone with Doug. He'll definitely have a talk with Rhett about this stuff. But he was already calling to tell me Rhett's complaints about you."

"Total bullshit."

"Scarlett. This isn't a game. If you keep pushing it, you're going to wind up in contempt of court. That carries fines and even jail time if the judge is annoyed enough. You've got to stop trying to piss him off."

She was quiet a moment and I was preparing for her to argue with me or just deny it altogether. Nope. Color me shocked. "Okay," she said, quietly. "I'll do my best."

"Perfect. Because if he keeps playing games like this and you *haven't* been? We can try to get him in trouble with the court. But as long as you are both antagonizing each other, we have no leverage. Make sense?"

"I get it."

"Good. Let me know how it goes."

"Count on it. Not like he can go a day without being a dick."

Goody.

After hanging up with Scarlett, I looked at my phone and had a text from Jonathan.

> *Hey Babe.*
>
> *Hey.*
>
> *So . . . when I stopped by the other night I got the feeling you were past the 'I need space because Jonathan is an asshole' phase and maybe we could hang out?*
>
> *Haha. Yeah. That was kind of a short-lived phase.*
>
> *How about lunch today?*

Well, now that I'd ended things with Dave, I needed to address the other elephant sitting on my chest, aka what to do about Jonathan.

As it turns out—I do eat lunch so that would be super :)
You kill me, Kiddo.

Sigh. Stupid, but "Kiddo" always got me. No idea why. I think it's the tall, in-control woman thing . . . who secretly likes it when a man wants to take care of her. And I guess *kiddo* sort of embodies that. Susan B. Anthony, I am not.

So I'll come to your office about lunchtime?
Sounds good.

Mags cleared her throat while I was staring at my phone, lost in thought.

"Hey," I said, setting my phone aside. "Looks like you finally get to meet that third arrow in my quiver. Thorn in my side. Whatever we're calling men these days."

"Ooh. The mysterious Jonathan is coming to the office?"

"Yep. We're having lunch."

Mags sat down in one of the chairs opposite my desk and looked serious. "Thinking about getting back together?"

I shrugged. Sighed loudly. "I told Dave I didn't want to see him anymore. I think I knew I was just killing time with him, and that's not really fair. So now I need to grow up and decide what I want with Jonathan." I propped my elbows on my desk and rested my face in my palms. "I'm just confused. I miss knowing what I wanted."

"Well, maybe you know more than you think."

I split my fingers apart and looked at her between them. Then I dropped my hands onto the desk. "But he was the love of my life."

"Was?"

"Is. He *is* the love of my life."

She gave me an annoyingly wise expression and nodded before heading out of my office.

CHAPTER *11*

A few hours later, my phone buzzed and Rita's voice came over my speaker.

"Kate, a Jonathan Alonzo is here to see you?"

"Thanks, Rita. I'll be right up."

I stood up and straightened my skirt and was smoothing my hair when I looked up to see Mags standing up in her cube, watching me with a smile. I stuck my tongue out at her and walked up to reception.

Jonathan's back was to me and he was studying the black-and-white cityscapes along the wall. He was in slacks that showed off his perfect ass and a polo shirt that made his shoulders look broad and defined. When he turned around and spotted me, I noticed his dark, two-day scruff covering his face and the way his hair was overgrown and curling a little by his ears.

He smiled big as he approached me and wrapped me in a

snug embrace. He gave me a quick peck on the cheek before pulling away. I looked over at Rita, who was busying herself, trying to pretend she wasn't watching us, even though she was.

Rita was sweet and friendly and not much younger than my mom. We'd chatted about our personal lives on several occasions, so she'd heard my Jonathan story. "Rita, this is my ex." Her eyebrows shot up before she could get ahold of them, likely making it clear to Jonathan that she knew a lot more about him than he knew about her. "Jonathan, this is Rita."

They shook hands. "Very nice to meet you, Rita."

"You, too, Jonathan. I've heard so much about you." Her eyes immediately opened wide and she appended "All good things!" to her statement.

Jonathan laughed. "That doesn't seem entirely likely, but thank you for saying so."

Rita blushed and I led Jonathan back to my office.

He whistled when he walked in and went straight for the window to admire the view. "Remind me again why you resisted taking this job in the beginning?"

"Yeah, whenever I *do* remember, I just look out the window and the blessed amnesia sets in again."

He turned to the side and noticed the pair of boxing gloves hanging on my coatrack. He gave one a twirl and raised his eyebrows at me.

"A gift from my coworker that witnessed my first KO. Well, technically it was our client's KO, I guess."

"Very nice."

He settled into one of the chairs across from my desk and crossed his ankle over his knee.

"Okay, I have to introduce you to my friend Mags or her head is going to explode." Mags had made three unsubtle passes by my office door already, so when she heard her name, she popped in.

"Hey, boss. Did you call me?"

I smiled at her. "Yes, I wanted you to meet Jonathan before your curiosity gave you an aneurysm."

"Aww. So thoughtful," Mags said.

Jonathan chuckled and stood up to meet her.

"Mags, great to finally meet you," he said, giving her that dazzling smile.

"You, too. I've heard so much about you," she said with an intentionally suggestive tone. Completely the opposite from Rita's polite greeting.

He laughed again. "Uh-oh. So, you're Kate's paralegal?"

"More of a minion, really," Mags said, lowering her eyebrows a tad. "Here to do her bidding."

"Glad to hear it," Jonathan said. "I've long felt that what Kate's life was missing were some devoted minions."

"And now she's poised for world domination."

"Well, with you on board, how could she fail?"

Mags nodded. "So, Jonathan, dating much?" You'd think I'd be used to the unpredictable shit that comes out of Mags's mouth by now. Turns out, no.

Jonathan's eyes got big. "Aren't I supposed to have a couple drinks in me before you start trying to pry that sort of information from me?"

"No time, really. We're on a schedule. So?"

"A little. Just trying to keep myself busy, I guess," he said, with a quick glance in my direction.

"But wasn't that the point of not re-upping with Kate?"

"Mags," I interjected. "That's enough. Leave him alone."

Now that I'm the one who can't seem to commit to Jonathan, it doesn't seem right to sit by while she browbeats him for not renewing our contract.

Jonathan ignored me, leaning in toward Mags when he answered. "Excellent question. It took me a little while to realize it, but I think I was unhappy with my job and it made me think I was unhappy with my life."

"So Kate was never the problem?"

"No. Never."

"Bummer, dude," Mags said, giving him a pitying look.

"Tell me about it."

"Well, it ain't over till the fat lady sings."

"True. But I think I hear her warming up."

No! No you don't, Jonathan. Suddenly, I just wanted that bitch to shut up. The fat lady. Not Mags.

"Quitter," Mags said, matter-of-factly.

"Maybe, but I don't want to just hang around making things harder on Kate."

"Okay. Stop!" I said, louder than I intended. "I'm right here. I'd appreciate you two not talking about my life as though I have no say in it."

Mags raised her eyebrows at me and then looked back to Jonathan. "Call me," she said quietly. "We'll talk about her some more." She made the *call me* hand gesture along with the request and slipped out of the office.

Jonathan turned to me with something like awe on his face. "I like her."

"Yeah. Everyone does," I said.

Just as I walked out of my office, with Jonathan trailing behind me, I heard Mags ask someone to hold.

"Hey, boss. It's Scarlett. She says, and I'm quoting here, 'We've got him by the balls.'"

I grunted. "I don't want to 'have him by the balls.' I want them to stop screwing with each other!"

"So, tell her you already left for lunch?"

"I'll call her from the car," I said grumpily.

Jonathan and I headed toward the elevator, rode it down, and then cut across the street to where his car was parked in a thirty-minute zone.

"Mexican okay?" he asked, before pulling away from the curb.

"Always." I took my phone from my purse and scrolled through my synced work contacts until I found Scarlett's number. "Let me call my crazy client back real quick."

"Go for it."

I dialed Scarlett's number.

"Hello?"

"It's Kate."

"Kate, we've got him."

"Uh-huh?"

"I've got him on camera ripping up my movie poster. That's destruction of property!"

"You mean the poster you taped up over *his* window?"

"Yeah. So?"

"That's not going to do it, Scarlett. You shouldn't have put anything up on his house in the first place."

"But I liked that poster."

"Then you shouldn't have used it to annoy him."

"Shit. That isn't fair."

"Like you said, he'll screw up again. Just take the high road or it won't do you any good when he does."

"Fine. Bye."

We disconnected and I closed my eyes and rested my head back against the seat.

"She sounds delightful," Jonathan said.

I smiled at him. "Practically Mother Teresa."

"That was definitely the vibe I got," he said, pulling in to the restaurant parking lot.

We were quiet on our way in, until we got seated, then he turned into Chatty Cathy.

"So, work sounds interesting at least?" he asked.

"It isn't dull."

"But better than you expected signing law to be?"

"I don't know. I'm not sure I really knew what to expect from any actual attorney job. It isn't as though law school teaches you anything about being an actual lawyer."

"Well, that sounds like a perfect use of two hundred thousand dollars, then."

"I have that same thought quite often," I said with a smile. "Usually when I'm sending in my student loan payment." He chuckled. "You're in a good mood," I said, tipping my head to the side a little.

"I am."

"Well?" I said, throwing my hands up. "Let's hear it!"

He pressed his palms to the tabletop. "Okay. You know how, for years, people have told me that I should open my own business as a consultant? You know, because with the last few companies I've worked for, they've brought me in when things were in the toilet and I've managed to turn things around?"

"Of course. Anytime you talk business, I always felt like people were taking notes."

"So . . . I'm gonna do it, Kate."

"Oh my gosh. That's amazing! You're going to start your own consulting firm?"

He nodded. "I put out my feelers that I was thinking about it, to the colleagues that have mentioned it in the past. I got fifteen phone calls back in the first two days. I have four clients ready to sign contracts with me right now."

"Wow. And, believe me, that 'wow' was for your courage in taking this leap. I'm not the least bit surprised that clients are lining up."

"Well, I realized I was just letting things pass me by. And I looked at you and the way you just decided you were going to law school and *did it*. I realized that I'd gotten so complacent. Settled for the status quo. You were never willing to do that." He was looking at me with his eyebrows lowered, as if seeing me differently. Or for the first time.

"This seems like news to you."

"I hate to say it, but it kind of is. I mean, I was proud of you for going to law school, and I knew it was a lot of work, but I never really acknowledged the leap of faith involved. Or the risks you were willing to take. Now that I'm taking some of my own, I guess I finally understand everything that was involved."

I nodded. "I'm glad." Admittedly, I felt a little let down. I'd always convinced myself that Jonathan knew me better than anyone. I guess there was a lot he didn't notice. Then I looked at him with wide eyes. "Are you planning to stay local?"

He shrugged. "I'm not sure. I'll definitely stay in California, but, so far, those clients that seem to be lining up are all closer to San Francisco. Still California, though, so you could still get a job at any law firm. You know, just in case."

He hadn't given up on us yet. Not if he was still considering logistics even in his new risk-taking phase. That made me happy. And confused. And strangely sad. So basically everything was clear as mud.

"So, what's involved? Have you created a company? Given your notice with your job?"

"I gave my two-weeks already. The company is being set up now."

"And?" I asked. "What's the name?"

He smiled, looking a little embarrassed. Then he squinted at me. "Alonzo Analytics?"

"I love it! People know your name, Jonathan. It makes sense to use it." I leaned in toward him a little. "And you know I'm a sucker for alliteration."

"Because you're a huge nerd," he said, grinning at me. "Although your love for alliteration may have crossed my mind when I came up with it."

I shook my head, overwhelmed by his new sense of direction and purpose. "Wow. Well, congratulations. I am *so* happy for you."

"Thank you."

By the time the waiter brought our food and left again, Jonathan was watching me closely. "So, I feel justified, since Mags asked me . . . Are you dating much?"

I set my fork down and shrugged. "I was dating this guy. Well, *dating* might be too strong a word. But I ended it. He mainly just gave me anxiety."

Jonathan smiled. "Pretty sure that's a red flag."

I nodded. "Well, he was supposed to be the uncomplicated answer. You . . . are so confusing. Even Adam I don't really know what to do with. But this guy was the easy one. I guess because it didn't matter enough."

"Adam mattered enough?" Oops. *Think, Kate. Before you say stuff.*

Deep breath. Nod.

There. That wasn't so bad. Until Jonathan looked back down at his plate and I felt like my answer had hurt him. Man, when I flip a switch, I really flip a switch, because just two weeks ago this was *all* Jonathan's fault. Now here I was, feeling guilty for hurting *him*.

Then Jonathan looked back up, pretending to be unfazed. "So you got rid of your *uncomplicated* route, huh?"

"Well, I'm not really one for killing time."

"No, you are not. So thank you for the eight years you spent with me."

My cheeks felt hot at that, and my stomach twisted uncomfortably. "It was a great eight years."

"I'm still hoping there might be more."

My cell phone vibrated on the table and broke the building tension between us.

I frowned at the unknown number on the screen. "Not sure who this is, so I should probably answer."

Jonathan just nodded agreement.

"This is Kate," I said.

"It's Scarlett." Those two words almost made me scream. Like a *getting pantsed at a seventh-grade dance* scream.

"Scarlett. How did you get this number?"

"You just called me, and this is the number that came up on my phone."

Shit. Stupid, stupid, stupid.

"Right. Well, I'm not in the office and this isn't really a good time. Is something wrong?"

"Something is always wrong—I live next door to an asshole."

"Scarlett, make it quick or I'll have to call you when I get back to the office."

"Fine. Rhett was out in the street, taking pictures of my house. That is totally against the law and an invasion of my privacy."

I sighed. "Scarlett, that's not illegal. If it was, we'd all be suing Google over Google Street View."

"Oh. I guess I didn't think about it like that."

"Okay, so call me at the office if anything major happens."

"K. Bye."

Once Scarlett hung up, I looked at Jonathan with the widest eyes I could manage without giving myself a headache. "Oh my god. What have I done?"

"That was your crazy client?"

I nodded. "I called her from my cell in the car," I said, pressing my fingertips to my temple, staring at my now blank phone screen.

Jonathan was trying to hold back a chuckle. "Rookie move, babe."

"Thanks for your support."

He shrugged, his mirth still evident.

After Jonathan paid the tab (yes, I offered but was vetoed, so, no, I don't feel like I'm taking advantage of him), we got into his car and headed back to my office.

As he drove, I looked over at him. He was tanner than the last time we'd been together, like he'd been spending time outdoors. And he clearly hadn't gotten a haircut since we split, almost six weeks ago. The five o'clock shadow was also apparently a regular thing now. The new Jonathan.

He pulled up in front of my office and turned to me.

"Thanks for having lunch with me."

"It was fun. Always is."

"So we'll do it again," he said.

"Jonathan, I want to say something to you . . . with all sincerity."

He lowered his brows and leaned toward me a little.

"Get a haircut," I said softly.

He smiled. "You're not the boss of me." I laughed. That was something he'd always said to me when we were together, to which I always replied, "We both know that's not true."

This time, I smiled and instead said, "This is true."

His smile faded a little. "That's easy enough to remedy, though." He pulled me across the front seat into a tight hug. I hugged him back, feeling an ocean of conflicted emotions that I didn't feel like I could possibly sort out. So I did what any woman in my position would do: I kissed him on the mouth, tweaked his nose, and got out of the car. Okay, maybe not what *any* woman would do. Whatever. I was improvising.

I stopped at Mags's desk and she looked up at me expectantly. "I called Scarlett back on my cell phone. She has my cell phone number. She *called* me on my cell phone while I was at lunch. Houston, we have a problem. We may need to move up the mercy killing."

"You called a client from your cell and didn't block the number?"

"You can do that? I don't know how to do that."

"You hit star sixty-seven before you dial. Seriously? You didn't know that?"

"Why would I know that?"

"Seems like the kind of thing they should teach you in law school."

"What happened?" Brad asked from behind me.

"Kate called a client from her cell phone without blocking her phone number."

Brad laughed. "Oh, Kate. Rookie move."

"So I've been told."

"Is it someone cool, at least?" Brad asked.

Mario, of the infamous punch, was actually Brad's client. "Hm. Could you imagine Mario having your cell phone number if he was living next door to John and they had filed restraining orders against each other?"

Brad's laughter came out in a loud bark. "Holy shit, Kate. I'd tell you to change your phone number, but I think this might require the Witness Protection Program."

I dropped my forehead onto the wall of Mags's cubicle. I felt a hand I assumed was Mags's pat the back of my head sympathetically.

I lifted my head and jerked a thumb toward my office. "Okay, well, I'm going to slink away now and rethink my life choices. You two enjoy your day."

I walked into my office and tried to get back into what I was doing before I'd left for lunch. I had my cell sitting on the desk and I caught myself glancing at it repeatedly, dreading the next ring that would confirm my worst fear—that Scarlett would never revert to calling the office and, of course, that I am the stupidest woman alive.

I was still looking at the phone when it buzzed, and I actually jumped a little. Then I watched it expectantly. One buzz. It was a text, not a phone call. Lucked out this time.

It was from Adam, so naturally it came with its usual dose of butterflies.

> *Good afternoon, Kate.*
> *Hey. Thanks for the burger the other night.*
> *Thanks for attempting to cook.*
> *Hey. I told you. I can cook the shit out of chicken. That night notwithstanding.*
> *Lol. Maybe I'll let you prove it.*

Uh-oh. Mayday. You'd think I'd have learned by now that I am absolutely not equipped to *casually* flirt with Adam. *So knock it off, girl.*

Apparently my delayed response signaled him to come to my rescue.

> *Okay. Or I won't. Don't have a panic attack.*
> *No panic attack. Maybe a few hives. A little shortness of breath. Definitely no panic attack.*
> *Haha. So I've got intel on my mom and Tony.*
> *Let's hear it!*
> *Let's hang out again.*
> *Resorting to extortion Mr. Lucas?*
> *By any means necessary Ms. Shaw.*
> *Well, I don't negotiate with terrorists.*
> *God you make me laugh. Come on, Shaw. Two buddies hanging out. I promise I won't hold your hand.*

Damn. That's some disappointing news, there.

Fine. But don't blame me if I go off the deep end and you wake up at a signing party because I drugged you and forged your signature on a contract.

You're worth the risk.

And now the tingles. Shit. What am I doing? Hm. I ask myself that a little too often these days.

Ok. When are we doing this?

Friday night?

Ok. And in case shit goes south, what type of token do you prefer?

Definitely the watch. I'm not really a cuff links kind of guy.

Perfect.

Alrighty. So I have a "hang out" session with my mad crush this weekend. I'm sure that's a good decision and won't have any negative repercussions whatsoever.

Mags walked into my office and stuck a sticky note on my desk that read **67 to block caller ID on your cell phone.*

"Day late and a dollar short on that one, honey."

"So," she said, perching herself of the edge of my desk, "I have a new intake that got routed to you. Woman's name is Luann Sykes and she caught her partner in bed with another woman. When can you meet with her?"

I tried to suppress a grunt and failed. "This is why I didn't want to do signing law. Every single person we work with is miserable."

"But then they come to you and you get to help them through a difficult time."

I scrutinized Mags a minute. "You really believe that?"

She shrugged. "Well, they come in miserable and they leave . . . slightly less miserable. I didn't say you were saving the world."

"Wow. I feel all warm and fuzzy inside. Do you think I could add that to my business card? Like 'Facilitator of slightly less misery' or something?"

Mags shook her head. "That doesn't exactly roll off the tongue. We'll brainstorm."

"Fine. I can meet with her tomorrow morning, if that works."

Mags hopped off my desk. "I'll set it up."

"Wear something cheerful tomorrow."

"It's Friday. I always save my most cheerful ensembles for Fridays," she said, with a wink.

My phone buzzed and I looked at it cautiously. Facebook notification. Friend request from Scarlett. I dropped my phone on the desk like it was a spider and pushed it away from me.

Mags frowned, picked it up, and looked at the screen.

"Ooh," she said, with a serious frown.

"It's not just her. She's the third client to try to friend me on Facebook. Why does this keep happening?"

Mags snorted a little through her nose. "Because you're the kickass facilitator of slightly less misery, woman."

I laughed.

"Do you want me to show you how to handle this?" she asked.

"Please."

"Okay," she said, holding my phone so that I could see the

screen. "You go into your friend requests, like this," she said, pushing the respective buttons.

I nodded.

"And then you click Ignore." Scarlett's request disappeared.

I rolled my eyes. "*I* could have done that. But now she'll *know* I ignored it. That is the problem."

"Just tell her it's an attorney rule."

I wobbled my head side to side. "She'd probably believe that."

"And maybe stop being so damn friendly with your clients," she said, heading back to her desk.

"Yeah. I'll work on that."

*

I had been home for about ten minutes when my cell rang. I did my ritual "Please don't be Scarlett" chant in my head and looked at the screen. Oh, it was Sandy. Much better.

"Hi, Sandy," I said, smiling even though she couldn't see it.

"Hi, Kate. Would it be any trouble if I stopped by real quick? I was hoping to get the measurements of your little back deck, because it needs to be replaced and I need the dimensions to get some bids."

"Of course. No problem at all."

"Wonderful. I'm only about two minutes away."

"See you soon."

We hung up and I ran upstairs real quick to change out of my suit. By the time I came back down, in shorts and T-shirt, there was a knock at my door.

I opened the door to Sandy's smiling face and, behind her, Adam's smirking one.

"Hi, you guys," I said, stepping out of the doorway.

Sandy wrapped me in a hug. "Hi, sweetie. I brought my helper. He's been making the rounds with me."

Adam stepped in toward me, once Sandy stepped back, and hugged me as well. "Hi, sweetie," he said, mimicking his mother.

I smiled up at him and gave him a quick poke in the rib. No mocking Sandy.

"Thanks for letting us drop in on you like this," Sandy said.

"Not a problem at all," I said again.

"Well, we'll do this quick and get out of your way."

"Please," I said. "You're not in the way."

Sandy walked through the kitchen and opened the back door to the deck. While Adam followed her to the door, I pulled out of the refrigerator a pan of chicken that I had been marinating. I turned on the oven, and just as I was sliding it into the oven, I heard Adam mutter, "Uh-oh."

I pointed a stern finger at him. "No input from you, mister."

"I just feel bad for the chicken."

"Well, shows what you know. This chicken is not going to turn out like the last one. This is my redemption chicken."

He started laughing. "Well, that does sound tasty."

I nodded. "And you don't get any."

His response to my snarky yet playful comment was to drop his chin and narrow his eyes, giving a look so ridiculously sexy, I almost forgot his mother was five feet away. "Not even a taste?"

My eyes shot open at the suggestiveness of the comment and immediately flicked over to where Sandy was standing, looking down at the deck, hands on her hips. Either she wasn't listening to us or she entirely approved of the flirting and was *pretending* not to listen to us. Either way, *I* got to pretend she didn't hear us.

Adam just laughed at my embarrassment and turned to his mom, holding out the tape measure.

"Thank you, hon," Sandy said, gripping the end of the measuring tape. They proceeded to do the whole deck-measuring thing, with Sandy writing down quick notations in a little notebook she had tucked in her pocket. After they measured the top of the deck and the height of the railing, Sandy walked down the few stairs to the little yard below and continued making notes.

Adam looked back at me, where I was leaning against the oven, and raised an eyebrow.

"What?" I asked.

"Not sure. I think she's trying to give us a few extra minutes of privacy so that we can declare our love for each other."

I grinned at him. "You go first, dear."

He laughed again and looked down at the floor, shaking his head.

I peeked into the oven and checked the chicken. No flames billowing. Always a good sign. I grabbed a fork from the counter and reached in to turn the chicken breasts over.

"Be careful, Kate," Adam said.

In true Kate fashion, as I glanced over to roll my eyes at him, I managed to connect my wrist to the edge of the metal baking pan. I jumped back, pulling my hand out, making the universal *Ow I burned myself!* sound of sucking air in through my teeth with a hiss.

"Shit, Kate. That was my fault." Adam grabbed me by the shoulder and guided me to the sink, where he turned the faucet all the way on cold. "Here," he said, reaching for the wrist

I was holding gingerly in my other hand. He stretched my arm out under the water and I did some more hissing sounds.

Adam was holding my wrist under the water with one hand while his other hand was behind my back. He looked down into my eyes. "Well, you weren't supposed to actually hurt yourself just because I distracted you."

"Yeah, you know I can't walk and chew gum," I reminded him. "I certainly can't cook and have a conversation."

He rested his forehead against mine just for a second, then pulled back and frowned at my wrist. "I'm sorry." He reached behind him and tore off a paper towel, which he soaked in the cold water before draping it across my wrist.

"Adam. Settle down. It's a little burn. Pretty sure this isn't going to be the end of me."

He lifted the paper towel and looked at my wrist. "I don't know—this could be serious. It could get infected, turn gangrenous, require an amputation." He smiled as he walked to the garbage can to toss the wet paper towel in the trash.

"Uh-oh," he said, looking into the trash can. "Man down."

I walked over and leaned past him to see what he was referring to. Oh. My broken wineglass with the tiger stripes. That was a gift from his mother. That I was still a little bitter at Dave for destroying last night.

"Oh. Yeah, Dave accidentally knocked that over last night."

Adam looked at me and narrowed his eyes a little.

I made a chuckle. "Just talking with his hands," I said, gesturing with mine. "That's all."

He nodded. "That's too bad. I know you love these glasses."

"I do. I need to find out where your mom found them so I can replace it."

Adam walked back over to me and pushed my hand back under the running water. I gave him a crisp salute with my other hand.

"Oh no!" Sandy said, coming in through the back door. "What happened?"

"Kate was cremating chicken and burned herself, with absolutely no help from me," Adam said. He pulled my wrist from under the water and looked at it closely. "And she did a pretty decent job of it."

I pulled my wrist away from his grip and looked at the burn. I had a tidy, straight line of little blisters forming across my wrist. It still stung, but it was a little numb from the cold water, so that was a plus.

"It's fine. Oh! I need to turn the chicken over."

"I'll do it," Adam said. "Back under the water," he said, pointing toward the faucet.

I put my wrist back under the cold water, and Sandy came and stood next to me, leaning over to look at my wrist. Adam picked up the fork I had dropped on the floor when I burned myself and set it on the counter. He opened a couple of drawers, found the forks, reached into the oven, without burning himself, and turned the chicken for me.

Sandy repeated the same thing Adam had done, tearing off a paper towel and soaking it in cold water. She folded it into a narrow band. "Here," she said, turning off the faucet and wrapping the cold, wet paper towel around my wrist. "I'm sure you don't feel like standing at the sink all night."

I smiled at her and went and sat down at the table.

She sat down next to me with a smile.

"So, I understand you had dinner with my uncle?" I asked.

She smiled her lovely smile and nodded. "I did. He's such a nice man."

"So . . . any plan of going out again?"

Sandy smiled at me. "I enjoyed the dinner very much." She narrowed her eyes, looking more like Adam. "Tony was delightful. But he's been calling, wanting to arrange another date, and I just want to keep things friendly. Not give him the wrong impression."

"Oh. That makes sense." Tony is screwed.

"Don't get me wrong," she added, with a cool hand on my wrist. "I really did enjoy spending time with him. I just am not looking for anything serious."

I nodded. "And he seemed . . . a little serious?"

Sandy wobbled her head back and forth. "I don't know. Maybe a little. Or maybe he wasn't and I'm just overly cautious. Who knows?" she asked with a shrug.

"Well," Adam said, putting his hands on his hips. "My damage here is done. We should probably go," he said, looking over at his mom.

"Yeah. We'll get out of your way. You sure you're okay?"

I laughed. "It's just a little burn. And, not surprisingly, it isn't even my first."

"That, I believe," Adam said. He walked over to me and dropped a kiss on the top of my head, resting his hands briefly on my shoulders. "I'll talk to you later."

"Bye, sweetie," Sandy said, with a smile.

I got up and followed them to the door. As they were walking down the walkway to Sandy's car, Adam called back over his shoulder, "Try not to burn the chicken. Again."

"Redemption chicken."

"Right," he said with a chuckle, as he slid into the passenger seat of his mom's car, giving a little wave through the window.

After they drove away, I hustled back inside to make sure Adam's prophecy didn't come true.

CHAPTER 12

I was booting up my computer the next morning when Mags sauntered into my office in a yellow fitted dress, wearing pumps with little yellow-and-white daisies on them. Mags's style was more like guerrilla fashion. I envisioned her closet having each outfit with its own pair of perfect shoes and jewelry hanging next to each ensemble. Take no prisoners. Match or be killed.

She did a hand flourish over her outfit. "Cheery enough?"

"I feel better already. Maybe you should go by the children's hospital on your lunch hour."

She smiled at me. "Luann will be here at nine a.m."

"Perfect. You definitely need to be the one to show her to the conference room, since you are visual Prozac today."

"You got it, boss."

I was still grinning as she walked back to her cube. I saw Brad approach her, with an even sappier grin, and, after a quick glance around, plant a quick kiss on her lips. So cute. So simple. Sigh. I want "simple" in my love life.

My cell phone buzzed and I answered it. Without thinking. Until I heard Scarlett's voice.

"Kate?"

"Scarlett. You really need to call the office phone. This is my cell phone."

"Whatever. This is an emergency. He's trying to kill me."

I frowned. "Scarlett, if you're genuinely afraid, you should be calling the police—not me."

"I thought I was supposed to call you."

"If he's chasing you with a knife? How would calling *me* help? Whatever. What's going on?"

"He's throwing peanuts around his backyard."

Nope. Not even answering. Too absurd.

"I'm allergic to peanuts!" she said in a shrill voice.

Pause. "Why . . . is he throwing peanuts into his yard?"

"He *claims* they're for the squirrels, but I think he's hoping that the wind will blow some peanut dust over here and kill me!"

I pressed my fingers to my temple. "I'll call Doug Simpson."

"Do it fast."

I hung up. Damn damn damnity damn.

I called Doug.

"Doug Simpson."

"Doug, it's Kate."

"Long time, no talk."

"Apparently Scarlett is seriously allergic to peanuts."

"Bummer. Peanut butter is delicious."

"Yep. And Rhett is feeding peanuts to the squirrels."

"Well, as long as he isn't feeding them to *Scarlett,* aren't we okay?"

I sighed. "One would think. But she's super allergic. And he's throwing them around his yard. And she's worried about peanut dust. Any chance he could feed them something that *won't* kill his neighbor if she accidentally inhales something?"

"I'll call him."

"Thanks so much."

About ten minutes later, Mags buzzed me. "Dot Hamilton is on the phone."

"Put her through."

I answered when my phone rang. "Hello, Dot."

"Hi, Kate," she said, sounding particularly chipper. Hm. Curiouser and curiouser. "So, I took your advice the other day and it worked."

"What advice? What worked?"

"The dating site idea. I went on there and I met the most amazing man."

"Dot, I said that *two* days ago."

"I know. There's no stopping true love." Oh god.

"You—you—you're in love?" I asked.

"Uh-huh. He's everything I've ever wanted, Kate. It's like we were made for each other."

Oh god. I think I already said that. "Um, Dot. You *just met him.* Don't you think that's a little fast?"

"Kate, I've spent more time talking to Sven in the last two days than I talked to Daryl during our entire contract."

Sven? Shit. I hope at least she didn't happen to mention

that she was coming into a few million dollars. "Well, that's important, but I really think you should pace yourself."

"To hell with pacing myself. I've spent my whole life being cautious. Time to take some risks!"

"Okay. I'm glad you're happy. I just don't want to see you get hurt."

"Sven will never hurt me." Of course not. Guys named Sven are notoriously good guys. If I'd ever known a *single* guy named Sven. Which I have not. "Anyway," she continued. "About the settlement. Daryl can keep Elvis."

My eyes went wide. "He can?"

"Yep. Sven made me realize that trying to hold on to Elvis was the same as holding on to the hurt Daryl caused me." I tipped my head back and forth a little. Not the worst advice ever . . . "And he came over last night with a gift."

"Dare I ask?"

"A beautiful chinchilla named Audrey!" She squealed with excitement.

"Well, that was sweet of him."

"I know! So, we need to get this settlement wrapped up so I can officially be single again."

"Okay. What about the clock?"

"Oh, it's his anyway. So, let's say he gets Elvis and the grandfather clock and he gives me the big-screen TV from the family room."

"Okay. Well, I'll call his attorney and propose that. You're *sure*, Dot? If we settle this and then things go south with Sven, we can't undo it."

"Honestly, Kate, you worry too much." Well, ain't that a kick in the head. "Call the attorney now."

I sighed so she could hear my reservation. "Okay, Dot. You sure you don't want to give it a couple of days?"

"I've already wasted too many days. I'm not wasting any more."

"Fair enough. I'll call you later."

"Thank you, Kate."

I hung up and called Beth.

"Beth Erickson."

"Beth, it's Kate Shaw. I have a counter that I think you'll like."

"You're shitting me."

"I am one hundred percent serious. I think. My head is still spinning a little."

"Well, let's hear it."

"Daryl can keep Elvis and she'll give him the grandfather clock and all she wants is the big-screen TV."

"What the hell?"

"I have no idea. She met a man named Sven. He bought her a chinchilla."

"Figures." It does? In what world? "Okay. Well, I'm calling him now, before she changes her mind."

"Good thinking."

We hung up and I looked up to see Mags standing in the doorway, frowning at me, clearly curious for the development on the Dot Hamilton front.

"Dot fell madly in love with a guy she met online two days ago and is willing to give up the guinea pig."

"Okay," she said with a nod, and turned to walk back to her desk.

"Oh," she said, turning back, "I just put Luann in conference room four for you, after being sure she got a full dose of this." She gestured to her bright yellow dress. "She seems fine."

"You're the best."

I scooped up my pad of paper and pen and headed to the conference room.

Luann stood when I walked in. She was about thirty, almost as tall as me, lanky, and pretty enough, in that "before" photo sort of way. Her hair was medium brown and stick-straight to her shoulders, and her skin was clear and makeup free.

I shook her hand and smiled encouragingly. "Hello, Luann. I'm Kate Shaw."

"Very nice to meet you."

I gestured for her to sit back down, and I took the chair kitty-corner from her. "I'm so sorry about the reason you're here. That must have been just awful."

She nodded and pushed her shapely lips together. "Yeah. Pretty sure he can have those sheets."

"Oh, god. You caught them in your bed?"

She nodded. "Yeah. In fact," she added with a frown, "he can have the bed, too."

I nodded sympathetically. "I'm sorry. So, you brought your contract, right?"

"Yes." She slid the pile of paper toward me. "I guess this is what I get for not listening to my mom."

I glanced at the papers and then back at her. Her brown, almond-shaped eyes were staring off into the distance, beyond my shoulder. Her eyebrows were delicately shaped and her eyelashes were long, despite the lack of makeup. I was rethinking my early assessment of her being plain.

"Mom didn't like him, huh?"

"She liked him. It was hard not to. He was so charming.

But he was too good-looking for me. She was just always suspicious."

I frowned a little, unsure of what the appropriate response would be in this scenario. "But you're very pretty, too." Yeah, maybe not attorney-like, but I always default to honesty. And sometimes I just speak before I think.

Luann laughed. "Thank you, but he's like *crazy good-looking*. He's a model. But just getting started, so he didn't have much money when we met."

I looked down at the intake form. Luann was a pharmaceutical researcher. I'm guessing that's lucrative. "So, you make a lot more money than he does, I'm guessing?"

"Yeah. I think that's why my mom was so suspicious of every man that seemed really interested." Luann slouched a little and shrugged with a pretty smile. "But you gotta be willing to take a risk at some point."

I nodded and smiled back. "Okay, well, let me review your contract and see exactly what we're dealing with as far as damages. Does he have an attorney?"

"Yeah. It was his attorney who drafted the contract. I *did* read it—I'm not a total moron. But I am a little worried now that I missed some things and that I'm going to end up screwed."

"Well, I'll go over it closely. Where are you staying?"

"With my parents. I know, super mature. Thirty years old and my relationship goes south and I go home to mommy and daddy."

"Lots of us have been there," I said.

Her eyes went wide. "Really?"

"Yep. Just got my own place a couple weeks ago. We're lucky to have good parents to go home to."

"Tell me about it. My mom hasn't even said 'I told you so.' The woman's a saint."

I laughed. "The best moms are." I held up the contract. "Do you think he'll deny that he breached? Any chance he'll lie and try to say you never saw anything?"

"Not sure, but it shouldn't matter. The girl he was with, Monica, had no idea he was signed, and she feels terrible. She called me and gave me her name and phone number in case there was litigation."

"Oh. That is definitely good. Okay. I'll give you a call once I'm up to speed."

"Great. Thanks so much, Kate. I feel like such a fool."

I put a hand against her shoulder. "We all do sometimes. But you're right—sometimes we have to take a chance."

She smiled and nodded at me.

She walked out of the conference room and I watched her go, head held high, shoulders square. She was kind of my new favorite client.

I walked back to my office and Mags met me at the door.

"So? What'd you think?"

"I really liked her," I said.

"Me too. Are you thinking what I'm thinking?" Mags asked, nodding continuously.

"I think the odds of that are against us, Mags."

She chuckled. "Well, *I'm* thinking that we need to match her with one of our other lonely heart clients."

I frowned. "Okay, (a) this is a law firm, not a dating service; and (b) so far we have angry rednecks and hairdressers not interested in the female persuasion. Not much of a dating pool. And she deserves someone good."

Mags nodded. "Point taken. We'll keep our eyes open for someone worthy."

"Well, I'm still on the high of pushing Dot Hamilton into what could potentially be a catastrophic train wreck, so I think I might hold off on any more matchmaking for a bit."

"Suit yourself."

I walked into my office and sat down. A few minutes later, Joe Markson was standing in my doorway, looking more spry than I'd ever seen him.

"What did you do?"

I stood. "Excuse me?"

"How on God's green earth did you get Dot Hamilton to settle?" he asked, walking in with a smile and putting his hands on the back of one of the chairs facing my desk.

"Oh. Well, I'm not certain it was a good thing, actually," I said, trying to steady my hands, since I talk with them whenever I'm nervous and they'd started waving around with my words. Pressing my fingertips to my desktop, I continued, "I sort of told Dot maybe she should try online dating instead of letting her life pass her by. And she met someone. Two days ago. And did a complete one eighty on the settlement."

Joe laughed, thankfully. And I could breathe again. I was more than a little worried I'd get my ass chewed for giving a client too much personal advice.

"Brilliant, Kate. Beth Erickson just called me to tell me that you had managed the impossible."

"Well, in all honesty, I'm a little worried about this man that Dot met. She's only known him for two days."

"Kate, you can't control people acting crazy. You gave her good advice: Move on and get a life. The fact that she took it to the extreme is not your problem."

I gave him a noncommittal nod.

"You got through to her when no one else has been able to for *two years*, Kate. It's a win. Take it."

I smiled. "Thank you, sir."

Joe left with a spring in his step and, I gotta say, I was even starting to feel pretty good about my victory.

I had a blinking red light on my phone, indicating I had a message. I pressed the button and listened.

"Hi, Kate. It's Beth. Daryl couldn't say yes fast enough. I already made the changes to the existing settlement agreement and I've emailed it to you. Any chance you can get Dot to sign it today?"

I checked my email and, sure enough, Beth had already sent over the revised settlement for Dot and Daryl. I reviewed her changes and they were correct.

I picked up my phone and called Dot.

"Hi, Kate," Dot said, picking up on the first ring.

"Dot, your offer has been accepted and they already revised the settlement agreement and sent it over. If you're certain, you can sign today."

"Fantastic. I'll be right over."

So that happened. What a weird day.

I had the settlement agreement printed by the time Rita buzzed me to tell me that Dot was here with her gentleman friend.

I headed to the conference room, and when I went through the door, I saw a completely new Dot Hamilton.

Dot stood and came to me, smiling, and gave me a quick hug. She was in a little white sundress that came below her knees, and her hair was loose and wavy. She looked ten years younger. Is this really what one good lay can do for you?

"Kate, this is Sven."

I turned to Sven and about fell over. I was expecting some tall, Norse god–looking guy. I was only right on the Norse part, because he was blond and blue-eyed. But he was about five foot seven and narrow through the shoulders. He had a light mustache and eyeglasses. He looked a little younger than her, maybe late thirties. He was wearing a sweater vest over a plaid shirt.

He shook my hand enthusiastically and snuggled up against Dot's side.

"Let's do this," Dot said, looking lovely, which is not something I ever expected to say about the woman.

"Okay," I said, putting the agreement on the table in front of her. I pointed out the couple of revisions Daryl's attorney had made, so that she could read them, and then I flipped to the signature page.

"And, if you're really sure, you can sign right there," I said, pointing to the signature line and holding a pen out for her.

She looked at Sven lovingly, took the pen from me, and signed the agreement. She tossed the pen onto the agreement and turned to Sven, who wrapped her in his arms and lifted her off the ground.

Great. I'm surrounded by people making love look like the easiest thing in the world today.

"Okay, I'll get this right back over to Beth Erickson so that she can get Daryl's signature. Once I have the final version, I'll get it to you."

"Kate," she said, looking at me sincerely. "I can't thank you enough."

"Good luck, Dot."

She and Sven left, arm in arm.

I went to the printer and scanned in the agreement and then emailed it back to Beth with the subject line "The Ark of the Covenant."

Someone knocked on my door frame and I looked up to see Jared standing there.

"I hear congratulations are in order," he said, beaming at me.

I held up the signed agreement. "Just got it signed."

"That's fantastic. Joe has been wandering around for the last half hour telling everyone how you worked a miracle."

"Well, at least he's not overselling it."

"Not at all. Well? We need to celebrate."

I nodded. This did seem like an occasion worth celebrating.

Mags appeared next to Jared. "Did I hear that we're going out to celebrate Kate's lifesaving settlement?"

Jared laughed. "It's a must. Tell your friends. Tonight after work?" Jared asked.

"I had some plans, but they should be transferable," I said, thinking of Adam's hostage negotiation scheduled for tonight. "Where should we go?"

"There's a new place called the Trunk that some of my friends just opened," Jared said, with his hands shoved in the pockets of his slacks. "Let's go there. It's at twelfth and K."

"Perfect. I'll let my friends know," I said.

"Okay. Say about six thirty? So we have time to go home and drop the suits?" he asked, with a light tug on his lapel.

"Even better," I said.

Jared tapped my door frame and walked away.

"You think Logek will come?" Mags asked.

"I'm going to call her. She's been lying low all week after the breakup. She needs to get out."

"Good. Brad and I are in."

I picked up my phone and figured I should call Logek first, since she might take more convincing than Adam.

"Hey, Kitty Kat," she said, answering on the first ring.

"Hey, sweetheart. How are you?"

"Angry. Which is an improvement from sad, so I'll take it."

"Good girl. So, you're coming out with me tonight."

"I am?"

"Yes. A whole group of us. One of my bosses and Mags and her guy . . . and Adam."

"Hm. The plot thickens."

"I just settled a case that they've been fighting over for two years, so one of my bosses said a celebration was mandatory. And I was sort of supposed to platonically hang out with Adam tonight, anyway."

Logek was quiet, and I got the feeling she was getting ready to fight me on it. "Logek. You've been hibernating all week. It's time to get out. You need some fun."

"Mmm," she moaned. "I'm not sure I'm ready."

"You're ready. You're fucking Logek McLean. No man gets more than a week of your sad time."

She laughed. "You really should have been a motivational speaker."

"It's not too late. Maybe that will be my next career change."

"Fine," she said with an exaggerated sigh. "What's the plan?"

"Meet at my house after work? Get to the bar about six thirty?"

"Okay. See you soon."

All in all, easier than I thought it would be. Next, I called Adam.

"What's up, Shaw?"

"Really, Adam? Are you really going to keep up this contrived buddy thing of calling me by my last name?"

"Not making it any more believable for you?"

"Not a bit."

"Good to know. So, *Kate,* what's up?"

"Change of venue for tonight."

"I don't think we'd picked a venue."

"I settled a big case, so Jared thought we should get a group together to celebrate."

"Oh. Okay. Where are we going?"

"I guess there's a new bar called the Trunk that just opened?"

"Oh, yeah. Some of my friends actually own that place." I'm guessing college friends, since Adam had mentioned knowing Jared Mann from college. "So, meeting there?"

"Yep."

"What time?"

"Six thirty?"

"Sounds good. See you soon, Kate."

When I set my phone down on the desk, Mags popped her head into my office. I gave her the thumbs-up and she smiled.

"Logek is meeting at my house. Do you want to meet there and have a glass of wine and then head over together?"

"Best idea I've heard all day. I'll let Brad know to meet us there."

It was already two o'clock by the time I was eating my lunch, which consisted of leftovers from what I'd made the night before. I was just putting my Tupperware back in my drawer when Tony came in and sat down in one of the chairs in front of my desk.

"So, darling, Joe tells me you settled that two-year-old case he had."

"I did."

"Did you kill the guinea pig?"

I chuckled. "No, Tony. No rodent killing necessary."

"What do you know? That was always my suggestion."

"Nice, Tony."

He smiled. "So, have you talked to your landlady at all?"

Oh man, do I *not* want to have this conversation with him. He was fidgeting with one of the cuff links on his shirt, not making direct eye contact.

"She was over last night to measure the back porch on my duplex. But I'm guessing that's not why you're asking."

He cracked his knuckles and looked a little flushed. "Well, we went out once. It was great. She said she'd go out with me again, but I haven't been able to pin her down on a date. I'm just wondering if I'm getting the shine-on."

"Oh. Well, I did sort of get the impression that she isn't looking for a relationship." I finished the statement with an awkward *sorry to be the bearer of bad news* expression.

"Hm. Okay. Well, I didn't ask her to move in or anything, so hopefully I didn't scare her off. This lady's got me ass over end, if you know what I mean."

I laughed. Tony "ass over end" was definitely a new position for him.

"Well, put in a good word for me if you get the chance, okay?" he asked.

I didn't have a lot of "good words" about Tony that ever came to mind, but his sincerity now made feel for the guy. "Sure, Tony."

He got up and left my office without another word. Insecurity was a new look for him. I think I preferred it to his usual macho womanizer crap.

Mags and I were part of the Friday five o'clock mass exodus from the building. Once we were outside, Mags turned to me before heading off toward her own car. "I'm going to run home and change and then I'll be over. Text me your address."

"Will do," I said.

I texted Mags as soon as I was in my car, and then I headed home. I'd changed into some jeans and a cute shirt by the time Logek was walking through my front door.

Looking at her, you'd certainly never know the girl had been nursing a heartbreak all week. Her blond hair was bouncy and her face was as perfect as it always is. I had one brief moment of wanting to go work on my makeup more after seeing her, but then decided that was silly. I was who I was. More makeup wasn't going to turn me into Logek. And I really was okay with that (despite my occasional flutters of Logek-induced insecurity).

"You look perfect," I said.

"I was just thinking the same thing about you."

She followed me into the kitchen and I was working on opening a bottle of wine when there was a knock at the front door.

"That's probably Mags."

"Cool," Logek said, heading out to answer the door.

I set three of my super-cute animal print wineglasses on my kitchen table and poured the wine by the time Logek and Mags reappeared.

Mags looked deliberately casual in some perfectly cut jeans and a plaid shirt that was what I would call "Hollywood flannel," since it was too sexy and fitted to be referred to as *just* a flannel shirt.

"Ladies," I said, holding out a wineglass to each of them. "Here's to . . ."

When I trailed off, Mags jumped in. "The assholes who help us recognize the good guys when they come along."

"Amen," Logek said with a laugh. She clinked our glasses and drank. "So, what case are we celebrating tonight?"

"I told you about the guinea pig case, right?" I asked.

"Yes. So you settled it? Or did the thing finally die?"

I laughed. "I *settled* it, thank you very much."

"Brilliant. How?"

"By advising a lonely fortysomething to try online dating," Mags said.

"Diabolical, Katie," Logek said with a chuckle.

"Hey. It was well-intentioned. And they actually look really happy together. So far."

Logek raised her glass again. "Here's to 'so far.'" We clinked glasses again and drank.

"So, Miss Kate," Mags said, turning her glass between her hands. "I wanted to ask you a question."

I frowned. "Of course. What?"

"These glasses are adorable," she said suddenly, raising her glass etched with zebra stripes up to the light to inspect it closer.

I looked at my own glass, with leopard spots. "Aren't they? Gift from Adam's mom. Well, my landlady."

"So cute," Logek agreed.

"So . . . was that your question?" I asked.

Mags made a half laugh, half snort thing. "No, sorry. I got distracted."

"Well, let's hear it."

"Brad and I want you to draft our contract."

My jaw fell open. "Oh my god, Mags! I'm so happy for you," I said, hugging her tightly.

"Good for you, girl," Logek added, also wrapping Mags in a quick hug.

"But you know I don't draft contracts. The firm has an attorney for that," I said.

Mags grimaced. "Please. Frank just opens form contracts and inserts people's names. And even that he manages to screw up sometimes. Besides, you're a friend to both of us. And you're obscenely fair, and you're so protective that you'll worry over every single provision like lives depend on it."

"Um. Thank you?"

"It's a compliment," Mags said with a big smile. "So you'll do it?"

"Of course I will."

Mags did a little happy dance while sitting, careful not to spill her wine.

"Have you ever been signed before?" Logek asked Mags.

"Nope. Came close a couple of times, but I always backed out when it came time to ink the contract."

"Can you teach me that?" Logek asked with a chuckle.

"Signed before, I take it?"

"Oh yeah. I'm what Kate calls a 'serial signer.' You'd think I'd learn."

"My mother always told me, 'Why buy the pig when you can get the sausage for free?' "

Logek and I both burst out laughing.

"Mags, you make so much more sense to me now," I said.

"So what made you decide to sign this time?" Logek asked.

"Finally realized this guy didn't make me feel like I was buying a pig."

"Aww. That's so sweet," I said with mock solemnity. "I think I might cry." I made the motion of whisking some fake tears away.

"Seriously. I think that needs to be on a T-shirt," Logek said. "So, first time under the big C-word. Nervous?"

"I almost said no. Didn't see the need. But it matters to him. And I love him." Mags shrugged.

I made an involuntary *aww* noise.

Then Mags added, "Besides, it's only seven years. I figure I can stick out anything for seven years."

My *aww* sound went away.

"I think," Logek said, looking a little more thoughtful, "that if humans were meant to mate for life, one of the bills to lengthen contracts would have passed by now."

Good point. Every few years, it seemed, there was a bill on the ballot to change the duration of the standard contract. Usually people trying to extend it to ten years. The occasional overambitious bill pushing for twenty years. Once in a while, we even get a push to change the contract to five years. Ultimately, the argument that everyone has the choice of whether or not to extend the contract kills the arguments to lengthen. And, good ol' traditional values always seem to defeat the argument to shorten the contract.

"But some people do stay together," I said.

Logek nodded. "I think people like the *idea* of being together forever. It just doesn't seem to work as well in practice."

Mags laughed. "Fuck forever. I'm good with seven years. I've never even had a pair of *shoes* I've kept that long."

"That is so sweet—comparing Brad to your love for shoes. Now I know it's serious," I said, smiling.

I finished the wine in my glass and looked at my watch. "Should I call a cab?" I asked. I looked at each of them for assent, reaching for my phone. "Six minutes," I said, setting my phone down.

Mags grinned. "Looks like we'll have time to finish that bottle of wine."

I divvied up the rest of the bottle among our glasses.

"So, did I hear you say that Adam is coming tonight?" Mags asked.

I paused, took a deep breath. "Yeah. He really wants to be friends, even though I've made it abundantly clear that I'm not feeling all that *friendly* toward him."

"He knows you're getting emotionally attached but he likes you enough to still want you in his life, regardless of the complications. What a dick," Mags said with a scowl.

"I'm so glad someone understands my plight."

CHAPTER *13*

Fifteen minutes later, we pulled up in front of the Trunk. There was a crowd milling around outside and I was a little worried there might be a wait to get in. To a bar. Seriously? This town did not have enough to do. The outside was pretty cool, though. The facade of the building had a rustic, nautical look, a little like what you'd picture a sunken pirate ship to look like.

We walked toward the front, winding our way through the crowd, to a thick-shouldered bouncer with a clipboard. For a bar. But I think I mentioned that.

"Hi. Is there really a wait to get in?" I asked.

The bouncer looked at me a minute and then smiled. "It's opening weekend, so it looks like everyone had the same idea."

"Oh. I didn't realize it just just opened." Because when you say a word twice, it apparently changes its meaning. The bouncer just shrugged his burly shoulders.

Suddenly Jared appeared behind him and tapped the bouncer's shoulder. "They're with me," he said.

"Oh, sure, Jared." The bouncer immediately opened the rope and let us through. Like movie stars. So *that's* what that feels like.

We walked through and I grinned at Jared.

"Pretty slick, boss man," I said.

Jared shrugged like it was no big deal. "Owners are college buddies. That's all."

As intimidating as Jared looked in his thousand-dollar suits in court, he certainly dressed down nicely. He was in nice jeans and a white button-down shirt that showed off his broad shoulders and narrow waist. It was the first time I'd seen him without a tie.

"Come on. Let's get you ladies some drinks," he said, smiling at each of us in turn.

"Jared!"

We all turned when we heard someone call his name. Brad was standing in front of the bouncer, who was looking over his shoulder at Jared. Jared nodded and Brad was let past the rope. I glanced at Logek and she was staring at me with wide eyes.

That's your boss? she mouthed to me.

I nodded.

Once Brad caught up to us and wrapped an arm around Mags's waist, we all walked toward the bar. The bar itself looked almost as though it had been salvaged from some old pirate ship. The amber lights above the bar were in the shape of bronze crabs and the bartenders were garbed in something pirate-themed, just subtle enough to be cool and not kitschy. Once I reached the bar and sat on a stool, I realized that, set into the wood of the bar, was an actual fish tank. I looked down at it, mesmerized for a moment, before I looked up at the pretty bartender who was smiling at me.

"This place is kind of amazing," I said.

"I agree," she said. She was African American, with high cheekbones and a perfect array of springy dark curls. She was wearing black-and-white-striped tights under little black shorts, with a white T-shirt and a red headband. She might not have looked like she was channeling "pirate" at all, except that she had an eye patch pushed up onto her forehead. "What'll it be, sweetie?"

"Gin and tonic with Hendricks, please."

"Put it on my tab, Jenny," Jared said, giving my shoulder a friendly bump with his own.

"Thanks, boss."

"You're welcome. First round is on me. And the second. What do you guys want?" he asked, looking at Brad and Mags.

Brad pointed at Mags. "Rum and coke?" Mags nodded. "And I'll have a Stella."

Jenny nodded at those requests and started bustling around. Jared turned to Logek.

"Oh, sorry. Jared, this is my good friend, Logek McLean," I said, with a gesture to Logek. "And Logek, this is Jared Mann, one of the partners at my firm."

They shook hands. Logek looked at Jenny the bartender and said, "Dirty martini."

Jenny winked at her, never slowing down as she reached for various glasses and bottles.

I looked at Logek and Jared, facing each other. Quite a pretty picture, actually. Jared with all his chiseled good looks and Logek being all . . . Logek.

"Logic?" Jared asked.

Logek wiggled her head side to side in the usual fashion. "Yeah, pronounced that way but spelled different."

"Interesting," he said. Then Jared tipped his head to the side a little and started to do his trademark staring thing.

After a minute, Logek snapped her fingers in front of his face. "Buddy, you're staring."

I chuckled, because she did in sixty seconds what I hadn't been able to do in a month—call him on his staring thing.

Jared smiling cordially. "I'm sorry—it's a bad habit."

"Apparently."

"Call it an occupational hazard."

"How so?" she asked, looking skeptical.

"As an attorney, I've seen a lot of people talk, but most people's facial expressions and body language end up saying a lot more than their words actually do. So I guess I spend more time observing people's actions—I guess I don't think about the fact that I'm awkwardly staring at someone."

"Hm. So what 'unspoken intel' did you pick up from me?"

"None," Jared said, tucking his hands into the pockets of his jeans and frowning a little. "You seem very . . . genuine."

Logek's face softened, her big, blue eyes widening. "Thank you."

Jared rubbed a thumb against the side of his jaw, thoughtfully. "I just don't see many people that put their real self out there. I can see why you're friends with Kate."

Logek looked at me and smiled. She turned back to Jared. "What's the point in putting on a show? The real you comes out eventually."

Jared nodded, looking a little mesmerized. So weird that this combination never occurred to me. Sure, Mags said Jared was scary, but scary was no match for Logek. And you take away the scary part and you're left with brilliant, handsome, thoughtful, successful . . .

Jared reached past Logek, picked up the drink Jenny had set down, and handed it to Logek.

"Thanks," Logek said, taking the drink from his hand. She sipped the drink, still watching Jared. "Dude, you're still staring."

Jared smiled broadly, warm and disarmed. "Sorry."

"I guess I'll let you off the hook since you bought this round."

Jared smiled at Logek and then turned to me, suddenly remembering my existence—and probably the fact that he was my boss—and looked a little embarrassed. I smiled approvingly. Far be it from me to discourage a worthy man's pursuit of my BFF.

I suddenly felt big, heavy hands resting on my shoulders, and everything inside me went liquid for a minute. Adam was here.

I looked up over my shoulder at him and he looked down at me, his green eyes familiar, his dark hair tousled, and, suddenly, kissing him in front of everyone felt like the most natural thing in the world. Thankfully, I'm not a total moron and I stopped myself from trying to kiss him. But I did lean back into his body a little before I could stop myself. He reciprocated by squeezing my shoulders a little tighter for a moment before reaching past me to say hello to the group.

Logek and Mags gave him a quick hug.

"Adam! I wasn't expecting to see you!" Jared said, clearly happy to see his old college friend.

"Long time, man," Adam said, shaking his hand. As he reached forward to clutch Jared's hand, he rested his other hand in the small of my back. And I really need to stop thinking about every little touch. *It doesn't mean anything, Kate. It's incidental.* And completely distracting.

"So, how do you know this crew?" Jared asked.

Adam looked at me. "I happened to meet Kate . . . what . . . about two months ago?"

Six and a half weeks. But whatever. Close enough. I nodded to Jared and Adam. "About that."

"And met Mags and Logek through her. I don't believe we've met," Adam said, extending his hand to Brad. Brad shook it, smiling.

"It was Brad's client that gave me the black eye," I said.

Adam raised his eyebrows. "So you knew you were going to have your hands full when she managed to get punched the first day on the job, I'm guessing?"

"Pretty much," Brad said. "But she took it like a champ, so we knew we had a keeper," he said, looking at Jared.

Jared shook his head. "I knew we had a keeper when she didn't want to sue the firm for getting hit."

I frowned. "Why would anyone sue for that?"

Jared laughed. "Are you sure you're a lawyer?"

I just smiled and set my empty glass on the bar and made eye contact with Jenny for another.

I looked at Adam. "And Brad and Mags are signing," I said, gesturing between the two of them with my finger.

Brad looked at Jared, wide-eyed. "We informed HR. We've been sure to follow the rules." Oops. Didn't think about that being untimely disclosure in front of the boss.

I looked at Mags and mouthed *Sorry*. She just shrugged like she couldn't care less who knew about it.

Jared ignored it like firm protocol was the last thing on his mind. As he turned back to Logek, I was pretty sure it was.

Adam must have caught the vibe between Logek and Jared as well, because he looked down at me with lowered brows. In response, I tucked up one side of my mouth and shrugged.

Adam gave me a last squeeze on my shoulder and wound his way over to a space at the bar, on the other side of Jared, to order his drink, which I suspected would be Scotch.

He had been over there a couple of minutes before I followed him with the excuse of looking for my refill. When I reached a spot next to him, I found Adam, relaxed with his elbow propped on the bar, and Jenny mirroring his position. Then I noticed just how gorgeous Jenny was. And I was right back to dreading this whole stupid friendship thing, which was likely a disaster in the making.

Adam looked at me, without surprise, and smiled.

"Have you met Jenny?" he asked.

I nodded, smiling at Jenny.

"Jenny is one of the owners. We went to college together."

"Oh! Well, then I didn't need to tell *you* this place was awesome—you already knew," I said.

"Well, *I* think it's awesome, but I was very glad to hear that you thought so, too," she said, giving me a full smile and a view of a cute little dimple at the corner of her mouth.

"So cool you guys finally did this, after talking about it for ten years," Adam said.

Jenny nodded, looking around the crowded room with a small smile. "My parents are less enthused," she said, looking back at Adam. "They aren't quite seeing how my bachelor's in marketing and my MBA were necessary to become a bar owner."

Adam chuckled. "It's all marketing and business."

"Well, I think they feel like the only good money they spent was on my bartending classes."

"This place will be a hit. Then they'll get it."

Jenny placed her hand over Adam's and gave it a grateful squeeze. *Don't think it. Don't think it.* Too late. Did they date? Were they a thing? Wait . . . what difference does it make? Adam already said he's never been in love. Perfect. So any other female he's known has never gotten any further than me. Well, as long as I'm not counting sex. Plenty of women have gotten further on that front. *Enough!* I shouted inside my head. *Enough obsessing over things you can't change for one night.* I know it's bad when I'm even annoying myself.

I smiled at Jenny. "This place is unique. I think you guys are really on to something."

"Thanks. Tell me your name again?"

"Kate," I said, reaching over and shaking her hand.

"So," she said, looking at Adam and then back to me. "How long have you two been together?"

"Oh, we're not," I muttered quickly.

Adam casually draped an arm over my shoulder. "Kate's my best friend."

I looked at him, with one eyebrow raised.

Jenny didn't seem to notice. "Oh," she said, nodding. "That's cool." She patted her hands on the bar top. "Kate, let me get your gin and tonic."

When she walked away, Adam turned to me. "You look pretty tonight."

"Thanks, bestie."

He chuckled.

Jenny was back a moment later with my drink and another

glass for Adam. "I gotta get back to work, but don't you dare leave without saying good-bye," she said to Adam, pointing a finger in his face.

"Promise."

Jenny hustled off, and Adam and I sipped our drinks.

"So, have you heard anything yet about the partnership?" I asked.

Adam looked down at his glass for a moment before looking back into my face. "Yeah, they ended up going with someone else. Said I'd be considered again for the next cycle."

I put my hand on his shoulder. "Oh, Adam, I'm sorry. That really sucks."

He gave me a bland smile and made a slight shrug. "Not a big deal."

Such bullshit. "Why do you do that?" I asked, showing all the frustration I felt.

"Do what?"

"Act like nothing affects you?"

He shrugged again in an attempt to reinforce his nonchalance. "What good would it do?"

"It doesn't have to do any *good*. That's not what this is about. You're entitled to feel things. To be disappointed."

"What's the point?"

"The point is that I *see* all of these feelings under the surface. Your denying they exist doesn't change that. It makes the words coming out your mouth meaningless."

Adam narrowed his eyes at me. He looked annoyed. "What good comes from sharing my disappointment? It changes nothing."

"It matters to me. What's the use of being friends if you don't talk to me about how you actually feel?"

"I don't want to be your friend just so I have someone to listen to me bitch and moan," he said quietly.

"But a real friend would never see it that way, Adam. When I look at you and I can tell you're feeling one thing but you *say* another? It feels dishonest."

"I'm not trying to be dishonest, Kate," he said, leaning down a little to be closer to my eye level. "I'm just trying to keep it simple."

"Well, people aren't simple. People are messy. I prefer messy."

He threw his hands up a little. "Fine. I'm disappointed," he said in a firm but hushed tone.

"I know you are."

He looked at me and his face softened. "They went with a guy that came from a big East Coast firm, who has only been with us for two years. He does have a lot of experience, but I had the best year of anyone with the company."

I shook my head. "Doesn't seem like that sends a good message to the longtime employees, to pass them over for a recent hire."

"Exactly." Adam ran his hand through his hair and took a drink from his glass.

"So, what are you going to do?"

"I don't know. When they gave me the news, they definitely wanted to soften it so that I'd stay. Told me I'd be the front-runner in the next cycle. It's just that these are the type of jobs where you're either on the partner track or you're not. Usually, if you get passed over for partner, it never happens."

"But they wanted to be sure you knew that wasn't the case where you're concerned."

He nodded. "We'll see. I just need to simmer a little and not make any snap decisions." He smiled at me. "But I'm still pretty damn disappointed."

"You have every right to be," I said. I reached out and laced my fingers through his. "Now, we're not going to read into this or overthink it or anything. But I don't know how to sit here with you—like this—and not hold your hand."

Adam laughed and wrapped me in a tight hug. He made a grunt noise. "Kate."

Not sure I can decipher his meaning in that one word, but I was beginning to believe he was sincere when he called me his best friend.

He let go of me and turned toward the bar again and took a long drink of his Scotch. He set his glass down and frowned. I leaned over to look at his face, and he glanced over at me and then poked his finger against the glass of the bar. I followed his finger down and peered into the fish tank.

There was a dissipating cloud of red in the water. As the cloud cleared, a pretty striped fish floated on its side, midway in the tank, dead.

Adam and I looked at each other. "Uh, Jenny?" Adam called out to Jenny, who was near the end of the bar.

"Yeah, sweetie?" she said, coming to stand in front of us, palms down on the bar.

"Any chance you have a piranha in your tank?" he asked, pointing to the carnage below.

"Damn. Drew!" she called out. A lanky guy with blond hair and thick-rimmed black glasses hustled over. He was wearing a red-and-white-striped shirt which, with the glasses, made him look a little more like Waldo than a pirate.

Jenny pointed to the dead fish in the tank.

"Shit," Drew mumbled.

Jenny looked up at us. "We've got a fish eater."

I raised my eyebrows.

"This is our third dead fish in two weeks," she added.

"Did you call the guy that installed the tank?" she asked, turning to Drew.

"Yeah. He said he didn't give us anything that should be eating the others. Just to keep our eyes open and figure out which one it is and he'll come and remove it."

"Keep our eyes open?" Jenny asked, sounding edgy. "There's one hundred fish in this tank, and when we're here, we're working. How are we supposed to babysit the damn fish?"

Drew shrugged, looking a little whipped. He glanced toward Adam.

"Hey, man," he said, breaking into a grin. "Good to see you. How ya been?"

"Good," Adam said, giving him a clap on the shoulder, bro style. Men are funny animals. "Congrats on the place. So awesome to see it come to life."

"Thanks. We're pretty excited."

"Drew, this is my friend Kate."

"Nice to meet you," Drew said, giving me a firm handshake. "So, I don't suppose either of you happened to spot our little Jack the Ripper tonight, did you?"

"Sorry," Adam said. "I only noticed it after it happened, because of the blood in the water."

Jenny responded to a beckoning from the other end of the bar, and Drew leaned in toward us and said quietly, "This tank was my idea, and Jenny wasn't thrilled with it. If I can't figure out which little fucker is eating the other fish, I'm never gonna hear the end of it."

Adam laughed, and I gave Drew a sympathetic smile.

Drew opened a cabinet behind him and pulled out a little net. He opened a panel on his side of the tank and proceeded to fish out the partially eaten carcass.

"Sorry, little fella," he said, dropping the fish into the trash can. "Good to see you, Adam. Nice to meet you, Kate," he said, before scurrying away to mingle with other patrons.

We both took one last look into the tank, I guess making sure no other fish-on-fish crime was being perpetrated, then we picked up our glasses and headed back to the group.

"Where'd you disappear to?" Logek asked, with a subtly suspicious look.

"We were getting a drink and Adam was introducing me to his college buddies," I said, making a vague gesture toward the other end of the bar. "And then we witnessed a massacre," I said, casually.

"Excuse me?" Mags asked.

"They've got a murderous fish in the tank eating its neighbors," Adam explained.

"Ew," Mags said, without inflection.

Jared frowned. "What kind of fish is it that's eating the others?"

"They don't know yet or else they'd get rid of it," Adam said. "I guess this is the third fish it's killed, but they've got a hundred in the tank, so they haven't caught it in the act."

Jared looked thoughtful.

"Why?" I asked. "Do you know anything about fish?"

"Yeah, I've actually kept a tank for years," Jared said.

Logek tipped her head at him, eyebrows raised.

"What? They're relaxing."

Logek smiled. "I could see that."

"I'm gonna go take a look at what they've got in there. See if I can help."

"I'll come with you," Logek said.

Adam and I looked at each other. I shrugged and nodded toward the bar, after Jared and Logek.

"Brad and I are gonna go play some pool," Mags said, gesturing toward the two pool tables across the room.

I looked at Adam.

"Well, what do you want to do? Go play fish detective or play pool?" Adam asked.

"Well, when you put it like that, who could pass up being a *fish detective*?"

"You're dark. You just want to see another fish get eaten."

"You got me. I'm just a dark and twisty soul."

"I learn new things about you all the time." He turned toward Mags as she and Brad walked away. "We'll catch up with you," he called.

Mags waved at us and kept walking.

I sidled up to the bar next to Logek, who seemed fairly engrossed in what Jared was telling her.

"That one—that's a Siamese fighting fish," Jared said, with a finger to the glass. "Let me know if you see another one. They're fine in a group of other kinds of fish, but you usually don't want to have more than one or they can be aggressive."

"He's pretty," Logek said.

I glanced at Logek. She was studying a fish in the tank, and Jared was studying her. Then he caught me looking at him and tried to cover.

"That one," he said, reiterating what he had told Logek.

The four of us focused on the tank, and within a couple of minutes I could see why Jared said fish tanks were relaxing.

"Ooh!" I said, pointing at a black and white, spiky-looking fish that swam in front of me. "Isn't that one?"

When I looked over, Logek and Jared were both looking at me.

"That's the one I just pointed out," Jared said with a slight smile.

"Oh. Oops."

"Wait!" Logek said. "There!" She pressed her fingertip to the tank and watched another fish with the same markings.

Jared smiled. "They need to get rid of the thugs."

Jenny stopped in front of us, eyebrows lowered. "Whatcha doing?" she asked.

"Looking for Jaws," Adam said, with a grin.

"Why?" Jenny asked, focusing on the tank. "Did you see something else?"

"You have multiple Siamese fighting fish in the tank. I read somewhere that they *can* turn homicidal if there is more than one in a tank," Jared said.

"Really? That's fantastic. I'll let our fish guy know to come get the damn things out of the tank. Thank you so much, Jared."

Jared shrugged, modestly.

"No, seriously," Jenny added, putting a friendly hand on Jared's shoulder. "Next round is on the house," she said with a broad smile, displaying gloriously white teeth.

"Well done, Holmes," Logek said to Jared, leaning into him lightly.

"I couldn't have solved it without you, Watson."

*

After a couple more rounds and a few games of pool, Mags and Brad were ready to say their farewells.

I hugged Mags, and then Brad. I was feeling pretty huggy.

"Again, congrats on the hamster case," Mags said.

"Guinea pig," I mumbled under my breath.

Mags laughed and ignored my correction. "I think I speak for all of us when I say, way to settle things without any animal slaughter, Kate."

"Oh stop. You'll make me cry."

Brad was in the middle of a friendly handshake with Adam, followed by Jared.

"See you Monday," I called out to them as they headed for the door.

I turned back to the remaining group, smiling.

"It might be time to get this one home," Logek said, wrapping an arm around my shoulder.

"You didn't drive, did you?" Jared asked, pointing a finger between Logek and me.

"Do we look like amateurs?" Logek asked.

"No, you certainly do not." Jared smiled and put his hands in his pockets again.

"Do you guys want a ride?" Adam asked. "I have my car." Of course. He was always sober and in control. No cabs for Adam.

"Sure," Logek said. "My car is at Kate's."

"How about you, Jared?" Adam asked.

"Oh, I'm in the other direction. I'll just grab a cab." He

looked at me. "This was fun. And seriously, congratulations. That was an awesome win today."

"Thanks, boss," I said, with a silly grin. "I appreciate that. And thanks for the drinks."

"Anytime. So, Adam, you'll call me about racquetball?"

"Absolutely." Then they did the manliest of handshakes. Psh. Alphas.

Jared turned to Logek and reached a hand out to her. "It was really great to meet you, Logek. Really. Incredible."

She gripped his hand and then took charge by leaning in and giving him a quick hug. "Likewise. Hopefully I'll see you around."

"That would be great," Jared said, with a nod of his head and small smile on his square jaw.

We walked to the door and waved a good-bye to Jared as he headed to a cab stopped at the curb. Adam's car was only a couple of blocks away and we were quiet during the walk there.

When we reached his car, Logek gestured for me to take the front seat, so I did. Logek climbed in the back and we pulled away from the curb, heading toward my house. As soon as we were driving, Logek sat forward from the center of the back seat, putting a hand on each of the front seats, and leaned her head in between Adam and me.

"Seriously. What was that?"

"What was what?" I asked.

"'Incredible to meet you'? 'Hope to see you around'?"

"Actually, I think *you* said 'Hope to see you around,' " I clarified.

"Not the point! It was *incredible* to meet me and then just . . . bye?"

I looked at Adam. He was listening but hadn't chimed in. "You've known Jared longer than I have. Any input?"

"You know Jared?" Logek asked. I guess I forgot to fill her in on their connection.

"We went to college together," Adam said. "We were friends, but not really close."

"Why?" Logek asked, leaning forward a little farther. "Is he weird? Creepy?"

Adam gave a small shrug while turning down a city side street. "Not weird. Just . . . odd. Hard to get to know. Does that make sense?"

Logek nodded. "But he seemed like he liked me, right?"

Adam nodded. I said, "Yeah, definitely."

Logek was nodding. "But he didn't ask for my number or anything. He has no idea if he'll ever see me again." I don't think Logek was accustomed to this phenomenon.

"He does work with your best friend. Maybe he figures he could just ask Kate?" Adam suggested.

Logek seemed to consider that, but I could tell she still wasn't satisfied. "I guess."

"You could have asked him for *his* number, you know," Adam added.

Logek looked at him like he hadn't used English. Logek was a strong woman, but needing to make a move with a man was still new territory for her. "Asked him?"

Adam chuckled. "I do believe that is done occasionally, yes."

Logek made a grunt noise and sat back in her seat with a flop.

"So, out of curiosity," Adam said, flicking his eyes toward his rearview mirror to look at Logek sulking in the back seat, "are you genuinely interested in him? Or just intrigued by a man that didn't immediately fall for you?"

Logek sighed. "You sound like Kate. Not *all* guys go for me."

"Okay," he said.

"But," she added, sitting up and leaning between us once more, "typically, when we hit it off and they seem attracted to me? Yeah. Then they do."

Adam gave an amused grin. "So is that a yes, you are interested in him?"

Logek shrugged and pulled her long blond hair up into a ponytail between her hands. She looked out the window for a moment before letting go of her hair and letting it cascade back over her shoulders. "He was interesting," she said matter-of-factly. "He's obviously attractive. He stares. He keeps fish . . ." On that list point, Logek frowned and shook her head at Adam, like she didn't understand it. "He's a little intense. He's just . . . interesting."

Adam shot me a quick, smiling glance before responding to her. "You mentioned that."

I woke up the next morning to my phone buzzing on the nightstand. I reached out with the blanket still over my head and grabbed my phone.

Scarlett. Crap.

"This is Kate."

"Hi, Kate. It's Scarlett."

I pulled my phone back and looked at the clock on the corner of the screen. 7:42 a.m.

"Scarlett, it's before eight a.m. On a Saturday," I said sternly.

"I have a clock. I know what time it is. But this is important!" I'm sure it's a matter of life and death. Again. "The bastard stole one of the cameras off my house."

I flipped the blanket back from my face and sighed. "Any chance it was the one pointed toward his bedroom?"

"Yes. It *was* that one."

"Any chance it was still pointed directly at his bedroom window?"

"Maybe."

"Because you never moved it, even though you agreed to in the stipulation?"

Scarlett grunted. "I really don't see what that has to do with him stealing shit off my house."

"Because. You were basically violating the order, still having it trained on his bedroom." I sighed then cleared my throat. "Scarlett, I can call Doug on Monday and ask him to ask Rhett to give the camera back."

"But he *took* it. How is that not illegal?"

"Then call the police and report a theft."

"I thought I was supposed to call you."

"How much was that camera?"

"I don't know. I think they were like thirty or forty dollars each."

"Okay. Well this conversation has probably already cost you more than that."

"I don't care about the cost of the camera!" she said, starting to sound shrill. "I care about dragging his ass back into court!"

I raised my voice, since I was beginning to think my calm approach was being lost on her. "I get that. But you were supposed to move that camera and you didn't. I've told you—repeatedly—you need to take the high road. That is the only way to get him in trouble. If you are doing everything right and not antagonizing him and he *doesn't* leave you alone, you'll have grounds. But as long as you are antagonizing him as well, we've got nothing. I don't know what else to tell you."

Scarlett was quiet when I finished, and I was a little worried that I might have gone too far. Where does yelling at a client fall on the bad lawyer scale? Then again, where does calling your attorney's cell before 8:00 a.m. on a Saturday rate on the shitty client scale? I'd say we're square.

"Okay," she said finally. "If you can get the camera back, I'll mount it somewhere else."

"Good. I think that is the right decision. I'll call Doug Monday and then let you know."

"Okay." Perfect. She was sulking again.

"I'll talk to you Monday," I said, when she went quiet again.

"Okay. Bye."

I hung up and covered my face with my pillow.

*

Monday morning, Doug Simpson beat me to the punch and called while I was still looking over new emails.

"Good morning, Doug," I said.

"Morning. Believe it or not, I'm not calling about Scarlett."

"You're kidding."

"Well, I'm not *only* calling about Scarlett." That makes more sense. "It took a little time, but I got Jennifer Roma to realize she wasn't going to get far with her breach of contract claim post deposition. She's willing to settle on the mutual termination provision."

I'd just back-burnered Jim Trainor's matter, since nothing was pending. Not to mention the fact that Jim's awesome referral, Scarlett, was eating up a lot of my time. "Oh," I said. "That's good to hear. I'll give Jim a call today."

"Great. Let me know."

"So . . . about Scarlett."

"Yeah. I guess Friday night she was on his front porch screaming about something."

"Pretty sure it had to do with Rhett taking one of the cameras off of her house."

"He did?"

"Well, it's the invasion-of-privacy one that's missing, so I think Rhett is a safe bet."

Doug chuckled. "Okay. I'll ask him to return it."

"Do you think that's safe? I mean, I'm not sure we actually want to encourage contact between these two."

"Fair enough. I can ask him to bring it to my office and Scarlett can pick it up here?"

"That'll work."

"I'll let you know."

I was looking up Jim Trainor's phone number when Jared appeared in my office.

"Hey," he said with a friendly smile.

"Hey, boss."

"Friday was fun," he said, walking farther into my office and leaning on one of the chairs in front of my desk.

"It really was."

"It was really good to see Adam again, too. We'd sort of lost touch over the years. Funny that you two ended up knowing each other." Funnier than you know. "And your friend Logek is . . . terrific."

Hm. Terrific. "She's the best," I agreed. Come on, Jared. You know you want to ask.

"Anyway, we should all do it again sometime."

"Absolutely."

"See you later," he said with a quick wave, and headed out of the office.

Almost like her ears were burning, I got a text from Logek.

> *Hey Kitty Kat. Want to grab lunch tomorrow?*
> *Tomorrow is no good. I have to be in court by 1pm.*
> *Wow. You sound so grown up and lawyer-y :)*
> *Haha. Goal achieved, then.*
> *How about Wednesday?*
> *Yeah—that sounds good.*
> *I'll come get you. I haven't seen your office yet.*
> *No ulterior motives there or anything.*
> *Kate. Whatever do you mean?*
> *Shameless.*
> *Your point?*
> *Why would I possibly have a point? See you Wednesday.*

I started reviewing Luann Sykes's contract. It was fairly standard, but the damages provision was a little vague. The better contracts have the mathematical formula for calculating the damages right in the contract—which is usually some measure of the combined incomes of the couple and the percentage contribution the contract provided the nonbreaching party, blah blah blah. Then there's a whole other calculation if the couple had children, which, thankfully, Luann did not. This provision just based damages on the maintenance of the current standard of living, which I was pretty sure Luann could maintain all on her own. Shit.

I grabbed her contract and headed to Jared's office. I poked my head around the corner and found him looking out the window, which was a first for him, since any other time I'd dropped by his office he was buried in paperwork and super focused.

"Hey. Can I bug you for a second?" I asked.

He quickly turned back to his desk. "Of course. What's up?"

"I was hoping you could read this damages provision and give me your thoughts on how to handle it."

"Absolutely," he said, extending his hand to me for the contract. I handed it over and he set it on the desk in front of him. I poked a finger quickly at the appropriate section of the page and waited quietly while he read.

"Ah. Yeah. I've seen ones like this. Here," he said, scribbling on a pad of paper. He ripped off the page and handed it back to me with the contract. "These are the cases you'll want at your fingertips. They're the leading authority that says just because she can maintain her current lifestyle doesn't mean she's not entitled to damages based on what his salary contributed to the partnership."

"Oh my gosh. That's perfect. Thank you."

"Of course. Anytime."

I gave him a grateful smile and headed back to my office to read these cases so that I could call Luann's cheating hottie's attorney properly armed.

While I was reading up on the cases, I remembered that I still needed to call Jim Trainor about settlement.

I dialed his number and waited.

"This is Jim," he said abruptly.

"Jim, this is Kate Shaw." Silence. "Your attorney."

"Of course. Hiya, Kate."

"So, as we expected after Jennifer's deposition, her attorney just called and said that she was willing to settle on the mutual termination clause."

"I've been thinking about that, though. She cheated. She admitted that it was before she found out about my DUI."

"Yes, but she didn't admit it was before you *got* your DUI—which is technically when *you* breached. Jim, I thought this is what you wanted . . . to just mutually terminate, with no damages."

"I think I'm entitled to damages."

See? Just when I start thinking my job isn't completely awful. Jim Trainor, ladies and gentlemen.

"You would be, Jim. If you hadn't breached the contract as well. But you did."

"But I think she breached first."

"Judges generally don't care who breached first if you didn't know about her breach. Which you didn't."

"I suspected."

"So you want me to go to a judge and argue that you thought she was cheating on you so that's why you thought it would be okay to get convicted of misdemeanor driving under the influence?"

"Well, not like *that*. In fancy lawyer talk, I bet it would sound a lot better."

"There are no fancy lawyer words for that, Jim," I said quietly, putting a fingertip to the bridge of my nose and closing my eyes. "My advice, as your attorney, is to agree to this settlement. The attorney fees you'll spend fighting this you'll likely never get back, because of your breach."

He was quiet. Then I heard him mutter, "Cheating bitch."

I'm gonna go ahead and assume that requires no response from me. "Fine."

"Fine? You'll agree to a mutual walk-away?"

"If that's my only option."

"There's always other options. I just believe it's your *best* option."

"Fine. If you think it's my best shot."

You can always tell when they want ironclad advice from an attorney so that they have someone to blame.

"I do think it's your best option. *But* it is ultimately your decision, Jim. If you want to spend the money to fight this, I'll fight it. It's my job as your attorney, though, to tell you that it would be a tough road, given the circumstances."

"Fine. You're telling me it's my only choice. I'll do it."

Son of a bitch. I sighed. Loudly. "It's not your *only* choice. Just the best choice." At what point do I get to stop playing tic-tac-toe with my client?

"Okay."

"Okay." I'm not stupid enough to give him another opportunity for a round of truth or dare. "I'll call you when the settlement is drafted."

"Fine." Jim didn't sound nearly as happy with me as he did the day I snared his ex during deposition. Oh well. I'll just have to find a way to live without his adoring approval.

I opened up a file and typed up some *highly* detailed notes of our phone conversation, including as much verbatim as I could. He's the type of client I could see one day forcing me to defend myself against a claim of malpractice. The joys of being an attorney.

I hung up with Jim and called Doug.

"Doug Simpson."

"Doug, it's Kate."

"Long time, no talk."

"Yeah. Jim Trainor agreed. Are you writing the settlement or am I?" I asked.

"Me. Jennifer insisted I make sure, and I'm quoting here, 'Jim's snake of an attorney doesn't slip something in there.'"

"Wow. Is it wrong that I'm flattered?"

Doug laughed. "If we aren't hated by the opposing party, we start to question whether we're really doing our job."

"Thanks, Doug. You're making me question all my career decisions."

"They didn't come up with a million lawyer jokes because people *love* lawyers."

"That should be on a plaque hanging up at the admissions office of every law school."

Doug chuckled. "Oh, by the way, Rhett's dropping Scarlett's camera off on her front porch while she's at work. I figured that would be okay. He didn't want to drive out to my office."

"Okay. I'd better warn her before she calls to tell me that he *trespassed* by stepping foot on her porch."

"Talk to you soon."

"You're jinxing us, Doug!"

He laughed again and hung up.

About an hour later, Rita buzzed me. "Um, Kate. Scarlett is here. She didn't have an appointment with you, right?"

"No. Damn."

"She was adamant that she see you, so I put her in conference room three. Do you want me to tell her you're in a meeting?"

Crap. "No. Don't worry about it, Rita. I'll take care of it."

"Sorry, Kate."

I smiled. "Not your fault, Rita. I blame Scarlett's long-term lack of psychiatric treatment."

Rita laughed and hung up.

I stopped at Mags's cube.

Mags looked up at me, expectantly. "Scarlett is here," I said. She frowned.

"Yes, no appointment. Just showed up," I continued. "I'm going to talk to her in conference room three. If I'm not back in fifteen minutes, I need you to come and interrupt and say I'm late for a meeting."

Mags saluted. "You got it."

I walked into the conference room and immediately noticed a pair of pink satin panties on the conference room table.

I just sat down in the chair across from Scarlett and didn't say a word. Not really sure how to open any conversation that starts with her bringing a pair of panties to my office.

Scarlett pointed to the panties, neatly displayed on the table between us.

I gave her my best confused expression.

"I found these in my laundry. In my *laundry*," she hissed.

I continued my confounded expression and waited.

"They *aren't* mine!"

What. The. Hell. "I still don't understand."

"It's proof! That's he's broken into my house!"

I started to ask *How?* but decided to just shake my head at her.

"Kate. Jesus. These aren't my underwear. How else would they have gotten in my house?"

"So . . . Rhett wears satin panties?"

"Of course not," she said. "I mean, one time, but—"

I cut her off, waving my hands between us. "Scarlett. Why would Rhett have another woman's underwear in your house?"

"To fuck with me?" she said, exasperated at needing to explain this to me.

This crazy train was officially so far off the rails, I couldn't figure out how she arrived at this conclusion. I shook my head again.

"Or," she continued, "it could be from when we were still together."

Still waiting, quietly.

"That would prove that he breached!"

"Didn't you *both* breach?"

"Which time?"

I threw up my hands. "I don't know, Scarlett. Which time are you talking about?"

She frowned at me. "Yes, we breached, but if he was screwing around, then his breach was worse."

"How long have you two been split up?"

"About four months."

"You really don't think you would have found these underwear in the laundry for *four* months?" I kind of regretted asking the question, because I was a little worried she would confess how seldom she washed her clothes.

"I don't know! Can't we run DNA on them or something? That would prove that he cheated!"

I instinctively leaned back from the potential DNA-carrying underwear on the conference room table. "I don't know what to say. DNA tests are very expensive and take a long time. You and Rhett settled your contract dispute months ago. I don't even understand what you think this could possibly change."

"It would be proof. I thought proof was what lawyers and judges wanted!"

"Proof that the underpants of an unknown woman ended up in your laundry without explanation?" I don't know why I continued asking questions. I was like a blind woman groping in an unfamiliar room, trying to find the damn light switch.

"That's why we need a DNA test! So she won't be unknown!"

"But unless she's in the database—usually for some criminal conviction—there would be no match!" I had inadvertently started raising my voice to match hers. Conversations with her were beginning to consistently have this effect on me. Apparently, third-grade playground rules applied.

"Oh, I'm sure she's got a record."

I went back to shaking my head. "Any chance you caught him on camera going into your house?"

"No."

"Scarlett, this isn't going to help us," I said, gesturing to the panties.

Scarlett just seethed at me.

I looked up suddenly, to the sound of the door to the conference room opening. "Ms. Shaw," Mags said. "You're late for the board meeting."

"Right. Thanks."

Mags closed the door but stood outside the window, pointing to the panties on the table.

I shook my head. "Scarlett, I have to go."

She snatched the panties off the table, thankfully, and wadded them up in her fist. "Fine. But he did this. I know he did."

I sighed. "I'm not saying he didn't. Or did. I don't know. I'm just saying that this isn't going to help your case."

"Fine," she said. She got up and walked out of the conference room, headed toward the front desk.

Mags walked into the room with a perplexed expression. She leaned onto the table toward me.

I pointed at the table where her hands were. "We might want to Lysol the table before putting your hands there."

She quickly snatched them away. "Yuck."

"Yup," I said. "*Board* meeting?"

"Like she's gonna know the difference. I could have said you were late for your swearing in as a Supreme Court justice and it would have had the same effect. She's only thinking about her own little world."

"Good point."

"Why did she bring you underwear?"

I tried to paraphrase what Scarlett had told me.

"But—" Mags started. "How . . . I mean, *why* . . ."

I shook my head at her. "It's not going to make sense to you because you aren't *insane*."

Now she nodded agreement. "Wow."

Wow is right. I pointed at the table. "I'm serious about the Lysol. Do we have any disinfectant?"

"I'm sure we've got something," she said, looking at her hands the way you would if they were covered in finger paint. She used her elbow to open the conference room door and went in search of a sturdy sanitizer. I didn't blame her. I felt like I needed a hot shower myself.

*

That evening, at home, I was eating salad from a bag (which is the best invention for lazy people who want to make attempts at healthy eating). As I channel surfed and sprinkled a few more sunflower seeds on my salad, my cell rang.

Sandy. "Hi, Sandy," I said, answering after the first ring.

"Hi, Kate. Am I interrupting anything?"

I looked down at my yoga pants and plateful of prepackaged salad. "Not a bit. What's up?"

"Would you mind if I dropped by?"

Normally, Sandy immediately declared her purpose, making this visit more of a mystery.

"Of course. Anytime."

"Wonderful. I'll be there in a few."

"See you soon."

I hung up and frowned at my phone. I finished the rest of my salad (feeling like a borderline health fanatic) and rinsed my plate. By the time I was done, there was a knock at the door.

When I opened it, Sandy was smiling on the doorstep, holding a little pink bag with tissue paper bursting from the top.

"Sandy, what did you do?" I asked, directing a worried glance toward the gift bag.

"See, I knew if I told you I had a gift for you, you would have made an excuse for me not to come by."

"Not true. I love gifts," I said, stepping aside and waving her into my apartment. "But you shouldn't have."

"That's what I meant to say," she said, setting the bag down on the coffee table. "You'd tell me I shouldn't have."

"And I would be right."

Sandy was actually in yoga pants tonight, too, or something similar, and a T-shirt. I'd never seen her dressed so casually. She tucked her dark hair behind her ear and, if it weren't for the gray streaks in her hair and the fine lines around her eyes, people would think we were the same age. She picked up the little pink bag and held it out to me, smiling.

I shook my head but accepted the gift gratefully. After pulling the tissue from the top, I withdrew another glass for my set—with tiger stripes. Surprised, I looked into her face.

"One of these just got broken!"

"I know!"

"How . . ." But before I voiced the rest of the question, I remembered Adam spotting the wreckage of the glass in my garbage can a few days ago. "Adam told you it got broken."

Sandy nodded. "And he even told me which one it was. Said you were heartbroken that you'd lost part of your set."

"I told him I wanted to find out where you got them so *I* could replace it. I certainly didn't expect you to run out and get me another."

Sandy waved a hand in the air, dismissing my concerns. "I only have a son, Kate. Let me have some fun buying pretty things."

After she said that, I gave her a quick hug. "How about we christen it and have a glass of wine?"

She did a quick look around my living room. "Oh, I don't want to intrude on your evening. I just wanted to drop that by for you."

"I insist."

She shrugged. "That would be lovely."

I grabbed a bottle of red from my kitchen and came back, after washing the new glass and grabbing a second one. I opened the bottle and poured some into both glasses for us.

After handing her a glass, I tapped the rim of mine to hers. "Cheers," I said. "To me having the absolute best landlady in the world."

Sandy laughed. "Thank you, Kate. And to the best tenant."

We both sat down on the sofa and took a drink. I looked at my glass and traced the zebra stripes etched into it with my fingertip. "Sandy, I have to ask. I mean, if it isn't prying. You are so incredible. How is it that you and Adam's dad didn't re-up?"

Sandy's face went blank a moment. "Well, Thomas died." When the shock registered on my face, Sandy put a hand to my forearm. "I assumed Adam would have told you."

"No, I mean, he just said you guys only had one contract. He never said why."

Sandy's face went slack a little and, for the first time, she looked every day of her sixty years. She looked at me a minute without speaking and I wasn't certain she was going to elaborate. Then she smiled, but it was that sad, wistful smile you usually only read about in books about unrequited love.

"Thomas and I signed and Adam was born a year later. Then, about the time we would have thought about renewing our contract, we found out he was sick. Cancer." She shrugged matter-of-factly. "So we spent the next two years doing the specialty circuit, trying experimental things. Even had it in remission for a couple of years. During that time, I brought up another contract, but Thomas was worried I'd be left with the bill for his care, so he refused. And then it came back and it was everywhere and he didn't have the fight in him anymore. He died when Adam was thirteen."

Without thinking, or being able to help myself, I reached out and grasped her hand. She smiled and held on to it.

"Thomas was . . . like no other man I've ever met. He was strong, but caring. So kind. He was the type that would drop everything to take care of those he loved. Which was funny, because when I first met him he seemed kind of stoic. Severe. But once I got to know him, he was the warmest man I ever knew." She sighed and smiled, and took another drink of wine.

I thought about her description and nodded. "Adam sounds like he takes after his father in that way."

"He might be, if he ever got close to anyone." She narrowed her eyes a little and leaned in toward me. "Is it me or does he not really date?"

I laughed. "Not really his thing."

"That's a relief. I was a little worried he was dating but just never wanted me to meet any of them. I just want him to be happy, so I try not to push, but he seems a little detached. Lonely, sometimes."

"I would've agreed with that when I first met him, but he doesn't seem so lonely to me now."

Sandy turned the stem of her glass, propped her elbow on the back of the couch, and rested her head in her palm. "I worry that I'm the reason Adam is the way he is."

"Adam is wonderful," I said with a laugh. "So, yes, you probably are the reason he is that way."

She smiled. "You know what I mean. He never gets close to people. I just wonder if watching me . . . stay in a relationship with a dead man for the last twenty years made him think it's not worth it." Sandy made a slight grunt. "Ridiculous. Thomas has been gone for twenty years and I just never let go. Every other man I've met is just a shade of him—not real enough for me to consider them as actual possibilities." Pretty sure Uncle Tony wasn't going to be the man to suddenly break that cycle. "But what if watching me pine away for the person I lost made him unable to love someone that much? So that he doesn't end up like me."

My eyes misted over a little. "Well, he recently told me that I was his best friend. So, while not romantic, he *has* gotten close to someone." She and I both laughed, and a tear ran down my cheek. "And I'm pretty sure he has turned out just like you in all the best ways."

CHAPTER 15

The next afternoon, I'd gotten to court fifteen minutes early and was waiting for Rochelle to show, when Dickhead, aka Richard Pope, sat down in the seat next to me.

"Dr. Pope," I said, not hiding my surprise.

"Ms. Shaw. How are you?"

"Um. Fine." I did a quick head swivel looking for Doug. "Is your attorney here?"

"Not yet. I wanted to talk to you."

"Dr. Pope, you're represented by counsel and I'm not allowed to talk to you."

He waved a hand in the air. "This isn't about the case. I'm fine with the child support. This is about Rochelle."

I frowned.

"I need her back. I know I made a mistake." I inadvertently raised an eyebrow. Think you mean to say *mistakes*, buddy, since there were several. "But there has to be some way she'll forgive me."

I leaned back from him, my entire body not wanting to have this conversation. "I really don't know what I could do. And whether it's about the case or not—I really shouldn't be talking to you at the hearing."

He sighed. "Fine." He got up and headed for a seat across the aisle before quickly turning back to me and adding, "I'll call your office later."

What the . . . what? No, no, no. Do the mental hospitals know there are this many crazy people walking around every day? Because I certainly didn't, until I went into signing law. Okay, and maybe a little while in television. More than a little. Whatever.

Rochelle startled me out of my reverie when she scooched past me and sat in the next seat.

"Hi, Kate," she said, with a big smile.

I did a quick, inadvertent glance toward Pope and he was watching her intently. I could almost picture the little red cartoon hearts in his eyes. One of life's hard-learned truths: you don't know what you've got till it's gone.

I looked back at Rochelle, and boy, was she gone. She didn't even seem to realize he was sitting three feet away. "Hi, Rochelle. You look . . . happy," I observed.

She shrugged and made a gleeful grunt. "*So* happy," she said. "It's weird the way a little distance can make you realize that you were never actually happy with them. Just too afraid to let go of the *idea* of them."

I nodded at her wisdom. "I guess I never thought of it that way." My mind quickly flickered to Jonathan. Nope. I was *actually* happy. No delusions there. I added, "I'm really glad it's working out for you."

She nodded and then faced forward as the judge entered the courtroom. We all stood when the bailiff told us to. Judge Stanford entered, looking severe in his black robe and prematurely annoyed with all of us. He sat down and straightened his glasses. I kinda hoped he wouldn't remember us from our clients' no-show a few weeks ago.

I glanced back just in time to see Doug slinking into the courtroom at the last minute, keeping his head low to avoid the judge's notice.

Judge Stanford didn't notice or didn't care and just started calling items on the calendar.

When our case was called, the four of us headed to the big kids' table. I sat down with Rochelle to my right and Doug sat with Pope to his left. I could tell Pope was whispering to Doug and Doug was trying to silence him.

"Ms. Shaw. So nice to see that your client could join us this time. And you, as well, Mr. Simpson."

Really, Kate? You thought there was a chance he wouldn't call you out on that? I felt my face grow hot. Per usual. Doug and I mumbled brief apologies.

Judge Stanford gave a quick glare to our clients. "Your motion, Ms. Shaw."

"Yes, Your Honor. As stated in the moving papers, a recalculation for child support is necessary, based on Dr. Pope's current income."

"Yes. This support order has been static for five years?" Judge Stanford asked, directing his attention to Doug.

"Approximately, Your Honor." I saw Doug hold a hand up

to Pope, who seemed to still be attempting to whisper in his lawyer's ear.

"Dr. Pope, you will hold your conversation. You should have had ample time prior to this hearing to discuss matters with your attorney," Judge Stanford said, without a hint of amusement.

Pope appeared to mutter another few words to Doug before finally holding his tongue. Doug sighed audibly. "Your Honor, it is my client's wish to withdraw our opposition to Ms. Britton's motion."

The courtroom went quiet at that.

"Mr. Simpson, may I address your client?"

"Of course, Your Honor."

"Dr. Pope, is this correct? You no longer wish to contest Ms. Britton's motion for an increase in child support?"

"That is correct, Your Honor. I want her to have whatever she wants."

I spared a quick glance at Rochelle. Damn, girl. You're going to need to teach classes or something.

Judge Stanford considered the statement for a quick second before picking up the relevant pleading in his hand. "Very well. Respondent's objection to Petitioner's motion is stricken at Respondent's request. It is the ruling of this Court that child support shall be ordered as prayed in the motion. Ms. Shaw, you will prepare the order for the Court's signature, pursuant to this ruling."

"Yes, Your Honor." I quickly shuffled my papers and lifted the relevant order in my hand. "Your Honor, I do have a proposed order already drafted on those terms."

"I would prefer if you included the request to strike the objection."

"Absolutely, Your Honor. I will revise it and submit it tomorrow."

"Thank you. Good day." And just like that, we were dismissed. Again. Stanford was a very abrupt judge.

We all filed out of the courtroom and, once outside, Doug reached out and shook my hand. "Thanks, Kate. Just send the proposed order over for me to approve as to form."

"Absolutely. I'll have it to you by tomorrow." I glanced at Pope and he was eagle-eyeing Rochelle, who was smiling, looking relaxed and lovely.

Rochelle walked up to Pope and took his hand between both of hers. "Thank you, Richard. I really do appreciate this not turning into an ugly fight."

"Of course," he said, earnestly. "I would do anything for you."

Rochelle responded with a look that, to me at least, resembled pity, and put a hand gently to his cheek. "I wish you all the best, Richard."

Pope frowned a little, like he was starting to catch on that his grand gesture may not have had the effect he was going for. "But . . . we'll talk, right?"

"Of course. You're Collette's father. We'll always be a part of each other's lives."

He still didn't seem satisfied, but that statement seemed to give him hope, so he nodded and squeezed her hand.

Rochelle and I turned and headed down the stairs and out of the building. Once outside, she turned to me, gripping my wrist.

"I can't thank you enough, Kate. You helped me more than you know."

I frowned, confused. "You did this all yourself."

She shook her head. "Don't underestimate your pep talks. Sometimes the right word when you need it most can change everything."

My face froze, and for a second I felt a little choked up. I put a hand to my chest. "I really appreciate that."

Rochelle surprised me by wrapping me in a quick hug before turning and heading the opposite way down the sidewalk.

Okay. So maybe signing law has *some* good days.

*

Mags buzzed me about 4:00 p.m. to tell me that, true to his word, Dr. Pope was calling for me. Dammit. And he wasn't even a client, so I couldn't bill him for my time. Not like I was going to bill Rochelle because her ex thought I could help him win her back.

I sighed. "Put him through, I guess."

"I can tell him you're in a meeting?"

"He'll just call back. I might as well get it over with."

"That's the spirit."

I picked up my phone when it rang. "This is Kate."

"Hi, Kate. It's Richard Pope."

"Dr. Pope, you have an attorney. I still don't feel that this is appropriate."

"The case is over. I'm not calling for legal advice."

And that's the problem with giving out personal advice. I'm apparently better at that than the legal kind. "I'm a lawyer, not a therapist."

"But Rochelle said you talked to her about us."

Crap. "I'm not sure what you think I can do for you."

"Tell me how to get her back."

"I'm not a magician, either."

Silence. Okay, maybe that was a little harsh. But seriously, unless this guy could get his hands on a time machine and go back in time and *not* cheat on Rochelle with half the women in town, I was pretty sure he was out of luck.

Finally he said, "But she was ready to take me back. You must have said something to her that changed all that." For the first time, I was realizing that he blamed me more than a little for Rochelle finally kicking him to the curb.

"I didn't change her mind. I just listened to her. She was upset. She needed to vent."

"No. That day at the courthouse, she was ready to sign. We moved back in together. And then suddenly she did a one eighty and ended it. I checked her phone. You were the only one she was talking to."

"Dr. Pope, forgive me for being blunt, but you cheated on the woman over and over again. I'm surprised you think she needed convincing that you weren't trustworthy. I'm sure she could reach that conclusion all on her own."

"But she didn't," he said, with a slight hiss in his voice.

"This conversation is over, doctor. I would advise not calling my office again."

The line went silent and I frowned at the phone. Yikes. I sort of dreaded the fact that Rochelle still had to share a child with that asshole.

I hung up the phone as Rita walked in with a smile and set an ivory envelope on my desk. "This was just dropped off for you by Dot Hamilton, along with her final payment."

I picked up the envelope and admired the pretty script

spelling out my name. I looked up and Rita made the *what are you waiting for* gesture with her hands. I smiled and opened the seal, sliding out a formal invitation to Dot's signing party.

"Well?" Rita asked.

I handed her the invite. "Apparently, Dot and Sven are signing."

"And you're invited," Rita observed, with an approving smile.

"Invited where? Who's signing?" Mags asked from the doorway.

"Signing party. Dot and Sven," I answered.

Rita handed Mags the invite on her way out of my office.

After looking the invite over, Mags fanned her face with it. "And you give *me* a hard time for matchmaking. Look what *you* did."

"Don't remind me," I said, taking the invitation back in hand. "Is there any possible way that this isn't actually a complete disaster waiting to happen?"

"Odds are slim, but not impossible. Maybe they'll have the chinchilla hold the tokens prior to the signing?"

"At this point, nothing would surprise me. Wanna be my date?" I asked.

"Ooh. I thought you'd never ask," she said with a grin.

*

I got to work the next morning, and by the time I'd logged into my computer, Mags buzzed me. "Scarlett's on the phone."

"She called the office? I guess that's a small victory, right?"

"Actually, she said she tried your cell but you didn't answer." I glanced at my cell phone on my desk and saw the missed call icon. Shit.

"Fine. Fine, fine, fine."

Mags chuckled and connected the call.

"This is Scarlett," I said.

"What?"

I looked up as Mags walked into my office. She set a cup of water on my desk and two little white tablets next to it that I was guessing were Tylenol. I saluted her and she walked back out.

"Kate. Sorry. Hi, Scarlett. I was thinking about you when I picked up the phone."

"Oh. So, I got home from work yesterday and my camera was on the front porch."

"I told you he was going to bring it back while you were at work so there'd be no confrontation."

"I guess."

"You wanted your camera back. He brought it back. I explained to you the problem with going after him over it when you hadn't moved it like you said you would."

"I know."

"Did you mount it again?"

"Yes."

"Not pointing at his bedroom, right?"

"No. More across the front of the property."

"Oh."

"I can see his front door."

"Oh."

"There's a woman over there."

"Oh?" I took the Tylenol and a gulp of water. "Aren't you at work?"

"Yes. You know I can see my cameras from the app."

"Right."

"She's pretty."

Holy crap. She's sniffling. She's about to cry. Over a guy that she claimed to hate.

"Um. Scarlett?"

Sniff. "Yeah?"

"Stop watching. It's not doing you any good to keep watching his every move if it's only going to hurt you. Just let it go."

"Let it go?" she shrieked in my ear. *Stupid, Kate. Know your audience. You got cocky after Rochelle's praise.* This is not Rochelle. This is something else. Entirely.

"Well—" I started.

She cut me off. "I can't let it go! You wouldn't understand. What it's like to really love someone. To have a soul mate. And to have it all go to shit."

My mind immediately went to Jonathan. *And* Adam. And I started giggling.

"I'm sorry," I said.

"What the fuck, Kate? This is funny to you?"

"No. Not at all. I'm sorry. You know what? My love life is a disaster. I shouldn't be giving advice to anyone."

"Hmph." Scarlett was quiet for a minute. "Disaster how?" Because everyone loves a train wreck as long as they're not on it.

"I wouldn't know where to start," I said. "Dumped at the end of a contract. In love with a contract killer. Ex wants me back." I laughed again. Because my dealings with Scarlett had passed the point of ludicrous and now it all seemed laughable. "It's a total mess. You're right. I don't get to give advice."

"No shit? A contract killer? Like, a murderer?"

Jesus, Kate. Shut your mouth. I started laughing again.

"No, Scarlett. Not a killer. Like a man who only goes after women under contract. A *contract killer*."

"Oh! I heard of them. I just didn't know they were a real thing."

Indeed they are. "Look, Scarlett, we aren't talking about me. We're talking about you letting Rhett make you crazy."

"He is," she said quietly.

"But we need to hang on to things that make us happy and let go of things that don't."

"Yeah. Okay. I'll talk to you later."

"Bye."

I hung up and tried to figure out exactly where that conversation went so far off course. I'd just spent ten minutes trying to reason with *Scarlett*. Not in my top ten best decisions ever. Not to mention, it was probably another rookie move to talk about my personal life with a client. Well, one of the crazy ones, anyway.

I managed to get a little work done on a complaint I was drafting before someone knocked on my door frame. I looked up to see Logek giving a quick wave to Mags as Mags sat back down at her desk.

"You were on the phone, so Mags came and got me."

Logek was in skinny jeans and a flimsy tank top, so she looked casually perfect.

"Great," I said, doing a quick save of my document and grabbing my purse. "Where do you want to go to lunch?"

"Oh, wherever." And then she widened her eyes at me and smiled.

"Hey," I said with a smirk, "how about we swing by Jared's office so you can say hi."

She shrugged. "Sure, if you don't think it'd be a bother."

"I'm not dignifying that with a response."

Logek laughed. I threw my purse over my shoulder, and Logek followed me through the office. I peeked around the corner to make sure Jared wasn't on the phone. He was reading through a pleading, alternating between highlighting things and scribbling notes in the margins with a pencil.

"Knock, knock," I said.

He looked up quickly and smiled. "Hey, Kate."

I moved over farther so Logek could fit in the doorway. She moved in next to me with a shy smile. "Logek came to meet me for lunch and wanted to say hello before we left." Logek gave me a quick jab with her elbow. Oh, right. Like I was taking all the credit for this "chance" meeting.

Jared stood, smiling, and came around his desk to stand in front of us. "I'm glad you did," he said, extending a hand to Logek.

They shook hands quietly. It was funny for me to see Logek this tongue-tied.

"It's nice to see you again," she said, finally.

"You, too. I had a good time the other night."

"Me, too."

"Kate," I heard a voice call. I looked up to see Brad standing a couple feet away from me. "Can I ask you a quick question?"

"Of course." I turned to Jared and Logek. "Back in a sec."

I walked over to Brad. "What's up?"

"I don't know. Mags just said I was supposed to call you away for a minute."

I rolled my eyes and looked at Mags, who was standing up in her cube so that I could see her smiling face. I shook my head at her. She sat back down.

"What's going on?" Brad asked, pushing his big glasses a little farther up the bridge of his nose.

"Mags is playing matchmaker again."

Brad frowned and looked toward Jared's office.

"Logek is here," I said.

"Oh," Brad said, finally grasping the situation. "Gotcha."

I walked back to the door and leaned in. "Um, Logek. Ready to go?"

"Yep," she said, turning back to Jared. "You sure you can't join us?"

"Believe me," he said, dropping his chin and looking up at her from his lowered brow. "I wish I could get away, but I've got a motion that has to be filed by the end of the day and it's nowhere near ready. Next time?"

"Of course," Logek said. "See ya."

"Bye," Jared said, putting his hands into the pockets of his slacks and smiling.

Logek and I started walking back toward the elevator. I looked at her and she had a puzzled look on her face.

She was still quiet when we reached the sidewalk in front of the building. "Mexican?" she asked.

"Of course," I said.

She pointed down the street. "Tres Hermanos is only a couple blocks."

"Perfect."

We started walking and she was quiet again.

"So? Did I miss anything when I was talking to Brad?"

"Nope. He just asked how I was. Little small talk. Otherwise, nada."

I smiled. "Why don't you just ask him out?"

"Because. He's had opportunities. He must have a reason, right?"

"I don't know. I told you, I don't really know him that well."

She snapped her fingers. "Is he signed?"

"Nope. I asked him that when I first started at the firm. He said a lot of signing attorneys end up too cynical to sign."

"He does like girls, right? I mean, he is awfully pretty."

"And well dressed. And his hair is perfect."

"Maybe I'm on the wrong team?" Logek reasoned.

"I don't think so. Mags didn't think so. But I really don't know for sure."

We walked into the restaurant, asked for a table for two, and sat down with our menus.

Logek picked up her menu but didn't actually look like she was reading it. "Text Adam. Ask him. I need to know if I'm making a fool out of myself."

I sighed.

"Come on, Kitty Kat. You'd be doing me a favor *and* I'd be giving you an excuse to text Adam."

I frowned at her, but pulled my phone out of my purse.

Hey. If you aren't busy, I have a strange question.
Like I could pass up an opening like that.

I smiled. Logek smacked her palm against the table. "Enough flirting. You're on a fact-finding mission, remember?" I laughed.

Are you sure that Jared's interests run toward the fe-
male persuasion?

Haha. Yes, Kate. I've known him to date many women. Can I assume this has to do with Logek?

Bingo. She came and met me for lunch (subtle, right?) and we stopped to say hi and he still didn't ask her out. She wanted me to make sure she wasn't . . . barking up the wrong tree.

Well, if it makes her feel any better, I've never known him to actually have a girlfriend. He always seemed to have a string of beautiful women around but they were never around long enough for me to need to remember their names.

Ouch.

But, remember, this was back in our college days. I can't really say what he's been doing in the last 10 years.

Hmm. True.

"Well?" Logek asked, throwing her hands up in the air.

I relayed my conversation with Adam.

"Okay. So it doesn't seem that his anticommitment thing has changed in the last decade, true?" she asked.

"Agreed," I said with a nod. "You know, Mags has the feeling he's a workaholic. Maybe that's it?"

"Does being a workaholic turn a guy that looks like that into a monk?"

I laughed. "I don't know. I'm just throwing out possibilities."

Logek grunted and picked up her menu again. "I'm gonna need a margarita."

After we'd ordered, I propped my elbow on the table and set my chin in my hand. "So. Have you talked to Derek at all?"

"He's texted, but I still haven't replied. Why do you ask?"

"You just seem like you're really looking for a distraction."

"A handsome, brilliant distraction that's playing hard to get," she corrected.

"Yeah, but maybe you should give yourself a little more time."

"I was only back with Derek for a couple of weeks."

"I know, but that doesn't mean he didn't manage to break your heart again."

Logek looked down at her glass of water and wiped the condensation from the side with her thumb. "He did." Then she looked up at me, looking very strong, self-assured, and Logek-y. "But I must have known somewhere deep down from the beginning that nothing had changed, because, maybe for the first time, I feel really *over* him. It hurt, but I guess it was worth it."

"Oh. Well, that is really good to hear."

The waitress set Logek's margarita in front of her and Logek took a long sip. "So don't worry that Jared is some desperate rebound attempt which I'll screw up, leaving you with work awkwardness."

I laughed. "That never crossed my mind," I said with feigned innocence.

"Sure it didn't. But Jared is nice."

"He does seem nice."

"And he's really pretty," she said, with a suggestive eyebrow wiggle.

"Let's not forget that."

"And at the rate I'm going, I might wrangle a date with him in about six to nine months."

"Well, every girl likes a challenge now and then." I took a drink of my iced tea. "Have you talked to Daniel at all?"

"No. I told you—he knew he was getting the brush-off when I started seeing Derek, and he just disappeared." She shrugged. "And that was for the best, anyway. There were no butterflies." She looked at me, doing her best Elizabeth Taylor impression, and added, "You know I can't live without butterflies, darling."

"And you think Jared is someone that can induce butter-flies?"

Logek sighed. "Oh, he already has."

*

I was back in my office an hour later. I'd read the cases Jared gave me, which I needed for backup on Luann's case. The cases were right on point, all three having to do with the non-breaching partner making more money and the contract terms surrounding damages being vague, at best. The consensus between the cases was that the vagueness in the contract didn't get the breaching party out of paying damages based on their contribution to the partnership.

I'd worked out the math on Luann's case and she made more than double what her cheating partner did, but, based on the ruling in the cases, I could still calculate his contribution and put it into the standard formula for damages. It wouldn't be a ton of money, but I didn't think that really mattered to Luann—just that it was fair.

I looked up the opposing counsel in her case, found his contact information, and dialed his number.

"Jonas and Unger," a woman said in a lilting voice.

"Hi, I'm trying to reach Greg Unger. My name is Kate Shaw. I'm the attorney for Luann Sykes on the Sykes–Langley matter."

"One moment, please."

The next voice that came on the line was deep and gravelly. "This is Greg."

I introduced myself again and told him I represented Luann. "Ty Langley gave Ms. Sykes your name as his attorney."

"Yeah, I'm not sure I'm actually retained yet. I mean, he came in and met with me but hasn't paid his retainer."

I didn't know what to do with that information, so I just moved forward. "Well, do you have any idea if he intends to just settle this amicably?"

"All he told me was that his partner wanted early termination of the contract but that he didn't know why. Since I haven't gotten paid yet, I haven't put much time into reviewing the contract and determining what Ms. Sykes's penalties might be for early termination."

Son of a bitch! I'm getting much better at being sure to keep those internal thoughts *internal*. "Um, Mr. Unger, Ms. Sykes walked in on Mr. Langley having sex with another woman. In their bed. That is why she's terminating."

"Oh. Well, that's not the way it was explained to me," he said, matter-of-factly. "You know what? I'm going to have to call Ty. I may not be representing him after all. Let me give you a call back."

"I understand. Please let me know."

Yikes. That was ugly.

My cell vibrated. Scarlett.

"Scarlett, this is my cell phone. I've asked you—repeatedly—to call my office phone. Please call me back." And I hung up.

My office phone buzzed a minute later. "Uh, Scarlett says you hung up on her?" Mags asked.

"I told her not to call my cell anymore." Then I may have growled. "Just put her through."

I made sure I'd clocked in on her time clock. If reason couldn't get her to stop calling me ten times a day, maybe receiving her first bill would. "Hello, Scarlett."

"Really, Kate? That's pretty childish."

"Scarlett, it is not a work cell—it's my personal cell. I've asked you to call the office but you won't listen."

"Fine. I have a grievance." Of course you do. "Rhett's whore walked out to her car in just a T-shirt and underpants."

"That may be tacky, Scarlett, but I don't see how it's a violation of the order."

"Because he's doing it to piss me off!"

"Not enough. It needs to be harassing you or coming onto your property."

"He *is* harassing me."

"Having a *nooner* is not barred by the order!" I said, raising my voice a little. I glanced up, and Jared was standing in my doorway with a smile on his face. "Call me if he actually violates the order. I have to go."

I hung up and put my fingertips to my forehead. "Sorry about that," I said, looking up at Jared.

"No problem. That's one of the funniest things I've heard all day."

"Crazy client."

"We get our fair share."

I nodded. "So, what's up?"

"How was your lunch?" he asked. Hm. Curious.

"Great."

Jared made a glance behind him to see if anyone was nearby, then he came around and sat in one of the chairs in front of my desk, propped his elbows on his knees, and laced his fingers together. "So, I . . ." He trailed off and looked behind him again. "Maybe I shouldn't talk to you about personal stuff while we're at the office."

His nervousness was kind of adorable. I laughed. "Then I wouldn't be able to work with Mags. And that wouldn't be okay, because she's a friend of mine now. And so are you."

He smiled at me. "Okay, but if this is in any way out of line, promise you'll tell me to go away?"

"Count on it."

"So, I have the feeling Logek is . . . interested . . . in me."

"That is a possibility."

"And she must think I'm completely crazy for not asking her out. Because she's beautiful. And funny. And . . . I don't know. Fierce," he said, squinting a little.

I laughed. "She is a little fierce."

"So, it's just that I don't date much. I work so much that I try not to date people I like."

I looked at him with a dumb expression. "I have no response to that."

He ran a hand through the side of his hair. "I just don't want to fall for someone and have it all go to hell because I work too much."

"Why do you work so much?"

"Because. I've worked hard to get to where I am. I've created expectations for myself that I'm always trying to live up to."

"But, Jared, you're a partner. A *named* partner. I could see it if you were a new associate trying to get on the partner track. But you've *achieved* that. Isn't *your* life supposed to start eventually?"

He looked at me thoughtfully. Stared a little.

"Fair enough. But a part of it is habit. When I have a big case, I kind of lose myself in it. I wouldn't want to subject someone I care about to that."

"Well, Logek is a big girl. She can probably decide what she can live with."

Jared appeared to chew on his lip a moment while he considered that. "Okay, honestly," he said, leaning in toward my desk, "I can't seem to stop thinking about her." When he said that, he lifted a finger and made a lazy circle in the air next to his temple.

I raised my eyebrows at him. Your move, boss.

He sighed. "I haven't really *liked* a woman in a while. But if you don't think it's a huge mistake, maybe it isn't?"

"No guts, no glory," I said with a smile.

He smiled back. "Could I get her number from you?"

"I thought you'd never ask," I said, pulling a Post-it note and scribbling her number on it. I held it out to him. "It's about damn time."

Jared grabbed the little yellow paper from me, grinning, and left.

I picked up my phone and texted Logek.

> *The eagle has landed. I repeat the eagle has landed.*
> *Am I supposed to understand that?*
> *No. I've just always wanted to say it. A certain smitten workaholic lawyer just asked for your number.*

Logek responded with a variety of shocked and excited emoji faces. Good god, there are a lot of emojis these days. Do we really need four just to illustrate varying levels of excitement?

Remember. You aren't allowed to make it weird. I work with him and I kinda like my job and don't want it to be awkward.
Wait. Did you just say that you LIKED your job??

So strange. I did say that.

Huh. Well, I'm sure a crazy client will call any minute to chase that thought right out of my head :)
You're such an optimist.

I set my phone down and Mags buzzed me again. "Greg Unger?"

"Yep. It's on Luann's case. Put him through." I picked up on the first ring. "This is Kate."

"Kate, Greg Unger."

"Hey. So, what did you decide?"

"I'm going to be representing him." No accounting for taste. Plus, his client's already lied to him. I had the sneaking suspicion I wasn't going to be a fan of Greg Unger. "Also, Ty says that Luann had stopped coming home before she showed up when he was in bed with the girl. He thought she'd already left him."

My stomach twisted in knots. Was my client lying to me? "I don't know anything about that, Greg. But I'm guessing that if they are both taking entirely contradictory stances, he's unwilling to reach a settlement?"

"Maybe a settlement based on mutual termination. Even though it sounds like your client bailed. If I were you, I'd get her to take that offer."

Yep. Not a Greg Unger fan. I've spoken to him for all of

five minutes and I'd bet, dollars to donuts, he's a dick. "Well, I'd say one of us is not getting the true story from their client and I'm inclined to think it's you."

"Suit yourself. If she wants the offer, let me know."

And he hung up.

I just sat there a minute, stunned. I dialed Luann.

"Hello?" she said, picking up on the first ring.

"Luann, it's Kate Shaw."

"Oh, hi, Kate."

"So, I just had an unpleasant phone call with Ty's attorney. Apparently, Ty is claiming that you hadn't been coming home, and he thought you'd left him by the time you caught him with that woman."

I could hear Luann breathing, but she wasn't saying anything. She took one more loud breath and blew it out slowly. When she spoke, her voice was steady and calm. "I work about sixty hours a week, sometimes more if we're close to a breakthrough on something. But I called him every night that I was going to be home late. I always texted him when I was leaving the lab, so he'd know, because he said he worried about me. Ironically, my phone had died, so I didn't text him the day I caught him with Monica. I guess that was the real reason he always wanted me to let him know when I was on my way."

"That's perfect. Sorry. Totally *not* perfect. What I mean is, do you think you can go online and print up your call history?"

"I'll check. I'm pretty sure I can. I'm not sure it has texts listed, though."

"Okay. I can attach the call history and hopefully that will be enough for his attorney to realize his client is lying to him. Then we'll make clear that the phone records will back up your story if this goes to litigation. Maybe that'll be enough to get Ty to come clean. And if he won't, we'll bring a complaint and, based on the contract, you'll be entitled to recover your attorneys' fees."

"God, I really hoped it wasn't going to get ugly. I just never realized he was such a good liar."

"The best ones have had the most practice. This isn't your fault, Luann."

"I know."

"Plus, Monica has agreed to help, and he told her he was single, which also makes him look like a liar," I added.

"Right. I gave you her contact info, right? I was hoping we wouldn't need it. Damn."

"You did. Let's see if we can get him to realize he's going to lose big if he keeps up this lie, and see if he'll agree to settle."

Another loud sigh from Luann. "Yeah. Thanks, Kate."

"Of course. I'm really sorry he's pulling this."

"You and me both."

I hung up with Luann and went and briefed Mags on the case.

"Oh my god, what a prick," she said.

"Right? I think I understand why Jared said a lot of signing attorneys end up too cynical to ever sign themselves. It's disheartening, realizing there are so many assholes out there."

"They're there, either way. You just get a front row seat as a signing attorney."

"I guess," I said, and gave myself a shake, trying to get the icky feeling off. No, it was going to require a shower.

CHAPTER *16*

Thursday night, after I had curled up into bed, my phone vibrated on the nightstand.

It was from Dave. Well, that was a pretty short-lived brush-off.

> *Change your mind yet?*
> *Sorry. Who is this?*
> *Ouch. Still know how to hurt a guy, beautiful.*
> *Just teasing. Lighten up.*
> *You're not the one that got dumped last week.*
> *There was no dumping. Just stopping it before it started.*
> *I had started.*
> *I'm sorry, Dave.*
> *So is that a 'no'?*

No what?
No, you haven't changed your mind.

Sigh. This breaking things off was supposed to put an end to my Dave stress. Apparently, Dave hasn't gotten the memo yet.

I really think it's for the best.

Then he went quiet. Guess a little reinforcement was all he needed.

My phone vibrated again. Okay, or maybe not.

Except it wasn't Dave. It was Adam. I frowned at the phone.

Come meet me for a drink.

I looked at the clock in the corner of my phone. 10:30 p.m.

Now? It's kind of late.
Oh. I didn't realize the old-folks' home closes its doors this early on Thursday nights.

I chuckled.

Well it does on 'Green Jello Night' . . . they don't want us getting frisky.
Yes. That. Frisky Kate needs to come have a drink.
Mr. Lucas. Have you been drinking?
Nope.
Uh huh.
Ok. One. Or four.

*What's the occasion for exceeding your ordinary iron
restraint?*
Birthday celebration.
Yours?
No. Come.

Crap. Let's see. I've been able to deny Adam Lucas a total
of . . . zero times. And it doesn't look like I'll be breaking that
streak tonight.

Where are you?
The Trunk.
*Well, I was kind of ready for bed. I've got to put my-
self together.*
Just throw on some jeans. You always look perfect.

Maybe someone stole Adam's phone?
I was in the middle of doing as instructed, donning a pair
of jeans, when my phone vibrated again.

Why aren't you here yet?

Impatient much?

It's been 5 minutes, Adam.
Oh. Haha. Well hurry.

I checked my reflection in the mirror and looked pretty
much the same as I had at the office that day, so I just ran a
brush through my hair, grabbed my keys, and headed out.

I lucked out and found some street parking near the bar. Apparently the bloom was not off the new-bar rose, though, because there were still some people waiting to get in, even on a Thursday night. Since Adam knew the owners, I figured I'd try my luck talking to the bouncer rather than waiting in line.

He looked at me and I smiled. He didn't.

"Kate," I heard someone call from inside. "Joe, she's a friend." It was Jenny, stopping her brisk walk back to the bar to rescue me from standing in line. By myself.

Bouncer Joe opened the rope, giving me a belated friendly smile.

As soon as I was in, Jenny hurried up to me and gave me a quick hug. Tonight she had a cloth headband holding her springy curls away from her pretty face and dark-brown eyes. She was in black skinny jeans and a red T-shirt, providing that cool yet subtle pirate vibe again.

"I'm glad you're here," she said with wide eyes.

I just gave her my best *And why is that?* expression.

"I told Adam he should text you. He did, right?"

"Yeah. He did. What's going on?"

"I mean, he isn't sloppy drunk or anything, but I'm not sure I've ever seen him drunk *at all*." She shrugged. "He just seems off. I thought it seemed like a BFF kind of job." She gave a brief squeeze to my shoulders, pointed toward Adam at the end of the bar, and bustled off.

As I approached Adam, he was simultaneously sipping from a glass and staring intently at his phone. My phone buzzed in my hand.

From Adam.

You better be on your way.

"Not 'on my way.' Here," I said, putting a hand on his wide shoulder.

He whirled around on his bar stool and his whole face lit up when he saw me. "Kate," he said, wrapping me tightly in his arms. I could smell the smoky sweetness of the Scotch on his breath. "You came."

"Of course I came," I said, my voice a little muffled, since he still hadn't released me from the hug. "So, what's up with you?"

He finally let go and sat up straight on his bar stool. "Nothing," he said with a smile. "Not now. Everything is perfect."

"Okay. Then what *was* wrong? Jenny said you seemed off."

His face mellowed at that. "Just a weird day."

I sat on the empty bar stool next to him. "Wanna talk about it?"

He took another drink from his glass. "Not even a little bit."

"Fair enough. But you know—"

He cut off what I was about to say by holding a hand out to Jenny as she passed us behind the bar. "Jenny, did you see? Kate is here."

Jenny smiled, her dimple showing at the corner of her mouth. "I did. I told you she'd come if you asked her." She put a hand gently to his forearm like she was talking to a child.

"We need a drink," he said, downing the remains of the glass in his hand. "Kate, gin and tonic, two limes?"

I exchanged a quick glance with Jenny. "Um. Maybe not tonight. In fact, you probably don't need another, either."

He frowned. He looked like he was about to ignore my suggestion and order, when Jenny piped in with, "She has a point, buddy. I think you've hit your sweet spot."

Adam frowned at her. "Pretty sure I've never been cut off in a bar before," he said.

"Well, this bar is run by *friends* who care about you, so consider it friendly advice rather than criticism." Jenny whisked away the empty glass in front of Adam and hurried off to serve other patrons.

"Well," Adam said, frowning at me. "I told you to meet me for a drink, but apparently that isn't going to happen. Here, anyway."

"That's fine. It's a little late for me to start drinking, anyway. How about I drive you home?"

"I don't want to go home." He sounded more sullen than I expected.

I leaned over a little, so he'd be looking at me instead of staring off in the distance. "Adam. Tell me what's going on."

He refocused on me. "I love your eyes."

Okay. He's drunk. Don't get carried away with the butterflies thing. Well, maybe just a few.

I put a hand on the side of his face, forcing him to focus. *Trying* to force him to focus, anyway. "Adam. Are you okay?"

His face softened. "You're my best friend, Kate."

Well, looks like this conversation isn't happening. Tonight anyway.

"Okay. You don't want to go home. How about my place?"

"Yes. Your place. Perfect. We'll have a drink at your house." He stood and took my hand, pulling me off my stool. He headed toward the door. As he walked past the bar, he held out a hand and called, loudly, "Jenny! Drew! Thanks, guys!"

Drew and Jenny looked over from their respective drink pouring and waved back to both of us.

As we headed toward my car, Adam suddenly stopped in the middle of the street. "Oh. My car is here."

I got behind him and gave him a push toward my car, in front of us at the curb. "We'll get it in the morning. You can't stand in the middle of the street."

He laughed a little. "Sorry." He walked to the passenger side and climbed in, once I unlocked the car.

I started driving us back to my house, and he rested his head back against the headrest. His eyes were focused on me, though.

"I'm so glad we met, Kate."

I smiled. Drunk Adam was definitely a whole new side to him. "So am I."

"No," he continued, more strenuously. "*I* am. You have *people*. I don't have people."

"Your mom is pretty awesome."

He smiled. "She is. But she's my mom. She has to be my people. But all my other people aren't really *people*. Does that make sense?"

Nope. "Sure."

"But now, you're my person. I have a person. Logek is your person and you're my person."

"And you're my person, too. You can have more than one," I said, giving him a supportive smile. Sure, he was drunk and borderline nonsensical, but I was pretty sure I knew what he was trying to say.

He smiled and closed his eyes. "I'm your person," he said softly.

I pulled up to the curb in front of my house and went around to the passenger side to help Adam out of the car.

Once he was on his feet, he actually seemed in worse condition than when we had left the bar. He draped an arm across my shoulder and I wrapped an arm around his waist. Once I had the door unlocked, I guided him to the sofa and sat him down. I closed the front door and dropped my purse and keys on the coffee table.

"I'm going to get you some water."

He was sitting, slumped down on the couch, watching me.

I grabbed a glass from the cupboard and filled it with cold water. "Here, drink this," I said, handing him the glass. He obediently chugged down most of the water in a matter of seconds.

I went to my room and grabbed an extra pillow and blanket, along with a couple of Advil from the bathroom, and went back downstairs.

"Okay, Adam. Take these," I said, handing him the Advil. "And finish that," I said, pointing to the glass of water.

He tossed back the hangover avoider and finished the glass of water.

I tossed a pillow on one end of the couch. "Slip off your shoes."

He did that thing where he used the toe of one foot to the heel of the shoe to push it off, and then repeated it on the other side.

Once his shoes were off, I walked between the coffee table and the couch and pushed his shoulders down till his head was lying on the pillow. Then I lifted his feet and guided them to the other end of the sofa. I looked at him, once he was lying down. He fit this sofa very differently than when I lay on it. His shoulders were almost as wide as the cushion, and he bent his knees to avoid putting his feet up on the arm.

He let out a sigh and draped one arm across his face, covering his eyes.

I brushed my fingertips across his forehead, pushing his

hair back. When I did, he reached out and gripped my hand, putting my fingertips to his lips, kissing them lightly.

Mayday. Shit. I pulled my hand away, with my heart in my throat. I picked up the blanket from where I'd set it on the coffee table, unfolded it, and draped it over him.

"My turn to get you coffee in the morning," I said quietly.

"Thank you, Kate."

I closed the curtains so that it wouldn't be too bright in the morning, turned off the lights, and headed upstairs.

For the second time tonight, I got into my pajamas and got into bed. To stare at the ceiling. And replay every drunken, sweet thing Adam said to me tonight. *Key word being drunken, Kate. He's drunk. Don't let your stupid, hopeful little heart read more into it.*

*

I woke up early in the morning, well before my alarm clock.

I tiptoed down the stairs in an effort to be quiet, but it was an old house and the steps seemed to creak louder the softer I attempted to step. I reached the living room and nearly got the wind knocked out of me by the sight of Adam sprawled across my couch.

I looked up the length of him but stopped where his T-shirt was bunched up, exposing several inches of his hard, tanned stomach. BFF, my ass. I'm pretty sure best friends aren't supposed to have quite this many naughty thoughts about their friend first thing in the morning.

One arm was under his head, making his bicep look flexed even in sleep, and his other hand was resting over his heart.

He had a slight crease between his eyebrows, making him look troubled.

Without thinking, I reached out a finger and put it against the crease, smoothing his brow. When I did, his eyes fluttered open. His green eyes scanned the room quickly and then settled on me.

He sat up slowly as I stood over him. He ran his hands over his hair and across his eyes.

"I'm going to put some coffee on," I said brightly. "How are you feeling?"

He cleared his throat. "Aside from embarrassed, you mean?"

"Yes, aside from that."

"Not too bad, actually."

"Advil and a glass of water before sleeping usually does the trick," I said, busying myself with the coffee maker.

"Kate. I'm so sorry."

I leaned against the door frame to the kitchen and frowned at him. "For what?"

"For . . . for getting like that. For drunk texting you. For making you come get me."

"Oh. Well, then I'm sorry, too."

"For what?"

"For getting like that. For drunk texting you. For making you come get me," I said, referring to the time he'd rescued my drunk ass from a signing party.

Adam smiled. "I think *I* texted *you* that time. And I think I offered to come get you."

"Details. I didn't expect you to judge me. Why would you think I would judge you?"

He shook his head. "I don't. I judge myself."

"Adam, we all have our days. It's kind of reassuring to know for sure that you are actually human, though," I said, giving him a wink and reaching for two coffee mugs. "Cream? Sugar?"

"I can get that," he said, standing up from the couch and coming into the kitchen. My kitchen felt particularly small this morning, once I had Adam in there with me, in socks and jeans, hair tousled.

Now that the coffee pot was full, I poured some into each of our mugs.

He added a little milk to his cup and sat down at the table, sipping it. I sat down across from him.

"So, wanna tell me what that was all about last night?" I asked.

Adam focused on his coffee mug. "I think I'm still a little too focused on being embarrassed you saw me like that."

I shook my head and grunted. "Enough. What kind of BFF would I be if I didn't get to see you all drunk and moody from time to time?"

He laughed. "I didn't know that was part of the criteria."

"Well, if my friendship with Logek is anything to base it on, it's actually an integral part."

"Well, I guess I'm in, then." He leaned back in his chair, holding his coffee cup in one hand. "You probably don't want to mention to Dave that I spent the night," he said with a humorless smile. "Guessing that wouldn't go over well."

"I'm not seeing him anymore, so I couldn't really care less whether he approves or not."

Adam leaned forward again. "Oh? What happened?"

"What do you mean 'what happened?' It's not like it was going anywhere, anyway. It was fine when we were just hanging out, but once he started pushing for more, I knew I didn't want more." I raised my eyebrows. "So, time to go."

Adam looked down and appeared to swirl the coffee in his mug. Without looking up at me, he asked, "So, it never became . . . more?"

I smirked at him. "No, Adam. We didn't have sex."

He did a lousy impersonation of being surprised by my declaration. "I wasn't asking *that*. Just wondering . . . how close you two were."

"Uh-huh."

He smiled at me.

I took a sip from my cup. "So, you mentioned over text that you were out celebrating a birthday. Any chance it was your dad's?" I asked softly.

Adam's eyes cut over to me immediately.

"Your mom was over the other night," I said. "She told me he'd passed away."

He nodded slowly but didn't say anything.

"I'm so sorry, Adam. I wish I'd known."

Adam shrugged and gave me a bland smile. "It was a long time ago."

I shook my head. "Don't do that," I said, pleading gently.

He looked at me. "You can be exhausting, you know that?"

"You'll get used to it," I said, giving him a wink.

He sighed. "Dad would have been sixty-five yesterday."

"I finally understand what you were saying when you said your mom never got over your dad."

"Yeah. That's been hard to watch. It was like a big part of her just died with him." He shrugged. "And she seems perfectly okay with living like that."

"Maybe she is. She seems happy, don't you think?"

Adam seemed to consider that. "Yeah, I guess so." Then he looked me in the eyes. "But you didn't know her before."

I nodded. "Fair enough. I don't think you can go through a loss like that and not have it change you."

"Exactly," Adam said, as though I'd hit the nail on the head.

I narrowed my eyes at him.

"What?" he asked.

"You just make so much more sense to me now."

He laughed a little. "Now? I thought you've been able to see through me since day one."

"Well, that's true." I said with a cocky shrug.

He chuckled again and looked at his watch. "I've got to get going." He shook his head. "Remind me not to go out and tie one on on a work night again, okay?"

"Check. I'll drive you to your car."

"It's only a few blocks," he said, walking into the other room and slipping his shoes back on. "It'll only take me ten minutes to get there."

"Still. It'll only take a minute to drive you there."

"Kate," he said, facing me and putting his hands on my shoulders. "You need to get ready for work. You've done enough. And I'm so grateful."

He wrapped me in a tight hug and kissed my forehead.

"I'll talk to you soon," he said with a wave, before darting out the door.

*

Later that morning, at the office, Mags buzzed me.

"Luann Sykes wants to know if she can come in and talk to you this morning."

I frowned. "Sure, I'm pretty open today."

"Alright. I'll get it scheduled."

I was making notes for myself on Luann's case, complete with the bits of evidence we had lined up to show that her ex was a lying piece of crap. My phone buzzed on the desk.

Jonathan.

Hey, want to grab dinner Saturday night?

I had a momentary rerun of my confused emotions where he was concerned.

Yeah, sounds good to me.
Great! How about 7?
Perfect.
I'll pick you up.
See you tomorrow :)

Okay. No sweat. That gives me a whole twenty-four hours to figure out what the hell I'm doing with my life. Now that Jonathan had his newfound ambition stemming from his start-up company, I had the feeling it would be pulling him away—geographically anyway. And he was still hoping I would be in for the ride. Sure, we'd been split up for almost two months and, if anything, I was more confused than ever about what I wanted, but I'm sure I'll be able to figure it all out in time for dinner tomorrow night. Piece of cake.

Mags leaned in my doorway. "Hey, Luann wanted early, and you said you were open, so she's going to be here in about fifteen minutes, okay?"

"Got it," I said with a nod.

Fifteen minutes later, I was heading to the conference room to find out what new urgent info Luann had for me. When I went into the conference room, Luann was in tan khakis and a polo shirt with the insignia for the laboratory she worked for embroidered on the breast, like she was headed to work after this meeting. Her straight brown hair was pulled back in a ponytail, and her face was still makeup free and startlingly pretty.

Her gaze was focused out the large picture window at the beautiful cityscape below. When she saw me, she smiled and extended her hand.

After shaking her hand, I sat down at the table across from her. "So, what's going on?"

She sighed loudly. "I've been giving this a lot of thought, Kate. A lot. And I don't want this."

"Want what?" I asked, letting the confusion show on my face.

"The fight." She sighed again and smiled at me. Her expression was so Zen-like, so peaceful, I almost had goose bumps. She shook her head. "Yes, I picked the wrong guy, and yes, he hurt me. We live and we learn. But now, I get to choose. And I'm not willing to give him *more* of my time. More time being hurt. Being angry." She flattened her palms to the table. "It isn't worth it. He isn't worth it."

I was nodding. Not like I could disagree with anyone displaying that level of maturity and self-possession. "But you realize you're entitled to damages for his breach of the contract. With the phone records and Monica as a witness, it shouldn't be difficult to prove—"

She cut me off by waving her hands in the air. "I get that. All of that. But, Kate, I don't *need* him. Or his money. I never did. And if I don't *need* the money, then what am I fighting for? Revenge? Justice? I don't need those things, either. Neither will add anything to my life."

My turn to sigh. "If you don't mind my saying, you are re-markable."

She smiled at me. "Thank you. I could say the same about you."

I returned her smile, gratefully. "So. I'm guessing then you are fine accepting the offer of settling on the mutual termination provision?"

"Precisely." She smiled, looking so content and certain with her decision.

I nodded once in agreement. "I'll call Ty's attorney today."

Luann stood and shook my hand again. "Thank you so much, Kate."

"I'll be in touch."

I watched Luann leave, admiring her even more today than I did after our first meeting. I realize she's younger than me, but I kind of want to be like her when I grow up.

I headed back to my office, and Mags was standing up, with her phone in her hand. "Greg Unger," she said.

I shrugged. "Good timing. I was just going to call him."

She put the call through to my office and I picked up.

"This is Kate."

"Kate. Greg Unger. So, I've talked a little more to my client, and he seems to think there may be some evidentiary issues he hadn't considered." No shit. "Anyway, he has authorized me to make a settlement offer of a one-time payment to your client of twenty-five thousand dollars, in exchange for a full release."

My eyes opened wide. "Um. Let me call you right back."

I hung up and ran from my office toward the elevator, try-ing to catch Luann. I stopped at Rita's desk. "Luann?"

"Sorry, Kate. She *just* got in the elevator."

I sighed, slipped off my heels, and ran for the stairwell. Ten floors. I can do that, right? Well, I mean, going *down* I can do that. I wasn't about to hoof it back up the same ten flights. I just wanted to catch her before she left the lobby.

I reached the bottom, giving myself kudos for only breathing a little heavy, since I'd been keeping up with my running. I burst through the door into the lobby and scanned the area while awkwardly slipping my shoes back on. I saw Luann's shiny brown ponytail just about to walk out the door.

"Luann!" I called. She turned, along with the few other people who happened to be in the lobby just then.

She turned to me with wide eyes and hurried back to where I was standing.

"Kate, what is it?" She put a hand against my upper arm, steadying me. Okay. So maybe I was breathing more than a *little* heavy.

"Sorry. Everything is fine. I just wanted to catch you before you left."

She looked behind me to the door to the stairwell. "So you came down the stairs?"

I tilted my head back and forth, neither confirming nor denying.

She smiled. "Well, what is it?"

"Ty's attorney called right as you were leaving. Ty realized he was going to get caught in his lie and offered twenty-five thousand dollars to settle."

Luann's face registered her shock. "Oh," she said.

"I know what you said, but—"

She smirked at me and cut me off. "Well, yeah, but I'm not a moron. I'll take it," she said, smiling.

I laughed. Then bent over a little at the waist, taking a few deep breaths.

"You know," she added, "you could have called me at the office, so you didn't have to race down multiple flights of stairs."

I shook my head. "Where would be the fun in that? And also, I don't want to give him a chance to change his mind."

Luann laughed and gave me a hug. "You're the best, Kate."

"Okay. Can I assume you don't want me to haggle for anything higher?"

"Nope. From where we were five minutes ago, it's found money. I'll take it as good karma."

I smiled. "Okay. I'll go accept the offer and I'll call you when it's settled."

"Great. I have to get to the lab."

I waved as she walked away and I pushed the button for the elevator.

When I stepped out of the elevator, Mags was standing at Rita's desk, and the look on their faces when they saw me was priceless.

Rita looked at my feet. "Glad to see you put your superhero shoes back on."

I gave them the ninety-second version of why I was running through the building like a lunatic, then headed back to my office to call Unger back.

"Greg Unger."

"Greg. Kate Shaw, again. Sorry about that. I was actually meeting with my client when you called, so I figured I could relay your offer to her before she left."

"Super. And?"

"And, since she would prefer not to waste time litigating the matter, she accepts the settlement proposal."

Unger sighed, I think louder than he meant to. "Great to

hear. I really think this is the best solution for all involved."
Meaning your client is getting off easy.

Taking a page from Luann's Zen handbook, I replied, "I
agree. This allows them to put it behind them."

"I'll draft the release and have it over for your review by
the end of the day."

"That would be great. Thanks, Greg."

I hung up with him and laughed. To myself. Alone in my office. I love it when my client's good karma comes with a twenty-
five-thousand-dollar pot of gold at the end of the rainbow.

CHAPTER 17

Friday night, Logek and I were curled up on my sofa, sharing a bottle of wine.

"So, give me all the Jared details," I said.

Logek smiled, pushing her hair back from her face with one hand. Her eyes danced a little. Ruh-roh.

"I told you we've been talking."

"Yes, and that is completely lacking in *details*! So spill it."

"The day you gave him my number, I kept waiting for a text. But, instead, he actually called that night. And we talked."

I nodded.

"For *two* hours."

My mouth dropped open.

"Exactly," she said. "I felt like I was in high school. We were suddenly talking about jobs, books, family. Everything. I

can't remember the last time I've just *talked on the phone.*
Who does that anymore?"

"You, apparently. Then?"

"Then we texted on and off throughout the day yesterday
and today, and we're going out tomorrow night." Logek finished brightly, with wide eyes.

"Oh my god! That's awesome. And I knew it would never
take you six months to wrangle a date with a man."

"Well, it was a pretty slow start."

"Worried at all about him being a workaholic?"

Logek waved a hand at me. "A workaholic is just a person
in need of a distraction." She shrugged. "I can be a hell of a
distraction."

I laughed.

She raised her eyebrows playfully. "So, what's new with
you?"

"Hm. I've got about twenty-four hours to figure out what
to do about Jonathan."

"You have plans?"

"We're having dinner tomorrow night."

"Well, he's the love of your life, right? What are you trying
to figure out?"

"The love of my life who dumped me."

"True. But he came to his senses quickly."

"I know. I'm having trouble putting a finger on exactly
what is keeping me from just taking him back."

"Maybe it's not a *what*. Maybe it's a *who*."

"Kind of tragic to pass on Jonathan for a platonic relationship with Adam."

Logek threaded her fingers through her hair again, propping

her elbow on the back of the sofa. "Yeah, but if your feelings for Adam made you realize that you don't feel *enough* for Jonathan anymore, then it's more a matter of whether you're settling for less than you deserve."

"I can't grasp the thought that Jonathan would ever be settling. He's amazing."

"It's not about whether he's great. It's about whether he's the match that lights your fire. If he's not, then taking him back would be settling. End of story."

"But I love him. I know I do."

"But maybe you're not—"

"Don't say it. It's too cliché."

"Tough shit. Cliché or not, maybe you aren't *in love* with him anymore."

"Clichés are stupid."

"And they're clichés for a reason. Because, usually, they're true."

"Adam and I are friends. He shouldn't be a factor in this decision."

"I agree," Logek said with a nod. "Right now, it's Jonathan or no one."

I focused on her. "Are you saying I should get back with him because he's the only option?"

Logek frowned. "Of course not. You know me better than that. I'm saying the opposite. I'm saying if he isn't your *everything*, then I think you should be on your own and wait for the person who is."

I rubbed my hand across my forehead. "He was always my everything. Maybe he still is and I'm just hurt over getting dumped."

"It's possible."

"But you don't think so."

She shrugged. "That's the million-dollar question, Kitty Kat."

*

I got up in the morning and ran a few miles through midtown. Running is definitely easier when you're preoccupied by thoughts of trying to decide on the course of your entire future. By the time I finished my loop and was running up my walkway, I was astonished that I'd been running for forty minutes.

I went upstairs to shower. After I was under the water and thoroughly drenched, I heard my phone vibrating on the bathroom counter. I peeked around the shower curtain at the phone. It was ringing, but I couldn't see the number. I had a brief internal debate over whether it might be an important phone call, before making a quick dive for the bath towel and practically falling on my face scrambling out of the shower and reaching for my phone.

Damn. Scarlett. Sigh. If I don't answer, she'll just keep calling.

"Hi, Scarlett."

"Kate. I know I'm not supposed to call your cell, but I just wanted to give you the good news."

Uh-oh.

"We're signing again!"

"Um. Really?"

"Yeah, really! He was just using that girl to make me jealous. He's here right now," she said.

"Hi, Kate," I heard from a masculine voice near the phone.

Wow. "Well . . . congratulations." I really didn't know how

to muster up any enthusiasm that the dysfunction twins were going in for their sixth contract. Seventh? I forget.

"Be happy, Kate. I know we were angry, but it's all better now."

Yep. That's why you have been through so many contracts with him. Who knew all you crazy lovebirds needed were dueling restraining orders and some surveillance cameras to rekindle your true love?

When I didn't answer, Scarlett continued. "Okay, have a good weekend. We'll call Monday to go over the particulars of our new contract!"

Can't wait. "Talk to you Monday."

We disconnected and I started drying up the water I'd dripped all over the floor trying to catch the phone call. I don't really draft contracts—Frank does that. I suppose I could. What am I saying? It's only Saturday. I give it fifty-fifty odds that the contract is off again by Monday.

*

That evening, I was dressed for my date with Jonathan and was just waiting for him to pick me up.

Jonathan pulled up to the curb in front of my car. I opened the front door as he got out of his car and came up the walkway toward me. He stepped in and wrapped me in a hug. Mm. Jonathan. It's funny how the fit and feel of someone's arms can be so familiar, so comfortable.

"Come in," I said, stepping aside. When he did, I closed the door behind him.

He stood in the living room, looking around it once again. "This place is great. It fits you."

I nodded. It did. But there was a weird finality about our split, having him standing in *my* apartment. "Are you going to keep the house?"

He shook his head. "I don't think so. It's too big." He turned from looking out my front window to give me a meaningful look. "And it's haunted."

"Haunted?"

"Yeah. By the ghost of my ex-partner. No matter where I am, she's there."

Oh. That's sweet. And sad. And I had no response.

"Shall we go?" he asked.

"Yep," I said, grabbing my purse and keys from the entry table. I followed him out the door and locked up behind me.

He opened his car door for me, like he always did.

We drove quietly for a minute before either of us spoke.

"So, how's the new business?" I asked.

"It's great. I can't believe how much I'm enjoying it. I think about my old job: too many hours, no proper work–life balance with that job."

"Yeah. It never seemed like the right fit. I'm so happy for you."

"Maybe if I'd figured that out sooner, it would have made a difference."

"How so?"

"Because. I was restless. Dissatisfied. I don't think you had anything to do with that, but I didn't realize it at the time."

"Oh."

He sighed. "I don't know. I'm just trying to figure stuff out."

"Me, too."

"How's that going?"

I shrugged. "I sort of feel like a sellout, doing signing law.

Makes me wish I hadn't spent four years telling everyone who asked what kind of law I planned to do, 'Anything but signing law.' "

He laughed. "Tough job market, Kate. People get that."

"Right. But that doesn't make me feel like less of a sellout, unfortunately."

"I guess I see your point. But maybe there is more to signing law than you thought when you used to bad-mouth it?"

"Maybe a little. I do have some clients I like working with."

"The crazy one on the phone?"

I laughed. "No, not her. Although she certainly has entertainment value."

He pulled up to our favorite little Italian café and we got out of the car.

"I haven't been here in months," I told him.

"I should hope not. This is *our* spot. It's off-limits if you're not with me." And he winked at me.

By the time we'd finished eating (and a bottle of wine), I'd recapped nearly every case I'd worked on at the firm to date.

"I hate to say it, but you sound like you're having fun there," he said.

I wobbled my head and smiled. "People are nuts. That certainly keeps it interesting."

"So. You mentioned that you aren't seeing that one guy anymore. Are you seeing anyone *else*?"

And here I was worried that the elephant in the room would just keep minding its own damn business in the corner. Since our lunch the other day, when Adam came up, I figured he must be on Jonathan's mind as a possible roadblock to us getting back together.

"Not really," I said, with a shake of my head. "I forgot what a pain in the ass it is being single."

He laughed. "I do have a solution for that, you know."

I smiled. He was trying to keep it light, but, inside, it was bringing me down. Because I didn't know what to do about it. I loved him. I knew that for certain. But I had feelings for Adam that seemed to make me question what I had with Jonathan at this point in our relationship.

I looked down at the table and played with my fork. When I looked back up, Jonathan was watching me. I swear, for all my subtlety, I may as well just think aloud. It's not as though it doesn't all show clear as day on my face, anyway.

The waiter slid the bill onto the table and Jonathan tossed a credit card into it and slid it back over to the edge. "Yeah, I'm definitely going to sell the house. It's silly to wait any longer," he said.

"Well, you have to do what's best for you," I said quietly.

"You were what was best for me." He signed the charge slip the waiter brought back and stood. "Shall we go?"

I nodded.

We drove to my place in silence. When he pulled up to the curb in front of the house, he turned off the car and reached over and grasped my hand.

"I don't blame you, Kate. I know it was me that got us here."

"I've been trying to make a decision. I don't mean to string you along. I'm just so confused over you," I said, looking into his face, which was partially illuminated by the streetlight.

He frowned. "Well, what are you confused about?"

"I love you so much," I said, putting fingertips to my heart without thinking about it. "So, if I love you, why can't I just decide to get back together?"

He looked at me quietly for a minute through the filtered light. "Because you love me, but something has changed," he finally said.

When he said the words, some dam broke inside me and tears started spilling down my cheeks. I nodded. "I don't know when it happened."

He pressed his lips together and his chin showed signs that he was struggling with his own emotions. He continued stroking my hand between both of his. He made a loud sigh and blew out a ragged breath, all the while focused on our hands rather than looking me in the eye.

"I love you, Katie," he said, with a cracking voice.

Tears were now pouring down my face. "I'm so sorry, Jonathan."

He looked up now, a few tears trailing down his cheeks. "Don't. Don't be sorry. I was so stupid. So fucking stupid. I let you down first. Things only changed for you because of my mistake."

"I love you, Jonathan," I said. I leaned toward him, verging on an actual ugly cry. "I'm so sorry that I'm hurting you."

He started brushing tears from my face, which was useless, given that I had plenty more where those came from.

"I'm so confused," I said, shaking my head. "I love you so much. You're one of my best friends. I don't understand why . . ."

"Why it isn't *enough*?" he asked.

When he finished my question, I broke down sobbing. He undid his seat belt, then mine, and pulled me onto his lap. He wrapped his arms around me and I cried on his shoulder while he cried on mine.

We sat like that for what seemed an eternity. When it was clear we had both stopped crying, he began to pull away slightly and I scooched back into the passenger seat. We both spent another minute drying our faces and wiping our eyes.

I made a steadying sigh. "I think I had trouble coming to this decision because I'm so afraid of not having you in my life."

Jonathan nodded. "I get that. You're one of my best friends, too."

He reached over and grasped my hand again. "But, I think, while you *love* me and I'm *in love* with you, it would be better for me to have a little space for a while. Because, right now, I don't think I can be around you and not want more."

A few more errant tears trickled down my face. I nodded.

He squeezed my hand then, hard enough to feel like the bones were rubbing together, making it hurt a little. It didn't matter, though, because everything else hurt, too.

"I love you," he said.

"I love you, too," I echoed, swallowing hard. Afraid we would fall into round two of the blubbering mess thing, I slipped my hand from his grasp and got out of the car. He stayed parked at the sidewalk until I was inside and had closed the door behind me. I watched him drive away before sliding to the floor to resume my breakdown.

After crying on the floor for a few minutes, I looked at my phone, wanting desperately to reach out to someone. Someone who would tell me everything would be okay. That I wasn't making a huge mistake. Or just someone to hold the pieces of me together for a bit.

Logek was on her first date with Jared tonight, so I definitely wasn't going to interrupt that.

Screw it. I dialed Adam's number. He answered on the first ring.

"Kate. How are you?"

"Okay. What are you up to?"

"Just hanging out at home, actually. Why? What's up?"

"Can I come over?"

"Of course. I'll meet you in the parking garage, okay?"

"Yeah. Perfect. See you in a few."

Out of the frying pan and into the fire.

*

I drove over to Adam's, doing some deep breathing, determined to stop the ridiculous heartbreak that had taken over. I was patting my cheeks dry, trying to look less blotchy, as I pulled into the parking garage of Adam's apartment building.

I parked in a visitor spot and got out of the car. I looked over and Adam was standing by the elevators, wearing long shorts and a T-shirt. His hands were buried in his pockets and he looked concerned.

As I approached him, he pulled his hands from his pockets, and the worry on his face wrecked me. A few feet from him, I burst into tears once again, and he started walking toward me. By the time we closed the distance between us, he had wrapped me in a suffocating hug, one arm tightly around my lower back and one across my shoulders so that his hand was on the back of my head, holding it against his chest.

"Oh, Kate," he whispered against my ear. "I knew you sounded upset."

I continued to cry against him for another minute in the (thankfully) abandoned parking garage.

When I stopped crying and pulled back from him, he brushed a broad thumb across my cheek. "Let's go upstairs."

I followed him into the elevator and then into his apartment.

"Want something? I have some wine."

I nodded.

I heard him moving around in the kitchen for a couple minutes before he came back, putting a glass in my hand.

I sat in an armchair facing his beautiful picture window and took a drink.

Adam sat down on the coffee table in front of me, resting his forearms on his thighs. He reached out and tucked a piece of hair that had fallen across my face behind my ear.

"Want to tell me what's going on?"

I frowned. Shook my head. "I barely know. I guess I ended things with Jonathan for good."

Adam looked surprised. "That's big."

I nodded, feeling like the crying was going to start again. "Yeah, but it was *my* decision. *I* was letting *him* go. So why does it hurt this much?"

Adam tilted his head at me, looking sympathetic. "Because he was a huge part of your life."

I nodded.

"And it's always hard to let go of someone who meant that much to us."

I nodded again, swallowing hard.

"But I love him," I said.

Now Adam nodded.

"But," I said, shaking my head, "just not the right way anymore." When I said it, more tears started falling.

Adam reached out a hand and rubbed my knee until I sniffed and got the crying in check once again.

"I've just loved him as long as I can remember," I said quietly. "I never thought that could change."

His hand was still absently rubbing my knee. He was looking at me like he was thinking about what I'd said. "Sometimes we can't control these things. Besides, Kate, it changed *after* he broke your heart. That doesn't exactly make you fickle, because your feelings for him changed after he ended things."

I sniffed. "He said the same thing. Kept telling me this was his fault, not mine." I started crying again. "He was so heartbroken, though. I just hated seeing him like that."

"Of course you do. He may have screwed up, letting you go, but he's still a good guy and it's only natural that you wouldn't want to hurt him."

I sighed and dried my face. Again. I chuckled a little and gestured at my puffy, tearstained face. "I just never expected to react like this. Not when I was the one ending it."

Adam smiled at me. "There's nothing small about what you let go of tonight. Letting go is hard. I completely understand why you're upset."

"Thank you. Sorry for dropping in on you like this. Logek is out with Jared."

"Oh, she is, huh? You definitely don't want to throw a monkey wrench into *that* date," he said with a grin.

"Exactly."

"I'm really glad you called, Kate."

I smiled and sighed, settling into the chair. I took a sip of wine and let the calm settle through me. "Wow, sorry for that whole display. Hope I didn't scare you off from wanting to be my friend."

He laughed a little and made an awkward smile that showed

his dimple. "I told you—I'm glad you came to me. You can come to me anytime."

"Be careful what you offer," I said.

I got some more uncomfortable smiles from him, coupled with some sporadic eye contact.

"Okay," I said, frowning. "Did I weird you out with my whole crying on your shoulder thing?"

He shook his head. "No, not in the least."

"Okay. Well then, what's up with you? You clearly have something on your mind."

"It'll keep," he said, shaking his head dismissively. "It's not the right time. You've had a rough night."

I sighed through my nose and smiled. "Actually, I kind of feel like I just needed to get it out. Now that I have, I feel a whole lot better."

He looked doubtful, so I gave him a reassuring smile. "Come on, Adam. This is what friends do. We share what's on our minds."

"Friends," he repeated. Adam stood up and walked to his picture window and gazed out toward the river. Then he abruptly came back to where I was and sat back down on the edge of the coffee table.

"Well, actually, you can help me."

I reached over and took his hand, frowning. "Anything."

He nodded. "So, you know me really well. You seem to get me."

"Sometimes better than you get yourself," I said, raising my eyebrow.

He smiled. "Exactly. So, could you help me understand something?"

I nodded and leaned closer to where he was sitting on the coffee table.

"Okay, there's something I've been trying to understand and, as many times as I turn it over in my mind, I seem to keep coming to the same conclusion." He pushed his hand through his hair before refocusing on me. "I think about you, Kate. All the time." He paused, letting his words sink in. "When I wake up in the morning, you're my first thought. When I go to bed at night, you're all I think about. Wondering how your day was. What you did. And I wish I was with you to hear about your day. Every day."

I became acutely aware of the little hairs standing up on my arms, and it seemed I could hear my heartbeat in my ears. And it's possible my mouth started to hang open a little as he continued speaking.

"And then, throughout my day, I think about a dozen things that I want to text you about. Because I think you'd find it funny. Or it would make you smile. Or because I want your opinion." He put his hands up in the air. "Or just because I get a rush when I see your name pop up on my phone.

"When I'm bothered by anything, all I want to do is talk to you. To see the look on your face when you tell me it will be okay.

"And I worry about disappointing you." He stopped a moment and swallowed hard before looking back into my eyes. "Kate, I haven't been with a woman since I met you." He shrugged. "Because I worry it would change the way you look at me. And I love the way you look at me. And I don't want to do anything to change that. Because it matters to me more than anything."

I was breathing heavily. He reached over and grasped my hand.

"What does it mean, Kate?"

My chest continued its obvious rise and fall, and my eyes felt misty, but with an entirely different emotion.

"What does it mean, Kate?" Adam repeated softly.

"It means, um . . ." My voice cracked and I cleared my throat. "It means that . . . you're in love with me." I finished the statement with all the awe that I felt.

Adam nodded. "Yeah, that's kind of what I thought it meant, too."

I laughed, and my breath came a little quicker.

Adam slid off the table and came to his knees in front of the chair I was still planted in. "So, I realize I'm a slow learner. Did I wait too long?"

I gave him a confused look.

"Well, I spent so much time telling you *not* to fall for me. Any chance I can change my position on that?"

I smiled. "Oh, don't worry. You never had a say in that, anyway."

"Meaning . . . maybe you love me, too?"

I slid onto my knees in front of him, wrapping my arms around his waist and looking up into that face that I had memorized the lines of. "I love you, too."

He had an odd moment of disbelief pass through his eyes before he lowered his face and kissed me. It was what I'd come to realize was an Adam Kiss. Part lips, teeth, and tongue, part frightening passion.

His hands were on either side of my face, tilting my head to match his rhythm as he invaded my lips, my mouth. Then his hands slid around to the back of my head and I felt his fingers weave their way into my hair, grabbing handfuls.

He stood suddenly, pulling me up with him. Circling his arms around my waist, he picked me up, managing to keep our lips in contact. I wrapped my legs around his waist as he carried me into his bedroom.

My heart was pounding in my chest. Does sex with Adam Lucas require a physical beforehand or anything? Because—in that moment—I was feeling a little faint. And flushed. Borderline delirious, really.

He laid me on the bed. His hands continued stroking my arms as he kissed my lips before trailing to my cheek and down to my neck. He stood and reached down, slipping off my shoes. I sat up and he reached for the bottom of my shirt, looking me in the eye a moment before stripping it off over my head.

I reached behind my back, unclasping my bra, and let it fall from my shoulders. No embarrassment this time.

His eyes took in my bare skin with such intensity that I started to tingle all over.

He put his lips to my shoulder. "You are so beautiful," he said, trailing his lips across my collarbone before moving down. Apparently, the months I'd known Adam had all counted as foreplay, because by the time he had his mouth on me, I felt like I might explode right then. I was light-headed, and my skin felt more alive than it ever had.

As Adam unbuttoned my pants and slid the jeans downward, I could feel his fingertips leaving little streaks of fire across my skin, beginning at my hips and continuing all the way to my ankles, where he pulled the jeans over my feet. He took a moment and planted a soft kiss on top of each foot before he stood, tossing my jeans aside.

I laid back on my side and watched him strip off his shirt. I'd seen him shirtless, but that was in the "forbidden fruit" context, since we were buddies. This context kicks that context's ass.

Then he slipped his shorts off and I got my full look at Adam for the first time. If only Michelangelo had had Adam to model for him. My eyes moved from his tight stomach and muscled legs to the man of the hour . . . and, for a moment, I had some genuine logistical concerns.

It must have showed on my face, because Adam smiled at me and chuckled. "Don't worry," he said. "We'll go slow."

Slow? I'm afraid if he touches me again I'll just bubble over and that will be all she wrote.

He climbed onto the bed next to me and everything inside began to tighten like a spring. He held himself over me and looked into my eyes. Then his gaze shifted down, across the rest of me. He took a deep breath. "I've never been with a woman I was in love with before," he said.

I smiled and ran my hand through the side of his hair. "Say that again."

He smiled, playful and sincere at the same time. "I love you, Kate." He kissed me briefly on the lips before his mouth began working downward, stopping at various points of interest like he was a tourist making memories. As his mouth moved over me, his hands seemed to have a separate agenda, taking in bits of me as though his fingertips were feeding off each new brush of skin. The combination of his mouth and his hands gave me the sensation that he was covering my whole body at once.

Each part under his mouth made me gasp and arch, while each section under the delicate touch of his fingers made me impatient and hungry for more. His mouth reached the point between my legs while his hands continued exploring my thighs, then down my calves. As expected, he'd barely begun before I reached my climax and everything went momentarily dark and sparkly like a night sky. I sat up quickly, putting my hands on the sides of his face, breathing heavy, dizzy.

His previously gentle fingers dug into my flesh a little deeper as his hands worked their way back up. He kissed my stomach and breasts as he traveled back up to where he was holding himself over me again. He pushed my arms up over my head and his hands gripped my biceps before slipping upward toward my wrists. Once there, he laced his fingers through mine and I thought about that night in his car, watching the bridge, holding hands, believing that this moment was impossible. But now, here we were.

He smiled at me. I felt him, down below, pushing lightly. "I feel like I should say something meaningful," he said, a little breathlessly. "But nothing seems big enough."

I laughed at that. "God, I love you," I said.

He shook his head. "You always know what to say."

And turns out, he lied, because from that moment forward, we didn't take it slow. With a wicked smile, he pushed into me hard, and I simultaneously thrust my hips up to meet him, and the intensity was an exquisite mixture of pain and pleasure.

He began placing kisses along my jawline, next to my ear, along my neck, while moving inside me. Then he looked at me with a worried expression.

In between harsh breaths, he said, "I mentioned I haven't had sex in a couple months, right?"

I nodded.

He was breathing heavier. He shook his head. "I'm not going to last," he said, giving a sharp thrust to make his point.

"I'm ready," I said, reaching up to plant a kiss on his perfect lips.

He wrapped his hands behind my waist and finished in a harsh, passionate rhythm that brought us both to the edge. And then over.

He grunted loudly, holding my hips tightly against him, his fingertips deep in my skin. I wrapped my hands behind his neck, letting out a sharp cry. When he finally stopped his movement, he put his hands on each side of my face, his green eyes fixed on mine. And it was that moment that undid me. Not his beautiful admission that he loved me or the aneurysm-inducing orgasms I'd just had. It was that look. And those eyes. And all the feelings behind them, which he was making no effort to hide from me anymore.

He dropped down onto me and I wrapped my arms around him while he did the same. I held him tightly against me, feeling this delicious moment was almost surreal. I ran my hands across his wide back, taking in his smooth skin with my fingertips.

He rolled onto his side, pulling me with him, so that we were face-to-face.

"Holy shit," he said, giving his head a little shake of disbelief.

I laughed, still breathless. "Agreed."

"Who knew that being in love made sex so much better?"

"Right? Had you known, you might have tried that whole 'falling in love' thing a long time ago."

He shook his head a little. "That wouldn't have been possible. I hadn't met you yet."

I let those words spread across my skin like honey, making everything feel warm and sweet.

He was breathing heavily, and his eyes seemed fascinated

as they continued across my face. "Kate," he said softly, as a complete sentence.

"Adam," I said, smiling.

"Kate."

I leaned my forehead against his. "You have *always* used my name more than anyone I've ever met."

"Have I?"

I nodded.

"Hm. I've always loved saying it. I guess now we know why."

I laughed and ran my hand up his bare arm.

"I just realized," he said, propping his elbow up to rest his head against his hand, "I'm part of a couple for the first time. Kate and Adam. Adam and Kate. You know, as in 'We should see if Kate and Adam want to come,' or 'Hey—Adam and Kate are here,' or 'Kate and Adam are running late again.'"

I laughed. "Running late because they had trouble getting out of bed, no doubt," I said, giving him a playful kiss on the mouth.

"I could see that being a very real problem," he agreed, lowering his brows.

"Oh my god," I said, touching my fingertips to my forehead. "I have to call Logek."

Adam laughed, rubbing his hand lazily up and down my hip.

"And your mother is going to be in shock," I said.

Adam smiled and brushed his knuckles against my cheek. "If by 'shock' you mean jumping up and down, calling everyone she knows, and knitting baby booties in case we ever have kids, then yes, she'll be in shock."

I laughed. "Exactly what I meant."

He let out a contented sigh and closed his eyes. His arms curled around me and pulled my body closer so that intimate portions of our skin were touching again. He opened his eyes and looked into mine with a serious expression.

"Kate, we can never sign . . ."

Oh.

"Or we can sign tomorrow. It makes no difference to me. Because I'm never going to let you go."

Oh. I blew out a little breath. I'm not going to cry. I'm going to *try* not to cry. Shit. I'm going to cry.

Kate Shaw, big game hunter. Brought down a unicorn.

EPILOGUE

Mags stepped into my parents' kitchen, smiling, and made a flourish down her dress. She was in a pale-yellow satin number that came to her ankles, with a slit up one side. Her dark hair was pulled back on one side with a sparkly clip, and she looked like she had just stepped out of a Ginger Rogers movie. Brad seemed to agree, because, as he moved in next to her, he looked so excited I thought he might break into song and dance at any moment. He was wearing a light suit with a narrow blue tie, along with his trademark black, thick-rimmed glasses, and seeing the two of them standing there made you question which decade you were in.

"Oh my god," I said, extending my arms to her. "You look so amazing."

"Mags," Mom chimed in from behind me, "you are stunning."

Mags was grinning widely. "Thank you. And I can't thank you guys enough for letting us have our signing party here," she said, looking at my parents.

My dad waved a hand in the air. "We are happy to. Ask Kate. We love throwing signing parties."

My mother was beaming, with her arm wrapped around my dad's waist. "We're so happy for you two."

Adam walked into the kitchen, carrying a case of wine. After setting it on the counter, he turned to Mags and Brad. He shook his head at Mags, appreciatively. "Wow. I would have expected nothing less from you." He reached in and hugged her and then did the one-arm man-hug thing with Brad.

Logek emerged from the back room and held out a hand to Mags. "Right? Did I nail her makeup or what?" Logek was everyone's go-to for special event makeup, and making Mags look like a 1940s movie star was probably the most fun Logek had had in a while.

"She is perfect," Brad said, putting a light kiss on her forehead.

Adam walked up behind me, wrapped his arms around my waist, and settled his chin on my shoulder. "It was very nice of you to invite my mom," Adam said, looking over at Mags and then back to my parents.

"Of course," my mother said, enthusiastically. "But you did warn her that my brother will probably be making puppy dog eyes at her from across the room all night, right?"

Adam chuckled and I could feel it vibrate through me. "Yes, I delivered your warning. She seemed undeterred."

"Happy to hear it," Mom said.

We all made our way to the backyard, and Mags made an uncharacteristic squeal of delight when she saw it. It was dusk, and the enormous patio was dotted with elegant tables draped in white tablecloths, with bright centerpieces of exotic-looking flowers. Every tree and post was wrapped in strands of white twinkle lights, and floating candles moved across the surface of the pool. Mags wasn't wrong—it was pretty spectacular. This is why Mom and Dad were the friends-and-family go-to when it came to hitting someone up to host a signing party.

People started arriving, and before we knew it the whole space was full of happy people, laughter, and music.

Mags and Brad had been surrounded by a steady throng of people for the last hour, so, when it seemed to be dispersing, I took an opportunity to steal a moment with her.

I grabbed her hand, smiling. "Having a good time?"

"Oh my god. The best," she said, squeezing my hand.

"And Kate, thanks so much for drafting the contract. It meant a lot to us," Brad said.

I smiled. "Of course. I was happy to. Especially since it conflicts me out from either of you asking me to represent you in a breach," I said with a wink, and they both chuckled.

Brad gave Mags a peck on the cheek and took her empty wineglass from her hand. "Another?" he asked.

Mags was too happy to give him a more Mags-appropriate smart-ass answer, so she just nodded. Logek slid in next to us and wrapped an arm around Mags's waist.

"Me too, Brad," Logek said, passing over her empty wineglass. He grinned and obligingly took the empty glass.

A photographer in a white shirt and a bow tie stopped in front of the three of us. "Could I get a picture?"

We squeezed in together, with Mags in the middle, and gave our best smiles.

"So," Logek said, after the photog walked away, "let's see it."

Mags turned over her wrist, displaying a small tattoo of the signature quill declaring she was signed. It was done in pale yellow and pink, so not too dramatic, but nonetheless permanent.

Logek shook her head. "You know, you only signed a seven-year contract." She lifted Mags's wrist a little. "This is gonna last a lot longer."

Mags just shrugged.

"Well, I think it's very *you*," I said.

"I agree," Mags said with a nod. "And how was I possibly going to accessorize a watch or bracelet into my outfit every day?"

Now it really made sense. One thing you never mess with is Mags's ability to flawlessly accessorize. That probably would have been grounds to cancel the signing.

"So, where's Jared?" Mags asked Logek.

Logek made a face. "We aren't seeing each other anymore."

I frowned. "What? What happened?"

Logek laughed. "Calm down. I'm just kidding." She pointed over my shoulder to where he was stopped, talking to Adam. "He was just running late."

Jared looked over, and he lit up when he saw Logek looking at him. Yeah. I didn't see this flame burning out for a while.

He and Adam made their way over to us. Jared, being the sensible litigator he was, congratulated Mags and told her how gorgeous she looked *before* he turned his complete focus to Logek, folding her in a tight hug.

Adam moved in behind me and wrapped an arm around

me so that his arm was across my chest and his hand was holding on to my shoulder. He casually pressed a kiss to my temple. Big inner sigh.

Brad came back and handed wineglasses to Logek and Mags, then he took Mags's hand. "They're playing our song," he said. I listened to the music, and it was some old-school slow song that seemed to fit perfectly with their clothing choices. She smiled at me and handed me her glass.

Brad actually gave her an elegant twirl onto the dance floor before they fell into something that looked suspiciously like a waltz. Who knows how to do the waltz these days?

"Damn, that girl's got style," Logek said.

"Come on," Adam said, standing in front of me. "You too."

I smiled and played pass-the-wineglass with Jared, since Logek already had a glass in one hand and her other was firmly occupied fiddling with the hairline at the top of Jared's neck. Jared took the glass with a smile.

Adam pulled me into the area where Mags and Brad and a few other couples were dancing. He gripped my hand tightly, tugging me against him. I reached my hands up behind his neck and laced my fingers together.

"Kate," he said, in a soft voice.

I grinned broadly. That will never get old. At my giddy smile, Adam chuckled and kissed me.

"This is a beautiful backyard," he said.

I did a quick look around and nodded agreement.

"Must have been a great place to grow up."

"It was. It was perfect."

He nodded. "Nice neighborhood, too."

I lowered my eyebrows a little and nodded again. "Very."

He lowered his head so that his face was closer to mine. "I

was just thinking. We might want to consider moving out this way. You know—if we're going to have kids, we need to think about school districts and stuff like that."

Oh. My heart was beating faster and I felt a flush creep up my neck. My mouth dropped open a little.

Adam smiled and his green eyes lit up a little. "Well?"

I looked around me, dazed. Mags and Brad were gazing into each other's eyes like the rest of us weren't even here. Logek and Jared were where we'd left them, talking close, laughing, and kissing intermittently. My parents were standing near the pool next to Sandy. They were all watching Adam and me dancing. Sandy waved, grinning, when I looked over.

I looked back at Adam and he hooked a finger under my chin and turned my face up to him. I smiled.

"This is a pretty great area to raise kids," I said.

Adam pulled me in tight against him and lowered his lips to mine, but instead of kissing me, he whispered against them. "Can I get that in writing?"

ACKNOWLEDGMENTS

Here we are again. I'm so glad you could join me. (I feel like I'm trying to seduce you while slipping into a smoking jacket. Am I the only one envisioning Christopher Walken on SNL right now?)

Since I got the husband out of the way in the dedication, I don't need to start with him this time (even though he probably deserves it for putting up with me for the last twenty years).

So I'm starting with my agent, Michelle Wolfson. I'm so grateful that you picked me. I'm so happy to know you. You may be small, but you are mighty. #WolfPack

To Whitney Ross for being such an amazing editor. Thank you for all of your insight and for sharing the same vision for Kate. To Amy Stapp, Alexis Saarela, and the other fantastic people at Tor/Forge for being consistently supportive, creative, and fun. It's been such a pleasure working with you all.

To Penny Lyon and Katie Copeland for (still) being eager to read everything I put in front of you. Writing—and life in general—is easier with you two at my back.

To my pop, Bob Lyon; my brother, Jeff Lyon; and my sister, Kelly Erickson, for being my cheerleaders through a difficult couple of years. We're making it. And she would be proud.

To so many friends, old and new, who were so supportive of *I Love You* *Subject to the Following Terms and Conditions*. From the bloggers and Instagrammers who loved it and talked about it, to the many friends, family, in-laws, and co-workers who posted pictures and reviews, and to all of you, friends and strangers alike, who reached out just to say "When the hell is book two coming out??" I appreciate every single one of you.

To my girls, Sydney and Alexa, just because I love you and you are amazing women.

To my uncle, J. R. Williams, for nothing in particular other than the fact that you gave me a bunch of crap for not being in my last acknowledgments.

And to you, Mom, always. Miss you every damn day.